5 GOOD Years

A MODERN TAKE ON BIBLICAL MASTERPIECE

DEUTINA IDISI

Warning

In "Five Good Years," vivid descriptions of bleeding, abuse, depression, anxiety, and near-suicide attempts are included, which may evoke a trauma response for some readers. If you find yourself experiencing similar feelings and need someone to speak to, please consider reaching out to one or more of the following services available in the United Kingdom, Kenya and Nigeria.

United Kingdom

Calm—Support for those feeling suicidal as well as those worried about someone
Web: https://www.thecalzone.net
Call: + 44 800 58 58 58 (from 5 p.m. until midnight 365 days a year)

Mind—For information and advice on mental health problems
Web: https://www.mind.org.uk/
Call: +44 300 123 3393 (from 9 a.m. to 6 p.m. Monday through Friday, except bank holidays)

Shout—Free 24/7 mental health text support
Text: "Shout" on 85258 (24 hours a day, 365 days a year)

The Samaritans—For if you are having a difficult time, feel suicidal, or are concerned about someone.
Web: https://www.samaritans.org/
Call: +44 116 123 (24 hours a day)

Kenya
Befrienders Kenya: for confidential emotional support.
Call :| +254 722 178 177 or +254 736 542 304 (Monday to Sunday, 9 am to 9 pm) for confidential emotional support.

Nigeria
Mentally Aware Nigeria Initiative (MANI): Visit their website at www.mentallyaware.org for information on mental health resources and support groups in Nigeria.

Nigeria Suicide Prevention Initiative (NSPI): Visit their website at www.nigeriasuicidepreventioninitiative.org for resources and support related to suicide prevention in Nigeria.

BASED ON A

true story

> *Consider it pure joy, my brothers and sisters, whenever you face trials of many kinds because you know that the testing of your faith produces perseverance. Let perseverance finish its work so that you may be mature and complete, not lacking anything.*
> **—James 1:2–4 (NIV)**

Contents

DEAR READER,

In the quiet moments of reflection, as I poured over the sacred texts that have guided generations, my thoughts were drawn to a story that, though ancient, resonates with a profound urgency in our modern lives. It's a tale that mirrors the struggles, hopes, and fears that many women face, particularly as we navigate the pivotal years between 30 and 35—a time often marked by society's watchful eye on the biological clock.

This period represents more than just a chapter in our lives; it's a crossroads, a crucible where dreams of motherhood, personal aspirations, and the realities of our biological timelines intertwine. With each passing year, the silent ticking of that clock grows louder, casting a shadow of dread over the joyous anticipation of nurturing new life. It's a shadow that many of us know all too well, a reminder of the pressure to conform to a timeline that may not align with our own journey.

As I delved deeper into the narrative of a woman from biblical times, who, for twelve long years, faced an affliction that isolated her from the world, I saw a reflection of the modern woman's struggle with the societal and biological pressures of fertility. Her story, though set in a time different from our own, speaks to the heart of what many of us feel—a blend of hope and fear, a battle between faith and the anxiety of 'what ifs.'

"*Five Good Years*" is born from this reflection, a narrative that weaves together the ancient and the contemporary, offering a message of hope and resilience to those who stand at the crossroads of life's biological timelines. Through the interwoven stories of the past and present, this book seeks to be a source of comfort and inspiration, illuminating the path forward with the understanding that each journey is unique and every moment of waiting is an opportunity for growth and self-discovery.

As you journey through these pages, my deepest wish is that you find solace in the realisation that, though the pressures of society and biology are real, your value and your journey are not defined by them. May the story of perseverance and faith from centuries past serve as a beacon of hope, guiding you to a place of peace and understanding, where the ticking of the biological clock is met with a strength and faith that transcends time.

This book is my gift to you, a testament to the legacy of wisdom, courage, and intentional living that we can all aspire to. May "*Five Good Years*" inspire you to embrace your journey, regardless of its pace, and to find joy and fulfilment in the moments, both big and small, that define our lives.

With warmth and solidarity,

Deutina Idisi

PROLOGUE

And there came a man named Jairus, a ruler of the synagogue. Falling at Jesus's feet, he implored him to come to his house, for he had an only daughter, about twelve years of age, and she was dying. As Jesus went, the people pressed around him. There was a woman who had a discharge of blood for twelve years, and though she had spent all her living on physicians, no one could heal her. She came up behind him and touched the fringe of his garment, and immediately her discharge of blood ceased. Jesus said, "Who was it that touched me?"

When all denied it, Peter said, "Master, the crowds surround you and are pressing in on you!" But Jesus said, "Someone touched me, for I perceive that power has gone out from me." And when the woman saw that she was not hidden, she came trembling, and falling down before him declared in the presence of all the people why she had touched him and how she had been immediately healed. And he said to her, "Daughter, your faith has made you well; go in peace."

—Luke 8:41–48 (ESV)

Within the sacred pages of the Bible lies a poignant tale—an account chronicled in Luke 8:41–48, depicting the woman afflicted with the issue of blood. Before our introduction, her existence had been a tapestry woven with threads of unrelenting misery and unbearable pain. Yet, in this biblical narrative, life hurled blows her way relentlessly, each one a merciless assault on her dwindling vitality and crumbling identity. Despite enduring excruciating suffering and depleting all her resources in pursuit of medical aid, her condition merely worsened. Indifferent to her plight, life continued unabated, casting her into a relentless cycle of trials.

For twelve interminable years, this woman remained shrouded in the shadow of her affliction—an ordeal mirroring the lifespan of Jarius's daughter when their fates converged in this tale. Under Mosaic law, the woman's constant bleeding rendered her ceremonially unclean, banishing her from society for seven days with anything or anyone she touched deemed contaminated as well (Leviticus 15:1–30 NIV). "Unclean! Unclean!" she would cry out, a desperate plea to those near, lest they share in her impurity. Consequently, she unwittingly became a public spectacle, a living testament to her silent agony. Though she might have preferred to grapple with her struggles in solitude, such solace eluded her. Can you empathise?

Her ailment stripped her of employment, intimacy, and participation in communal gatherings, including religious congregations. In this biblical account, her identity fades into obscurity, overshadowed by the relentless torment of her condition and the suffocating shame it imposed—an unfortunate reality for some in our contemporary society.

Though history affords no formal diagnosis, we can speculate on the woman's affliction. In our era, her condition might align with menorrhagia or haemorrhage stemming from prolonged menstrual or postpartum bleeding. Symptoms include extended menstruation, debilitating cramps, blood loss, and potential anaemia, rendering normalcy an impossibility. In the technological age, 50 per cent of women diagnosed with menorrhagia remain unaware of its cause (Oehler and Rees, 2003). Oehler and Rees further elaborate on this topic in their comprehensive review article, 'Menorrhagia: An Update,' published in *Acta Ob-*

stetricia et Gynecologica Scandinavica, which provides valuable insights into the diagnosis and management of this condition.

"Five Good Years" draws inspiration from two women: the biblical figure with the issue of the blood and a contemporary counterpart, Zawadi. Zawadi, a woman of the present, possesses a name, an identity, and a voice. Her name, originating from Swahili, translates as "Gift" in English.

This literary work aims to provide a contemporary interpretation of the biblical woman's struggle—a narrative intended to offer wisdom and solace, particularly to those entrenched in adversity, providing a glimpse of hope amidst life's storms. Confronting mortality and unspeakable agony, the ageless words of wisdom, "Teach us to number our days, that we may gain a heart of wisdom" (Psalm 90:2 NIV), resonate profoundly. The hope is that you won't wait for a terminal diagnosis before choosing to live authentically and intentionally. The uncertainties of tomorrow emphasise the value of this fleeting moment. Selah.

The deep aspiration is for this work to empower you to stand resolute in the truth amidst the harshest trials—a challenging yet transformative space.

Living isn't solely existing; it's the legacy we carve into the lives of others. "Five Good Years" serves as a gift to you—an offering cherished twice by the giver and the receiver. Enjoy the journey through these pages, and may you pass this gift forward.

Year 0

Chapter One

GOOD RIDDANCE

> *You are enough.*
> **—Unknown**

"**G**ood riddance to bad rubbish!" The words reverberated in Zawadi's mind, sharper than the scalding tea she had accidentally spilt on the pristine white tablecloth. Her hand trembled as she fumbled with the spoon, missing the saucer entirely. Meeting her father's gaze, she felt a warmth flush across her forehead. Tension gripped her jaw, twisting her smile into a grimace. Breakfast, typically a sanctuary of familial connection, had devolved into a battleground of unspoken tensions. In the ensuing silence, her father's usually invaluable words hung heavy in the air, weighing as heavily as a ton of bricks, his piercing stare leaving her feeling exposed and hollow.

Tightly woven hairstyles, fashionable Bata shoes, and the ubiquity of pinafore uniforms characterised the era. Barney's whimsical tunes on VHS tapes echoed through bustling streets lined with salon cars and the distinct silhouettes of TV aerials dotting households. Lushly carpeted houses and drapes punctuated the landscape, their robust appearance mirroring the resilience of the times.

Television screens flickered with mesmerising black-and-white contrasts, capturing the collective attention of families. Makeshift antennas adorned rooftops, reaching out in an analogue dance. The air carried the scent of pomade, a hallmark of grooming rituals, while "Big" exercise books held the weight of knowledge and creativity within their ample pages.

Zawadi's *Book of Bible Stories* was a cherished literary companion, weaving tales of morality and faith into the fabric of daily life. *Super Story* unfolded on screens, captivating audiences with its narrative allure. Amidst routines, the ritual of savouring *Chocomilo* and spreading *Planta* margarine on bread added a touch of comfort to breakfast tables.

Eddy Grant's music provided a soundtrack to the era, while boy band posters adorned teenagers' walls, capturing the essence of youthful admiration. Fashion choices embraced bold shoulder pads and nostalgic, puffy, ill-fitted church dresses. These elements defined the era, each contributing a note to the symphony of memories echoing through the collective unconscious.

Breakfast, in the lavish embrace of her family, was the pinnacle of Zawadi's day, an opportunity to bond with her father, the orchestrator of their household. The telltale sign that her dad was ready to kick-start his day came from the subtle yet distinct fragrance of *Davidoff Cool Water* cologne that wafted through the air, lingering on his clothing and handkerchief, carrying his essence for weeks, a comforting reminder of his presence.

Her dad's man purse always boasted crisp, fresh banknotes that he whimsically called "mints." The scent of his cologne was a giveaway; anyone handling the cash would immediately know its origin. Approaching her tenth birthday, Zawadi hoped to receive some "mints" from her dad that morning.

Her father's meals, a regal feast, showcased the meticulous coordination between her mother, the cooks, and the housemaids. Every detail, from the impeccable table dressing to the precise cutlery arrangement, was a spectacle of perfection.

A well-rehearsed routine unfolded once Zawadi's father settled at the dining table. Her mother attended to his needs, pulling out his chair and tucking a white napkin into his shirt collar, ensuring no food would mar his attire. As the morning ritual progressed, Zawadi prepared tea and poured water for her father.

Amidst this carefully curated routine, a hiccup occurred. Zawadi's attempt to impress with a new tea-making technique, drawn from a television demonstration, unfolded like a muted symphony.

The customary morning ritual of savouring nostalgic flavours was typically a highlight for Zawadi. However, on this particular day, the allure of familiar breakfast delights held no sway over her. Consumed by panic, she found that any thoughts of food or her birthday were inconsequential.

Zawadi set about making what she believed to be a quintessentially British cup of tea, her methods hilariously flawed. She started with tepid water from the morning's earlier use, convinced that boiling it twice would unleash a stronger essence. The teapot, cold and unwelcoming, received a few teabags — a mishmash of green and black tea — tossed in without ceremony. Ignoring the traditional boiling fervour, she poured water just off a simmer over the teabags and immediately stirred vigorously with a spoon, as if coaxing the flavour out by force. In a final act of tea sacrilege, she squeezed lemon into the murky brew, then dolloped cream on top, creating a curdled spectacle. Each swirl was a testament to her enthusiastic, albeit misguided, tribute to British tea culture.

In a swift movement, her mother, sensing her daughter's unease, placed another cup on the table and began crafting a new cup of tea. Zawadi, well-versed in the art of tea making, had recently been captivated by a portrayal on TV. Eager to impress her dad with this novel approach, she endeavoured to replicate it, but the outcome proved far from her intentions.

She sidestepped gracefully, coming to a standstill, fixating on her mum as though witnessing the alchemy of tea for the very first time. "Sorry, Daddy," she uttered, uncertainty lingering in the air as his eyes remained locked on the unfolding morning news on TV. His silence after taking a sip hinted at his satisfaction.

With furrowed brow betraying a lingering startle, Zawadi withdrew discreetly, the purpose of the stealthy retreat being to ensure that her dad's morning remained undisturbed. The beads of sweat that had formed on her brow bore testament to the tension she felt, which intensified as she navigated her brother's room strewn with a new collection of books acquired from the library, each step a delicate dance between literature and family dynamics.

OOPS! WHEN SLANG HITS HARD:
A SIBLING REALITY CHECK

Zawadi said, "'Good riddance to bad rubbish!' What does it mean? Is it a compliment?"

Jaali, her brother, asked, "Who told you about this phrase?"

"Dad!" Zawadi answered.

Jaali said, "I'm sure he was playing with you. You know how Dad is."

"But what does it mean?" Zawadi asked.

Jaali's dismissive tone stung Zawadi. 'Erm, you are no good and unwanted,' he remarked, his words hitting her like a slap.

Zawadi's curiosity led to an unexpected revelation in this brief exchange, causing vulnerability. Jaali attempted to downplay the seriousness, attributing it to their father's playful nature. In contrast, the stark truth in Jaali's response hinted at an unsettling reality for Zawadi, making her question her place and worth in her father's eyes.

Zawadi's chin touched her chest, feeling the dampness on her blouse—a fusion of sweat and tears. In a surge of emotion, she slammed the door and raced towards her room, which seemed an unattainable refuge on this day. Time crawled, and Jaali's calls echoed like distant underwater murmurs. Desiring solitude, Zawadi shut herself in, allowing the tears to flow freely.

FAMILY TIES AND TATTLES:
THE COST OF A SECRET SPILLED

Two weeks earlier, Zawadi's older sister, Firyali, had taken her siblings, including Zawadi, for a swimming outing. Zawadi had promised secrecy but succumbed to verbal diarrhoea, revealing to their mum embellished details of Firyali's intimate encounter with her boyfriend. Zawadi's parents disapproved, emphasising the family's value of modest behaviour until one completes one's education and attains readiness for marriage.

The aftermath diverged from previous instances of her offending Firyali. A coldness enveloped the house, a pervasive emptiness that lingered with all of Zawadi's siblings around.Firyali, seemingly irritated by Zawadi's playful nature, bore the brunt of their parents' disappointment. Zawadi's apology seemed futile, her feelings seemed invalidated, and the "*Best-Behaved Girl*" award from school felt like a distant fiction.

A week later, hope emerged as Firyali announced a family swimming trip. Zawadi, delighted by the idea of restored relations, eagerly prepared by packing her swim towel and bathing suit. Changing from her Sunday best into a casual outfit, she hoped to find reassurance in Firyali's actions.

As Zawadi approached the car door, Firyali forcefully shoved her aside to make way for Ava, her boyfriend's daughter. With delicate care, Firyali lifted Ava, seated her on her lap, and affectionately patted her hair.

"You are not going anywhere with me," Firyali declared to Zawadi in a resounding voice. "Learn to keep your mouth shut and not disclose everything you witness, and I might think about taking you out again. Get out of there; let me close my door!"

The door slammed shut in Zawadi's face, narrowly missing her tiny fingers. Zawadi's heart sank as she watched her siblings nonchalantly pile into the car and drive away. Their laughter faded into the distance like a distant echo. The space beside her felt vast and unforgiving, a stark reminder of her isolation. Tears welled up in her eyes, blurring her vision as she fought to keep her emotions in check. With each passing moment, the weight of her loneliness grew heavier, threatening to crush her spirit. The guards closed the gates, indifferent to her distress. The veins in her neck visibly strained as tears streamed down her face; she was fervently hoping her wailing would compel her family to turn around, forgive her, and invite her to join them. In her desperation, she uttered a prayer, seeking a saviour to shield her from the profound pain in her heart and chest. The security guards, empathetic yet powerless, looked at her with pity.

Everything felt surreal to Zawadi, as if she were having an out-of-body experience. Standing there, staring at the gate for what seemed like an eternity, she finally accepted that her family were not coming for her.

Questions swirled in her mind, as follows:

Why am I different?

How can I fix myself?

Why does everyone hate me?

What did I do wrong?

I thought everyone deserved forgiveness. Is that not what the teacher taught in Sunday school? I have yet to use my daily forgiveness quota of seventy times seven that Jesus prescribed.

These were the unanswered questions haunting her. She wished she could express that her siblings had disappointed her by not protecting her and choosing a stranger over their baby sister. The familiar notes of "Another Sad Love Song" by Toni Braxton played in the background, a melody that never resonated as deeply as it does at this moment. Heartbroken, Zawadi believed she had lost her place as the baby of the house.

LONGING AND LOVE:
NAVIGATING THE GAPS IN A SIBLING BOND

As the youngest in the household, with a considerable age gap setting her apart from her older siblings, she often had found herself navigating the expanses of time in solitude. Her brothers and sisters were either engrossed in the routines of boarding school for their secondary education or immersed in the academic pursuits of university life. Each departure turned into an emotionally charged ordeal for Zawadi, characterized by mini panic attacks in the lead-up to her needing to say goodbye, with tears streaming down her face as she watched her siblings drive away. To alleviate her pain, her mother would extend comfort by inviting her into the house, serving her favourite meal, and offering reassurance that everything would be OK.

Despite the challenges of being alone at home, Zawadi's siblings consistently reassured her, promising swift returns laden with gifts. Yet, their empty promises left Zawadi yearning for their presence, each occasional phone call or letter serving as a feeble substitute for their physical absence. They visited every three to six months, and their stays were limited to two weeks. Despite their brevity, Zawadi cherished every fleeting moment with them, savouring the warmth of their familial bonds amidst their departures.

Her older siblings, especially her brothers, embodied coolness, trendiness, and athleticism within the fabric of their familial ties.Their presence inadvertently attracted the attention of girls vying for their affection, leading to a cascade of attention that benefited Zawadi. In their quest to win the affection of Zawadi's brothers, these girls extended their friendliness towards her, inadvertently adding emotional depth to her unique journey.

The tapestry of her family dynamic weaves threads of longing, with each visit from her siblings serving as a bittersweet reminder of their physical absence. As they departed, Zawadi clung to the remnants of their presence, cherishing the memories and moments shared during their short stays. Despite the temporary nature of their visits, the love and camaraderie they brought filled the void left in their wake, providing Zawadi with fleeting moments of solace amidst the solitude of their absence.

NIGHT WHISPERS:
SECRETS AND SHIVERS IN A FAMILY DRAMA

Auntie Afaafa played a crucial role in filling the void that Zawadi felt in the absence of her siblings, serving as a maternal figure and bridging the emotional gap. Despite her initial trepidation about Auntie Afaafa's strict demeanour, Zawadi's sentiments evolved, transforming fear into genuine love and appreciation. Auntie Afaafa's unique blend of strictness and affectionate care contributed significantly to Zawadi's life. Her warm presence possessed the remarkable ability to transform their house into a proper home, offering comfort and security, especially during the times Zawadi's mom was away.

Auntie Afaafa behaved like a second mom, ensuring Zawadi's neat appearance, cooking delicious meals, and offering life advice. Her strict adherence to early bedtimes, set at 9 p.m., reflected a disciplined routine that required Zawadi to rise at 6 a.m.—early to bed and early to rise. The routine remained consistent, whether a school night or a weekend.

Yet, one night, the familiar routine was disrupted by loud voices in the corridor, waking Zawadi. The generator's hum made it challenging to decipher the words, but it seemed a heated argument involving her mom, Auntie Afaafa, and perhaps her dad. The confrontation escalated, demanding someone to leave immediately.

Trembling in confusion, Zawadi curled up in her bunk bed, fearing a potential threat. Tears streamed down her face as she grappled with the distressing sounds and unsettling possibilities. The possibility of a robbery or something more sinister gripped her as her heart raced.

The feeling of security that Auntie Afaafa usually provided seemed shattered at this point, leaving Zawadi vulnerable and afraid in the sanctuary she had called home.

Zawadi's dad, a formidable presence with a hidden arsenal of guns and bullets under his bed, usually provided security in their home. The sight of those forbidden boxes filled with ammunition was a familiar yet unsettling reminder of her father's preparedness. Every morning as Zawadi cleaned his room, she inevitably noticed the boxes tucked away, their contents concealed from view. Yet, instead of offering reassurance, they added to her sense of vulnerability on this particular night, casting a shadow over her usual feelings of safety.

Despite the unreliability of the police force, the proximity of Zawadi's family's house to a police station and the presence of heavily armed guards at the estate gates added a layer of assurance. Faced with a tense situation involving her parents and aunt, Zawadi, paralysed by fear, clung to the hope that her dad's preparedness would be enough for him to handle any potential intrusion.

Terrified to venture outside her room, Zawadi remained huddled in her bed, listening to the escalating voices outside. The tension in the air was palpable, suffocating her as she struggled to make sense of the chaos unfolding in her once-serene home.

As the commotion continued into the night, Zawadi questioned her family's stability and the safety of her surroundings. The familiar walls of her room seemed like confining barriers, trapping her in perpetual fear and uncertainty.

As dawn broke, the voices outside gradually subsided, replaced by an eerie silence that hung heavy in the air. Zawadi, exhausted from a sleepless night filled with fear and apprehension, cautiously emerged from her room, her eyes scanning the corridor for any signs of danger. On Sunday mornings, the lively commotion of the crew setting up canopies and musical instruments for the church in the garage heralded the start of Zawadi's day. Yet, as she heard the familiar sounds this time, she hesitated, waiting and listening for any signs of abnormality, such as shouting or crying. The air remained calm, to her relief, leading her to believe everything was normal; otherwise, the family wouldn't be preparing for church.

In a rush, Zawadi made her bed and headed to the bathroom, conscious of her mum and aunt's emphasis on cleanliness. The consequences of being caught wandering around the house in an unclean state with an unmade bed were not something she wanted to face. Yet, as she navigated through her morning routine, an unusual quietness enveloped the house, a marked departure from the usual bustling atmosphere. The sight of her parents in the living room, their faces worn and haggard, filled her with relief tinged with anxiety. Sensing a palpable stiffness in the air, Zawadi couldn't shake off the feeling that today was different. An unspoken tension lingered, casting a shadow over the customary preparations for church.

As the youngest in the family, Zawadi understood it was wise not to pose too many questions, particularly in moments of tension as elders could see curiosity as a form of disobedience. Despite sensing something was amiss, she held her burning questions and waited for her aunt to clarify the situation.

The sombre atmosphere weighed heavily on Zawadi's heart as she sat in the pew, trying to focus on the sermon. The familiar hymns and prayers seemed distant, drowned out by the turmoil within her family. She stole glances at her parents, their strained expressions betraying the facade of normalcy they tried to maintain.

Auntie Afafa's absence added to the mystery. Normally a pillar of strength and wisdom, her missing presence spoke volumes about the severity of whatever had transpired. Zawadi wondered what could have happened to cause such tension and worry.

As the church service continued, Zawadi's mind raced with questions. What had happened? Was someone sick? Was she in trouble? The uncertainty gnawed at her, and she longed for the comfort of answers.

Despite her attempts to find solace in the familiar surroundings of the church and her family's presence, the unease persisted, casting a shadow over everything. The former warmth of her home felt distant and unfamiliar, eclipsed by the weight of the unknown.

Surrounded by turmoil and uncertainty, Zawadi clung to the hope that her family would overcome their differences and restore the sense of security and stability that had previously defined their home.

After the service, Zawadi sought answers from the housemaid about her Aunt Afaafa's whereabouts. The housemaid revealed that her aunt had left the previous night after a heated argument with Zawadi's parents.

Devastated by the news and struggling to cope with the sudden departure of her beloved aunt, Zawadi went to her mum's room seeking solace.Her mum, though, offered little comfort, stating that her aunt would return, but not anytime soon. The abrupt loss left Zawadi feeling abandoned and fearful of facing the loneliness that would quickly permeate her at home.

Throughout the day, Zawadi remained inconsolable, as her mum tried to reassure her and offered her favourite meal. The pain of losing those she loved and the recurring theme of abandonment intensified her resolve to build the family she idealised.

DADDY DRAMA: ZAWADI'S ROLLERCOASTER FROM TEARS TO TRIUMPH

The slow descent of Zawadi's swimming bag down her shoulders went unnoticed until it hit her toes, jolting her to reality. Still reeling from the emotional turmoil of her siblings leaving her behind, she felt undone.

"Daddy! Daddy! Daddy!" Zawadi's anguished cries echoed through the house as she rushed inside. Her father, concerned, instructed her to wipe away her tears and share who had hurt his baby. After she had recounted her painful experience with her siblings leaving her behind, he reassured her, saying, "Don't mind the actions of your siblings. You know Daddy can do anything for you, right?"

Zawadi, still tearful, nodded in agreement. Her parents had returned from the United States the previous week, and her father invited her to his room. There, he showered her with an array of gifts—chocolates, toys, a computer gadget, diamond-studded earrings, her favourite cartoon character watch, and school stationery. Zawadi's tears transformed into a radiant smile; she felt like a princess.

Her father spoke with love and promise: "Make sure you remain a good girl and get good grades, and I will ensure you have the best life of your dreams. I will also pay for your education to the highest level you wish and send you to any country you choose. I will make you the envy of your siblings, don't worry. Do you trust me?"

"Yes, Daddy!" Zawadi exclaimed, her voice quivering with emotion. She wrapped her arms tightly around her father, feeling the warmth of his embrace and the weight of his words sinking deep into her soul like an anchor. With each squeeze, a ray of optimism ignited within her, cutting through the darkness of her pain and disappointment like a beacon of light.

Zawadi's anguish melted away in that moment, replaced by a profound sense of security and belonging. Despite the upheaval in her family dynamics, she knew deep down that she would always be Daddy's little girl. With a silent vow, she promised to rise above the challenges and carve out a chosen path. Her father had become the saviour she had longed for, and she was determined to make him proud.

HEARTSTRINGS AND HOPE: ZAWADI'S PATH FROM REJECTION TO RESILIENCE

In the here and now, the memory of her father calling her "rubbish" over a cup of tea had left Zawadi in tears and questioning her worth. Feeling dethroned and worthless, she had seen herself as odd with her skinny frame, dark skin, nappy hair, and peculiar walk. Her odd laugh, reminiscent of *Chucky* from the movie *Child's Play*, intensified her sense of isolation. She believed that no one treasured children who were like her.

Zawadi's heart sank as she observed her stepsister—a captivating mixed-race child with long, flowing curls—receiving all the attention and luxuries that were once exclusively hers, courtesy of their shared father. The feeling of displacement hit her like a sudden blow, twisting her insides with every passing moment. She struggled to contain the tears that threatened to overflow, the sting of rejection burning fiercely in her chest. It was as if the love her father had previously professed for her had evaporated, leaving her feeling dethroned and uncertain in her own family.

The family dynamics had undergone a profound shift, and the love that used to feel unwavering seemed fragile and uncertain at this moment. Yet, amidst this emotional turmoil, Zawadi found solace in her mother's steadfast love and support. In the reassuring embrace of that enduring connection, Zawadi found a sanctuary untouched by the intricate nuances of shifting family dynamics.

Drawing on the teachings of forgiveness from Sunday school, Zawadi embraced the ethos of her county, known for its "Big Heart," and forgave her dad and siblings. With resilience and grace, she vowed to rise above the challenges and carve out her path, stoked by her mother's love and support and her unwavering faith in her strength.

In her reveries, she envisioned a warm, loving home where mutual appreciation abounded. Inspired by her mother's impeccable homemaking skills and the imagery of her dream wedding, reminiscent of *"The Father of the Bride,"* Zawadi cherished creating a sanctuary filled with love and warmth. This vision fueled her determination to pursue her dreams and build a life in which happiness and contentment prevailed. With eager anticipation, Zawadi looked ahead to adulthood, aspiring to become the woman capable of realising her dream.

Chapter Two

THE RITE OF PASSAGE

Periods are red; she feels blue.
—Unknown

"**A**unt Flo is here! Fetch a whole chicken for Zawadi. Today is a special day, and she deserves to savour it all by herself," Zawadi's mother exclaimed with excitement, her voice filled with urgency and anticipation as she instructed the housemaid.

Earlier that day, Zawadi had confided in her mother about her discomfort, describing the cramps in her lower belly and the discovery of blood-stained bedsheets upon waking up. In response, her mother had equipped her with super-strength pads and delved into lessons on the menstrual cycle, emphasising its significance as a rite of passage into womanhood.

In her quest for acceptance and identity, Zawadi eagerly anticipated the defining moment she would hear her mother say, "You are now a woman!" She wore her newfound status as a badge of honour, compensating for her perceived lack of excellence in academics, sports, or other activities. Society had instilled in her the belief that a woman's defining trait was her ability to procreate.

Zawadi's journey into womanhood was fraught with challenges and contradictions. Despite society's emphasis on womanhood as primarily tied to procreation, she struggled to reconcile this expectation with her own identity as a tomboy. As puberty began, she navigated a world that suddenly scrutinized her body and actions through the lens of her gender.

The arrival of Aunt Flo, brought forth a cascade of emotions and experiences. While some revelled in it as a rite of passage into womanhood, others greeted it with trepidation or barely acknowledged its existence. Unfortunately for Zawadi, she became entangled in the throes of physical and emotional turmoil during Aunt Flo's visits, transforming what should have been a natural process into a harrowing battleground of pain, discomfort, and shame. The pervasive societal stigma surrounding menstruation served to exacerbate Zawadi's tribulations.

The warm gush between Zawadi's thighs signalled Aunt Flo's arrival, and Zawadi instinctively knew it was the start of a bloody war. While she hoped the initial cramps would be Aunt Flo's brief and painful announcement of her arrival, reality proved to be a nasty and excruciating experience. Aunt Flo visited monthly, bringing along pain, vomiting, leg paralysis, depression, and embarrassment stuffed in her suitcase. Aunt Flo stayed for at least five days at a time.

A hushed, unspoken stigma surrounded her during Aunt Flo's visits, branding her as "filthy" in the eyes of those around her. Zawadi felt relegated and marginalised to isolation until Aunt Flo's departure, signifying her return to societal standards of cleanliness. The peculiarities of Zawadi's heavy flow added an extra layer of complexity to this monthly ballet. Despite using super-plus pads and tampons, she needed to change every hour, leading to inevitable moments of soiling herself. Zawadi was amused by women who described their flow as heavy while opting for thin pads.

RISING THROUGH THE RITES: ZAWADI'S JOURNEY FROM SCHOOL TRIALS TO MEDICAL TRIUMPHS

Zawadi's daily routine became intricately entwined with the waxing and waning of Aunt Flo's unpredictable visits. Aunt Flo sometimes surprised her by coming a couple of days early or late, catching Zawadi off-guard. Staining her uniform was embarrassing, especially in a mixed boarding school with a requirement for all-white uniforms. On such days, she would signal to female students for the dark blue cardigan, part of the school's uniform, which she would then tie around her waist to disguise the stains—a telepathic call of duty. Girls were prohibited from talking to boys, saving Zawadi from explaining her predicament. The blue cardigan became her saving grace, disguising the bleeding until she returned to the hostel.

Boys perceived Aunt Flo as an affliction—an illness they couldn't comprehend—being oblivious to the nuances of this natural cycle. Their lack of understanding intensified the difficulty, turning Zawadi's monthly journey into a more formidable ordeal. In the midst of these trials, she navigated the complexities, determined to challenge stereotypes and emerge from the shadows of societal misconceptions.

As time passed, the cramps intensified, but Zawadi, remembering her mum's pep talk about embracing motherhood, mustered every ounce of courage to handle the pain with pride. She often reassured herself, saying, "You are no longer a girl; you are a woman and must behave as one. You are grown, and the pain comes with the territory."

Despite the pain, the school expected productivity from her during Aunt Flo's visit. Her grades suffered as she missed classes and study times, known as *"preps"*. During exams, Aunt Flo's visit almost guaranteed bad or average grades. In severe cycles, Zawadi ended up in the sick bay, unable to keep anything down, including water, and requiring an IV for hydration.

Boarding school was three hours away from home, and Zawadi had to grapple with the setbacks of Aunt Flo's monthly visits without the support of her understanding mum and sister, who had faced similar experiences. Despite pleading with doctors at the school's sick bay and the family hospital for a solution, she received Panadol (acetaminophen), Buscopan, and suggestions such as hot water bottles and warm baths. Unfortunately, hot remedies were impractical at her boarding school, located in a cold, mountainous region where Zawadi spent six years. The school, a Catholic missionary institution, adhered strictly to military-like protocols, including 4:30 AM cold showers with a bucket and bailer under the open sky, prolonging her agony. Soaking in baths on holidays always looked like a crime scene, which Zawadi diligently avoided. As she continued to articulate the adverse effects Aunt Flo had on her quality of life, the doctors proposed that pregnancy was the sole solution to halt the pain and heavy bleeding.

Zawadi's friends often teased her about her love for love, but she was still too young to discuss marriage with her parents, though she eagerly anticipated starting her own family.In an African household, where education is highly valued, titles such as medical practitioner, engineer, or lawyer carry significant prestige. As a result, many Kenyan families make considerable sacrifices to send their children overseas for university education, where excelling in these esteemed fields is expected. This investment is driven by the belief that an international education provides a better chance at both a superior education and a prosperous living.

Growing up in a Christian home, Zawadi's parents frowned upon the idea of her having a boyfriend. If marriage was her sole way out of this painful life experience and a means to start her dream family, she knew she had to excel at school to bring a man home. She awaited her knight in shining armour to sweep her off her feet. Knowing her mum had married at age sixteen, Zawadi believed she could convince her parents to let her marry early once her ideal partner arrived.

After graduating from high school with flying colours, Zawadi was ready for the next big step—college. With better science grades and indecision about her future career, her parents suggested she use her science-inclined brain to study medicine or engineering. Medicine was the preferred choice, considering there were no doctors in the family, making it a significant accomplishment. Her dad was willing to support her all the more, as having the first doctor in the family would add another feather to their cap.

Zawadi moved away from home to South Africa to attend medical college, residing with her homestay parents. Certainly! It was her first time far from home, and she was ecstatic to travel and discover new worlds and experiences. Yet, little did she realise the challenges that awaited her in what she would call the "Wild, Wild West".

Chapter Three

SHATTERED INNOCENCE

> *I can be changed by what happens to me,*
> *but I refuse to be reduced by it.*
> **—Maya Angelou**

Zawadi's consciousness surged like lightning, jolting her from a hazy abyss. Blinking away the blur, she was encircled by three unfamiliar faces, a visceral rush of panic gripping her chest. Instinctively, she whispered fervent prayers, an urgent plea for divine intervention to shield her from the looming threat.

In her mind, vivid and haunting memories of her tumultuous past surged forth. Scenes from African horror tales flickered in her thoughts, amplifying her mounting fear. In that vulnerable moment, she yearned for the steadfast protection of her oldest brother, realising the sanctuary of her parents' strict upbringing—a bastion against the cruel whims of the world she found herself thrust into currently.

The recollection veered to a time steeped in isolation and longing for recognition within her family. Zawadi felt like an invisible spectre, reluctantly invited to familial gatherings solely through her mother's persistent cajoling or monetary persuasion. The passage of time had failed to mend the deep-seated wounds of neglect, leaving her feeling abandoned and voiceless despite her silent prayers for solace.

Then, her cousin Scarlett emerged like a beacon of hope amid her darkness. Determined to fortify their bond, Zawadi showered Scarlett with gifts, burying past grievances to cement their fragile alliance.

The night hung heavy with the weight of rebellion as Zawadi, driven by a genuine yearning for acceptance, conspired with her cousin Scarlett to venture into uncharted territory. Their clandestine scheme worsens as they relentlessly seek validation, a desperate attempt to break free from suffocating societal norms.

In Scarlett's bedroom, adorned with opulent trappings, Zawadi underwent a makeover. Carefully curated ensembles were selected, and a delicate touch of makeup illustrated her features. Together, they orchestrated a seamless escape, orchestrating a getaway vehicle to whisk them away at the stroke of midnight. With clandestine arrangements made with housemaids and security guards, they slipped through the shadows, navigating past the initial barrier like phantoms at night.

Their hopes of an exhilarating escapade came crashing down as they neared the second gate. A sudden blaze of light pierced the darkness, laying bare their covert machinations. Panic surged as they realised the source of the illumination—a stark reminder of their doomed endeavour. The revelation that Zawadi's oldest brother stood sentinel over their folly struck like a thunderclap—a harbinger of impending retribution.

The arrival of Zawadi's formidable brother amplified the peril, sending fear coursing through their veins. Fueled by sheer desperation, Zawadi and Scarlett bolted with a velocity driven by primal instinct, seeking sanctuary in the guardhouse. Alas, they failed in their efforts; someone had marked them. The thunderous roar of her brother's vehicle reverberated through the night as he barrelled towards them, fists clenched in a menacing display of fury.

"Where do you think you're going? I'll catch you! I'll catch you!"

In a frantic bid for survival, Zawadi and Scarlett surged through the gates, their strides mirroring the nimble grace of a panther in flight. Zawadi's background as a competitive 100-meter sprinter in high school came to her advantage during this ordeal, lending her the speed and endurance needed in this critical moment. They were teetering on the precipice of physical exhaustion. Driven by the spectre of impending doom, they sought refuge within the confines of their home, a desperate gambit to evade the storm that loomed on the horizon.

Zawadi's lithe frame proved advantageous as she manoeuvred through the labyrinthine corridors of her parent's room, swiftly slipping through the broken Crittal door. Her movements were fluid and elusive, reminiscent of a phantom haunting the shadowy recesses of the house, much like Tom in "Tom and Jerry". Concealed within the darkness, they evaded detection with the precision of seasoned fugitives.

Meanwhile, her brother's frantic footsteps echoed like a drumbeat, his voice a thunderous clarion call demanding her surrender. Amidst the cloak of darkness, Zawadi remained motionless; a statue shrouded in silence, her resolve unyielding confronting impending reckoning.

As Scarlett bore the brunt of their audacious escapade, enduring the stinging lash of her brother's retribution, Zawadi nestled amidst the cold embrace of the tiled floor, a solitary carton of noodles her makeshift pillow. The silent vigil of the night bore witness to her steadfast resolve, an unyielding determination to brave the tempest until the sanctuary of her mother's return offered a reprieve from the disruption of their reckless dalliance.

The virtue of Firyali before marriage cast an ethereal glow upon Zawadi's aspirations, a shimmering guiding light illuminating the path towards her envisioned nuptials. In a solemn pledge to her parents and Firyali, Zawadi vowed to safeguard her purity until the sacred exchange of vows.

Amidst the hallowed halls of boarding school and the hallowed precincts of academia, Zawadi remained steadfast in her convictions, reserving tender gestures solely for her love interest. Though beset by a storm of internal conflict, she steadfastly upheld her vow of abstinence, her resolve unshaken in the crucible of temptation.

FROM DARKNESS TO DAWN: ZAWADI'S JOURNEY THROUGH TRAUMA TO TRIUMPH

But the echoes of her past transgressions dissolved into insignificance as the stark reality of her present predicament engulfed her. Surrounded by assailants, her innocence ravaged in an act of unspeakable cruelty, Zawadi contended with a maelstrom of fear and powerlessness. Despite the steely fortitude her father and brothers instilled, she acknowledged the futility of resistance, reluctantly acquiescing to their vile machinations.

As her assailants collapsed in the wake of their iniquity, Zawadi moved urgently, staunchly concealing the crimson tide that trickled down her trembling limbs. Unaware of the true nature of her plight, she mistakenly attributed the bleeding to the onset of her menstrual cycle, fervently praying for respite before the crimson tide could swell to an uncontrollable deluge.

In a last-ditch attempt for freedom, Zawadi quickly pulled on her jeans, clutching her phone tightly in her trembling hand. With a determination hardened by hardship, she dashed into the night, a solitary figure navigating the maze-like streets of the embattled community. The familiar sights of her beloved neighbourhood twisted into a haunting scene of abandonment at this moment, a stark reminder of her profound disconnection from the sanctuary of her childhood memories.

Spotting a parked cab, Zawadi dashed towards it, urgency lacing her words as she pleaded, "Please, can you take me home?" She did her best to explain where home was, her voice quick and anxious, as she tried to convey the address to the driver amid her distress.

The cabbie's response sent a shiver down her spine, his words lingering ominously in the night air: " It costs a fortune. Do you know where you are, at all?"

Trembling, Zawadi whispered, "Soweto?"

Terrifying tales of this part of town flooded her mind, amplifying her fear – fear for her safety, fear of the unknown, fear of the horrors that awaited.

Zawadi's voice was desperate as she begged, "Sir, I have no cash on me. My phone's worth at least a grand; take it. I'll pay you and tip generously. Please, trust me. Otherwise, keep the phone."

As Zawadi hesitated at the cab's door, her heart raced uncertainly. Would her friends notice her absence at all? The lack of missed calls or messages on her phone sent a shiver down her spine, amplifying the fear gripping her soul. The memory of waiting in the club, vulnerable and alone, haunted her. The thought of someone spiking her drink lingered like a sinister shadow, casting doubt on her every move. Despite her homestay parents sharing similar values to her own, Zawadi couldn't shake the regret of her escape while they were away for the weekend.

Sinking into the cab's seat, Zawadi felt the weight of despair settles around her like a suffocating cloak. In the solitude of her room, she sought solace in painkillers, a futile attempt to numb the relentless ache gnawing at her core. The scalding water of the shower mirrored her desperation to cleanse herself of the shame, guilt, and trauma consuming her like a relentless tide.

As darkness descended, Zawadi curled up in bed, her tears staining the sheets as she grappled with the crippling sense of irreparable damage. Memories of feeling endangered at ten years old resurfaced, a stark reminder of her vulnerability in a world devoid of safety. Seeking guidance, she turned to a medical acquaintance under the guise of helping a friend in need.

"She should go to a sexual health clinic, get checked for any potential risks, and consider emergency contraception and post-exposure prophylaxis," he advised.

Cutting ties with friends who offered no support, Zawadi faced her ordeal alone, grappling with conflicting emotions as she toyed with the idea of seeking closure from the cabbie. The consuming thought drove her to believe reconnecting with him would somehow absolve her of guilt and convince her parents of her innocence.

Amidst the turmoil, Zawadi hoped that dawn would eventually break through the darkness. Determined to find strength in her suffering, she searched for a glimmer of silver amidst the shadows. The burden of her shattered innocence lifted from her shoulders like a weight being lifted, granting her a newfound sense of liberation from the unattainable ideals that once shackled her.

Expelled from her homestay, Zawadi was adrift in a sea of misunderstanding, battling anxiety as she struggled to adapt to her new surroundings.Longing for the familiarity of home, she confided in a pastor, finding solace in prayer and the promise of redemption through faith.

Determined to rebuild her life, Zawadi decided to marry, seeking solace in starting a family and leaving behind the sins of her past.Though her ordeal tarnished the mantle of purity, she embraced a life of abstinence, seeking absolution for the pain, guilt, and shame that haunted her. In search of a fresh start, Zawadi made her way to the United States, greeted by a few siblings eagerly awaiting her arrival.

Chapter Four

DADDY'S LITTLE GIRL

> *There is this girl who stole my heart and she calls me Daddy*
> **—Unknown**

Enlivened by her determination to earn her father's pride, Zawadi pursued academic excellence with unyielding resolve. In her pursuit, she stumbled upon a potent painkiller during her time in the States, offering relief from her chronic period pain. Despite its efficacy, the relentless bleeding persisted, leaving her weakened and weary. The question of why doctors hadn't recommended this solution earlier gnawed at her mind.

The rigors of medical school, particularly the unsettling encounters with blood and corpses, proved too much for Zawadi. Opting for law—a field where her family believed her argumentative skills would thrive—she faced escalating pain that disrupted her academic pursuits. As the elusive goal of achieving a first-class degree seemed to slip further from her grasp, each visit from Aunt Flo became more disruptive.

Taking a gap year to circumvent the typical postgraduate Catch-22—needing experience to land your first job, but being unable to get a job without experience—Zawadi applied to law firms. Guided by her mother's superstition that an itchy right hand foretells financial gain, she nervously awaited responses. To her astonishment, she secured a position at a prestigious law firm, igniting a spark of blessing and excitement.

During her internship, Zawadi triumphed by meeting challenging qualifications and experiencing a profound sense of accomplishment. Nonetheless, Aunt Flo persisted as an unwelcome disrupter, causing her to miss work and vital meetings. In a male-dominated industry, discussing periods remained taboo, leaving Zawadi unable to explain her frequent absences. Fearing judgment, she played the sick card too often, feeling like she was racing with a burden on her back, struggling to keep pace with her peers.

Zawadi's employer dashed her hopes as the one-year mark approached by failing to offer her a job upon graduation. Her plans

crumbled, leaving her heartbroken, rejected, and feeling inade-
quate. Despite giving her best effort, Aunt Flo seemed to cast a
shadow over her aspirations.

Feeling powerless as others thrived, Zawadi, typically a glass-
half-full person, sought solace in the positive aspects. She built
a healthy savings account for the home she hoped to make with
her prince charming.She also explored fancy restaurants during
her internship, showcasing her love for fine dining, finding some
consolation.

Yet, news of her father's worsening health—a cancer diagnosis—changed everything. Zawadi's dad received the diagnosis
during his visit to South Africa while she was still pursuing her
studies there. Determined to be by his side and nurse him to
health, she decided to take a break and return home. She sought
reassurance that her father could make everything okay despite
her disappointments in the United States.

With her father's reassuring words that all would be well, Zawadi gathered herself and returned to the United States to complete her program.

FRIDAY THE THIRTEENTH

The phone rang, and Zawadi's heart sank. Her mother's call at
this hour hinted at something serious. Unsure of what awaited
her, she hesitantly answered.

"Zawadi?" her mum said.

"Yes, Mum."

"Where are you?" her mum asked.

"I am on a road trip, Mum. Decided to get away for the weekend."

Mum's tone carried an unusual weight, signalling that the
news might not be ordinary.

"Please stay strong after what I'm about to tell you."

"OK, Mum. I'm listening," Zawadi replied. Foreboding crept over her as her mother uttered the words she feared.

"Your dad just passed."

The words pierced through Zawadi's heart, leaving her breathless and shattered.Her dad had left Kenya as a passenger for treatment, but now he would return as cargo, as he had to be buried in his home country.

"Stand strong, Zawadi," her mum said. "I will call you later."

"OK, Mum. Are you OK?" Zawadi asked.

"I'm fine. I'll call you later."

"OK, Mum."

The phone call ended, leaving Zawadi struggling to come to terms with the sudden loss.Her mother's resilience was remarkable, but Zawadi knew the toll her father's illness had taken on her. The news was devastating.

Zawadi's father, formerly a vibrant and influential African pioneer, was accustomed to hosting kings, queens, and dignitaries. Yet, his relentless commitment to his vast and weighty vision left him little time to savour life's pleasures. Zawadi wished he could have enjoyed the fruits of his labour and appreciated life as the lover of joy he was.

Watching her father's decline into a mere shadow of his former self was heart-wrenching for Zawadi. A man who had been robust and larger than life became emaciated, losing the ability to carry out essential functions. As his health deteriorated rapidly, the family made the heartbreaking decision to capture a poignant family photo during Zawadi's last visit home. Including all the children and in-laws they gathered around him, their faces etched with both sorrow and love, seeking to preserve his memory for eternity. Despite the gravity of the moment, Zawadi's mother meticulously made adjustments to present him as dignified as possible, as he faded away before their eyes. Each click of the camera shutter captured not just a moment frozen in time but the profound bond of a family united in both joy and sorrow.

Her father, often quoted as saying, "Something must kill a man. I don't need rest; I'll find rest in death. There will be plenty of time then," found solace in his acceptance of life's inevitable end. Embracing his philosophy with stoic resolve, he faced each day with unwavering courage, refusing to succumb to despair confronting his declining health. His unwavering acceptance was a beacon of strength and resilience, inspiring those around him to cherish every moment and live life to the fullest, in the shadow of mortality. Zawadi, though grieving, took comfort in the belief that he could now rest in peace. She prayed that his earthly struggles would earn him a heavenly crown.

The phone slipped onto Zawadi's carry-on bag nestled between her legs. Resting her head on the seat before her, she sought refuge to conceal her emotions. She listened to Beyoncé's "Ego" on repeat on her iPod, drawing parallels between the song's celebration of confidence and how she saw her father — a man of immense strength and unwavering pride. The beat offered a brief escape from the torrent of painful emotions as tears flowed uncontrollably. With another ten hours left on the bus journey and it being the middle of the night, returning to university was not an option. At pit stops, her eyes locked with those of other passengers, yet no words were exchanged, except for a man who walked past and gently squeezed Zawadi's shoulder—a silent gesture of solidarity, even as he remained oblivious to the specifics of her struggle.

Recollections of her father's promises flooded her thoughts. At ten, he had assured her of a future filled with success and happiness. His commitment to funding her education to the highest level and sending her anywhere she desired had forged a sense of security. As Daddy's little girl, she had pledged to make him proud. But at this point, the anticipated moments of his witnessing her graduation, walking her down the aisle, and providing for her future were irreversibly lost.

Her father's absence, who had always been her steadfast supporter, created a profound void. She had worked hard for years in school, aiming for his acknowledgement with a proud "Well done, Zawadi!" At this moment, that acknowledgment would forever remain an echo in her memories. The gaping hole left in her life begged the question of whether anyone could ever fill that void left by her father.

With brothers dispersed across different US cities, their lives busy with families and assisting their mother, Zawadi sought solace in a late-night call to her best friend, Ruhiu. Their friendship blossomed during her visit to Kenya for her brother's wedding. After their initial meeting during the Thanksgiving service, Zawadi had entrusted him with her purse, a test of character that he passed admirably.

Ruhiu, having experienced grief himself, became her pillar of support. Through long daily conversations and his unwavering presence during her father's funeral in Kenya, he proved to be the friend she needed. Their unbreakable bond offered Zawadi comfort during her darkest hours.

Ruhiu may not have replaced her father, but he provided a sturdy shoulder to lean on during Zawadi's darkest moments. As she bid farewell to her first love, her father, during the solemn procession behind the casket, a friend from high school reached out to hold her hand. In that moment, the friend's words and presence were a timely source of strength, offering solace amidst the overwhelming grief. As Zawadi held her father's stone-cold hands for the last time, she whispered her final goodbye, a poignant tribute to the man who had been her pillar of support throughout her life.

"Adieu, Daddy. I hold your memory close, wrapped in the echoes of the pet names you lovingly bestowed upon me. Mum carries those endearing monikers presently, embodying the warmth you instilled in our home. Our promise, forged in moments of laughter and shared dreams, remains etched in my heart, and I am steadfast in honoring my part of the pact.

I am determined to carve a path of success, a legacy reflecting your pride in our family name. With each step forward, I aim to build a life that others will admire, reflecting the values you instilled in me. As I embark on this journey, your spirit guides me, a silent presence urging me to reach greater heights.

Though you may be gone, your love remains an enduring beacon, lighting the way as I navigate life's twists and turns. Until we meet again, know that your legacy lives on in the footsteps I tread and the dreams I chase. Farewell, Daddy, and thank you for the gift of your unwavering love."

Chapter Five

THIRSTY

> *In recent black and internet slang, "thirsty" describes a graceless need for approval, affection, or attention, so raw that it creeps people out. Thirst signifies a fundamental unmet need and the sheer desperation to satisfy the need for something or someone. The word is used in a derogatory way, indicating that someone is overreaching.*
> **—Unknown**

As Ruhiu's eyes blinked uncontrollably, he reached for his drink and slurped for longer than usual before finally gathering the courage to speak.

"Are you sure?" he asked, his voice tinged with uncertainty.

"Of course!" Zawadi replied with unwavering determination.

She had just asked him to marry her, and his hesitation was palpable.

"But I don't know if I can afford a wedding or if your family would accept me," Ruhiu confessed, his doubts evident in his tone.

"Why don't you leave that to me?" Zawadi responded reassuringly. "All you need to do is get the ring, and then the life we always wished for can finally become a reality. You shared with me the experience of missing having a family and sitting alone in your room with a bottle of Coke the day you graduated, with no one to celebrate with you. It would bring me immense joy to compensate for the lost time, considering all the trauma you faced as a child, losing both parents at such a young age. We both deserve happiness and solace at this point in our lives. Won't you agree?"

"Of course," Ruhiu answered, grinning with excitement and terror, evident in his expression as they clinked their glasses, sealing the deal.

A week after the funeral, Zawadi and Ruhiu went out for lunch. Ruhiu was shaking and seemed to have bugs in his pants, sweating profusely despite the cool air-conditioned room. Zawadi knew something was amiss, and then she noticed his leg gradually lowering to the floor.

"Baby, I promise to be your rock," he said, his voice trembling with emotion. "I would never let anyone come between us. Believe anything about me, but never believe anyone who says I betray this love we share. You are the one I want for the rest of my life. We will ride and die together, just like Bonnie and Clyde. We will have a beautiful family, make loads of money, and see the world. Nothing will be able to come between us. You are my home, and I am yours. You have my heart, my body, and my soul. Let's make it official. Zawadi, will you marry me?"

Zawadi wrestled with a surge of uncertainty, questioning whether her idea of marriage was born out of genuine desire or a desperate attempt to fill the void her father's absence had left behind. Committing to Ruhiu triggered an inner conflict between her longing for familial stability and the fear of rushing into a decision driven by emotional neediness.

For years, Zawadi and Ruhiu had navigated their relationship and found a comfortable equilibrium, keeping their connection rooted in friendship. Ruhiu persistently desired to elevate their bond, but Zawadi's hesitation always met his advances. As marriage loomed ahead, she stood at a crossroads, torn between the familiarity of their existing dynamic and the uncharted territory of matrimony.

Recalling her pastor's counsel on marrying one's best friend as a key to enduring matrimony, Zawadi sought solace in the foundation of their companionship. Ruhiu had been a constant in her life, a confidant through joys and sorrows. Amidst the uncertainty, she convinced herself their love could blossom into a lasting union.

Suppressing her doubts, Zawadi attributed her apprehension to mere cold feet, a natural response to the enormity of the decision. Despite the impending change, she reassured herself that their lives wouldn't drastically differ from the harmonious existence they had cultivated thus far. In thinking this, she pushed aside the nagging question of whether her motives were genuine or driven by a desperate need for stability.

In this delicate dance of emotions, Zawadi chose to silence the inner turmoil, allowing the anticipation of a shared future to override her lingering doubts. As she embraced Ruhiu's proposal, she clung to the belief that their friendship, which had withstood time, would be the bedrock for a successful marriage.

She said, "Yes!"

FRIENDS TO FIANCÉS

They had transitioned from friends to fiancés, a journey marked not just by a change in their relationship status but by the deepening of their understanding and commitment to each other. This evolution from friendship to a romantic partnership underscored the strong foundation they had built together—rooted in mutual respect, shared experiences, and a profound connection.

As friends, they had learned about each other's quirks, supported one another through challenges, and celebrated successes together. These experiences, which had woven a rich tapestry of trust and companionship, became the bedrock upon which they built their future engagement. Now, as fiancés, they were poised to merge their lives even more intimately, planning not just a wedding but a life together filled with dreams, goals, and shared aspirations.

The transition also brought new dynamics and responsibilities into their relationship, prompting discussions about deeper subjects such as family planning, financial goals, and personal aspirations. Each conversation, while sometimes challenging, reinforced their bond and highlighted the importance of maintaining open communication, a trait they had cultivated during their friendship.

This natural progression from friends to fiancés enriched their relationship, making their engagement not just a formal commitment to marry but a celebration of a partnership that had already proven resilient and fulfilling. As they prepared for marriage, they cherished the unique path that had led them here, knowing that their strong friendship would continue to be the cornerstone of their union.

They hugged, cried, and kissed. Having Ruhiu by her side for a lifetime was what she needed, and she was over the moon. Filled with euphoria, Zawadi went home and shared the exciting news with her mum and siblings who were around. She thought they would be happy that she was getting the extra support she needed to get her through the grief. In the aftermath of the funeral, she grappled with the notion that there might never be a perfect time to share the news of her impending marriage. The weight of grief hung heavily in the air. Still, she felt compelled to seize the moment before returning to the United States. She wanted to deliver the announcement in person and proudly showcase the modest yet meaningful ring Ruhiu had given her.

LOVE UNDER SCRUTINY: ZAWADI'S STRUGGLE FOR FAMILIAL ACCEPTANCE

Zawadi's ring, though not opulent, held an unparalleled value in her heart. Ruhiu, having just secured his first job after university, offered it as a symbol of commitment that transcended material wealth. With the anticipation of her family's support, given their conduct as friends and her commitment to maintaining her innocence, Zawadi believed the revelation would elicit joy and encouragement.

To her dismay, the family's reaction was far from what she expected. Disappointment etched across their faces, and doubts lingered about Ruhiu's intentions. Firyali, whom Zawadi held in high esteem, delivered a cutting remark that shattered her expectations, questioning the significance of the "small ring" from a "small boy".

This unexpected response hit Zawadi like a ton of bricks. She had hoped for validation and praise from Firyali, anticipating her commitment to a secure relationship would be celebrated. Instead, the harsh reality thrust her into a profound depression, accentuating her melancholic temperament and amplifying her persistently low mood. She carried a long face throughout her trip, a visible manifestation of the emotional turmoil she was grappling with. This gloomy cloud hung over her until she returned to the United States to resume her undergraduate studies.

Zawadi's frustration escalated into emotional outbursts in the following months as she defiantly asserted that Ruhiu was her ideal partner. She threatened to run away if her family denied her wish to marry him. Drawing parallels to her parents' humble beginnings that eventually led to prosperity, she questioned why her family couldn't envision a similar trajectory for her and Ruhiu.

BEYOND DREAMS AND DOUBTS: ZAWADI'S PATH TO LOVE AND LEARNING

As Zawadi navigated the emotional turmoil, she clung to the belief that her love and commitment, coupled with Ruhiu's genuine intentions, would eventually win over her family's approval. Reconciling her aspirations for marital bliss with familial expectations became an arduous test of her resilience and determination.

Despite Aunt Flo's persistent predicaments, Zawadi's determination to establish a solid foundation for her future home with Ruhiu burned brightly. Her aspiration to mitigate his potential financial shortcomings by excelling academically, securing a promising job, and facilitating Ruhiu's relocation to the United

States fuelled her drive. Beyond her aspirations, she saw her achievements as a tribute to her late father and a promise fulfilled.

Doctors presented a unique approach, suggesting that Zawadi consider having a baby as a solution to her health problems. Though that was not an immediate option, the doctors administered quarterly contraceptive injections as respite, granting her the freedom to pursue her dreams unhindered.

Zawadi's heart overflowed with gratitude for the unwavering belief her older sister Kioni's fiancé had in her capabilities. Her academic journey reached its pinnacle with first-class honours in law, followed by a master's degree in entrepreneurship. These accomplishments not only established her as a trailblazer but also shattered barriers within her African family. Standing proudly as the first among her siblings to graduate with first-class honours, Zawadi left an indelible mark as a beacon of educational achievement, pioneering the path for her family as its first generation of educated members.

Despite initial reservations, Zawadi's family gradually softened their resistance to her marriage aspirations. Reluctantly, they acknowledged her success thus far and believed she had applied her critical thinking skills to the decision to marry Ruhiu. Without their awareness, her singular focus on academia and her limited social exposure veiled a subtle naivety that would complicate her path to matrimony and affect her judgment.

This concealed naivety, masked by her academic brilliance, emerged as a significant hurdle to navigating the intricacies of marriage. The road ahead promised moments in which Zawadi's intellect would clash with emotional complexities she had not yet navigated, turning the journey towards matrimony into an unexpected voyage of self-discovery and deepening her connection with Ruhiu.

Excitement surged as Zawadi received her family's blessing, marking the beginning of a joyous chapter in her and Ruhiu's lives. The looming prospect of ending their long-distance relationship added to the anticipation. Wedding arrangements were set in motion, blending legal, spiritual, and social elements. They gave notice of their intent to marry at the local registrar, engaged in pre-marital counselling at their church, and captured their love in a a pre-wedding photoshoot. The photos were meant to be shared on social platforms, used for personalisation on wedding favours for the guests, and prominently featured on the wedding program. As Zawadi began exploring this uncharted territory, her family's approval carried the weight of unspoken expectations. The contrast between her academic prowess and veiled naivety set the stage for a complex journey towards marriage, testing her adaptability and compelling her to harmonise idealised visions with the multifaceted realities of married life.

A crucial decision emerged as Zawadi stopped taking injections a year before the wedding, in anticipation of starting a family with Ruhiu. The ensuing six months of continuous bleeding challenged her resolve, yet the doctors' assurances ultimately proved valid as her periods normalised.

The forthcoming fairy-tale wedding became a collaborative labor of love, with her mother and Firyali investing their discerning taste and meticulous attention to detail to ensure a cherished celebration. Having conquered academic feats and familial hurdles, Zawadi embraced the impending marriage with hope and unwavering optimism. However, her aunt Nadia's request for a private sit-down that night, once the guests had departed, cast a shadow of anxiety over her. The aunt's stern demeanour and the timing of the discussion made Zawadi apprehensive about the nature of the conversation, stirring a mix of unease and curiosity.

Chapter Six

FOUR WEDDINGS

> *Home is the starting place of love, hope, and dreams.*
> **—Unknown**

Before her wedding, Zawadi embarked on a Daniel Fast, adhering to a strict vegan regimen that excluded animal products, processed foods, caffeine, and alcohol for twenty-one days. With her heart set on a union sanctified by her parents, spiritually endorsed, and validated by church tenets and societal norms, she envisioned a vivid tapestry of life unfolding. Amid the jubilant celebration of impending matrimony, the vision of settling into their future abode, either graced by a serene white picket fence or fortified by a sturdy iron fence in Africa, symbolised the triumphant realisation of Zawadi's meticulously crafted vision for a prosperous life. The transition from love to marriage and the anticipation of nurturing a family mirrored

the age-old adage: "First comes love, then comes marriage, then comes the baby in the baby carriage."

Zawadi and Ruhiu's wedding celebration comprised four ceremonies:

- ⚕ "The Introduction"
- ⚕ The Traditional African Wedding ("Trad"), where Ruhiu's family paid the bride's price to Zawadi's family.
- ⚕ The Civil Ceremony
- ⚕ The Enchanting White Wedding

TALES BY MOONLIGHT

On the eve of the white wedding, Zawadi's aunt Nadia, a custodian of conventional wisdom, delivered advice steeped in societal expectations, emphasising obedience to her husband and upkeep of the household regardless of the challenges. This counsel stirred deep conflicts within Zawadi, as her aunt also offered her the chance to back out, assuring her of support. Caught between tradition and her personal beliefs, Zawadi found herself on the brink of a transformative journey of resilience, self-discovery, and the pursuit of her truth.

That night, haunted by her aunt's words, Zawadi's mind reeled with flashbacks of Ruhiu's controlling behaviour during an encounter with a childhood friend. His overreaction had escalated to forcibly removing her to her sister's house, where she wept herself to sleep. This incident prompted Zawadi to reassess their joint religious engagements, particularly their participation in the Sunday evening music service affectionately known as Jaz, where they donned matching t-shirts as a symbol of their unity and devotion. Though they eventually reconciled following Ruhiu's apologetic gesture, the fallout from the episode left a profound impact on Zawadi. It tested her resilience and commitment, forcing her to confront the fragility of their relationship. Despite the turmoil, Zawadi ultimately chose forgiveness, viewing the incident as a momentary lapse rather than a permanent rift.

From her childhood, separation anxiety had insidiously woven itself into Zawadi's life, manifesting in physical symptoms like trembling hands, shortness of breath, and a pervasive sense of dread. These symptoms intensified as major life events loomed, especially her wedding, often misunderstood by those around her but reflective of her profound internal struggle.

HARMONY AND DISCORD: ZAWADI'S WEDDING DAY OF JOY AND JITTERS

On the eve of their white wedding, after the traditional ceremony, Zawadi discreetly left her parents' house to practice a surprise song for Ruhiu, hoping to create a joyous memory. However, her efforts were overshadowed when she spotted Ruhiu and his friends dismissively eating at a fast-food restaurant, still in their heavily adorned wedding regalia. Their casual disregard for the sanctity of the day, combined with Ruhiu's unfounded complaints about the wedding food and doubts about her capabilities as a wife, deeply wounded Zawadi. Watching them indulge carelessly while she prepared to pour her heart into a performance meant to celebrate their union left her feeling abandoned and humiliated.

The narrative of their wedding unfolded with intricate details: pink rose bouquets and petals imported from South Africa adorned each table, a live band serenaded the guests, and a choreographed dance by the bridal party captivated all. Zawadi's heartfelt rendition of Beyoncé's "Dangerously in Love" was a highlight, though initially overshadowed by Ruhiu's impulsive act of sweeping her off her feet, which later turned into a touching, joyous gesture as the couple settled back into their celebration. In this magical moment, Zawadi disclosed that the song was behind her seemingly suspicious moves before the wedding. Her revelation dispelled any lingering suspicions Ruhiu may have harboured about her actions. In the middle of the euphoria and celebration, they shared a tender moment that momentarily erased the tensions that had preceded their union.

Zawadi's stepping out of her comfort zone, especially considering her shy nature, added a layer of significance to the performance. Singing in the choir from a young age had not fully prepared her for the vulnerable situation of rendering such a personal and emotional song in front of a large audience. It stood as a poignant expression of love, a gesture that transcended her usual reserve, and it marked a unique and memorable moment in their wedding celebration.

The weeklong festivities, resembling a joyful festival, featured daily parties, including the hen do and bachelorette eve, each resonating with diverse food and drink. The culmination of Zawadi and Ruhiu's union offered the new bride a profound respite from the persistent separation anxiety that had haunted her for years. The "Mr and Mrs" title, bestowed upon them by the pastor, fulfilled her longing for belonging and rootedness. Yet, despite this joyous occasion, Zawadi was constrained by her shyness.

As the moment arrived to seal her vows with a customary and celebratory kiss, she hesitated, aware of all her guests' eyes, including the pastor's, upon her. This moment of vulnerability, though challenging for her, added a layer of authenticity to the ceremony.It reminded that despite the grandeur of the celebration, Zawadi remained true to herself, navigating the delicate balance between tradition and personal comfort.

As the village women performed the customary village tradition, the final rite involved handing over Zawadi to Ruhiu, with the community carrying her suitcases on their head as a symbolic gesture that ushered her into Ruhiu's home. These suitcases contained traditional wrappers from the women's club her father supported, intended for her to sew into freeform, comfortable formal attire in anticipation of potential pregnancy. A tumult of emotions overwhelmed Zawadi; tears marred what should have been a joyous occasion. This act by the village women held profound significance, symbolizing not only her permanent detachment from her father's house but also her formal union with her husband. Tradition stipulated that this union could only be reversed by death, at which point her husband's family would return her to her father's house. The deeply ingrained weight of these cultural rites intensified Zawadi's emotions, adding layers of solemnity to what was meant to be a celebratory journey.

WEDDING WHIRLWIND: A NIGHT OF MIXED EMOTIONS FOR ZAWADI

The wedding night, designed to be the pinnacle of the weeklong festivities, unfolded with a bittersweet tone as Aunt Flo made an untimely appearance. The celebrations, steeped in cultural richness and familial traditions, collided with the unsettling realisation that Zawadi was stepping into a lifelong commitment with a man who had displayed red flags both during their dating period and after the traditional wedding. This sobering realisation cast a shadow over the joyous atmosphere, stirring a profound sense of unease within Zawadi. The weight of her emotions found an outlet in tears as the contrast between the cultural exuberance surrounding her and the private apprehensions within her heart became starkly apparent.

The clash between the outward festivities and the internal turmoil painted a complex picture of emotions on a night meant to mark the joyous union of two lives. Her anxiety previously believed to have been banished forever, surprisingly resurfaced, challenging the narrative she had constructed for herself throughout the elaborate ceremony. Somewhere in her heart, Zawadi harbored the sinking feeling that she had made the biggest mistake of her life, a sentiment worsened by the realization that she would have to live with its consequences indefinitely. Amidst her confusion and internal turmoil, she managed to maintain her composure, silently praying that her suspicions were unfounded and that her distressing thoughts and feelings would soon pass.

HAPPY NEVER AFTER

Days after the wedding, Zawadi contended with post-event blues. The silence of her phone, which previously rang incessantly, and the absence of the anticipated high after saying "I do" left her frustrated and questioning the stark contrast between reality and the romanticised fantasies she had harboured.

Zawadi's world began to shatter two weeks after the wedding, as the violent intrusion of someone with a gun to her head, exposing her and her husband's vulnerability in an unsafe neighborhood, abruptly awakened her from her newlywed dreams. The theft of her wedding ring marked the beginning of a nightmare that shattered the illusion of the honeymoon phase. Her mother, silent with a look of confirmation, took charge, initiating plans to relocate the couple to a safer part of town, belying the celebratory atmosphere of the lavish wedding attended by hundreds of well-wishers.

A BRUTAL AWAKENING

Ruhiu's sudden and drastic behavioural shift plunged Zawadi deeper into a disorienting reality. Demanding to be addressed as "Lord," citing biblical references, and enforcing servile practices, Ruhiu's preferences oscillated unpredictably, leaving Zawadi in constant confusion. From body image preferences to inappropriate remarks, Ruhiu's inconsistent desires eroded Zawadi's sense of self, leaving her feeling disconnected and unattractive.

The compliance with washing Ruhiu's feet and the distressing act of bleaching her skin to align with his preferences became a symbolic struggle for Zawadi. A few weeks after the wedding, the tension reached a harrowing climax in the confined space of the car, and the dark clouds of violence followed the couple into the bedroom upon their return home.

In a nightmarish escalation, Zawadi grappled desperately to shield her face as Ruhiu, adorned with his wedding ring on the left hand and other rings on the right, subjected her to a brutal barrage of slaps. Each strike echoed the emphatic assertion of his authority as her husband, a stark contrast to the love and partnership that marriage should embody. The symbol of their eternal union became a weapon. The sacred space meant to symbolise unity had turned into a battleground of pain and fear, leaving Zawadi shattered and questioning the foundations of her once-cherished dreams.

In the aftermath of her ordeal, Zawadi was in a desolate state with bloodshot eyes, a broken pinkie finger, and overwhelming pain coursing through her body. Curled up in a fetal position on the bed, she sobbed, the pillow soaked with her tears and snot. Amid her despair, she reached out to the memory of her late father, muttering his name in a desperate plea for solace.

As her eyes struggled to open, she surveyed the room around her. Each item she had meticulously selected and shipped from the United States, with months spent reviewing colours and patterns, was meant to create a beautiful and cosy home for their family. Yet, instead of being comfortable, the space felt like a hellhole—a stark contrast to her imagined picturesque vision.

ECHOES OF DOUBT: ZAWADI'S TURBULENT JOURNEY INTO MARRIAGE

As Zawadi wrestled with doubts about her self-worth and the viability of the relationship, memories of past trauma, including her sister's slamming a door against her fingers, haunted her. The echoes of her father's absence intensified her emotional turmoil, prompting questions about the strength she believed she possessed. In this moment of profound despair, she questioned whether her perceived strength was a mask for an underlying weakness. Completely drained and unable to see a way out of the tumultuous situation, Zawadi stood at a crossroads, confronted by the harsh realities of her marriage and the formidable tests ahead.

The haunting melody of "Dangerously in Love" that Zawadi had passionately sung during their wedding echoed with a sour tune at this moment, mirroring the ominous undertones that had stealthily invaded her life, love, happiness, and marriage. Caught within the unraveling nightmare, entangled in its web, Zawadi struggled with her situation.

The symbolic act of performing a Beyoncé song during the wedding, a gesture meant to celebrate love and commitment, took on a cruel irony at this moment. The sweet notes that formerly resonated with the promise of a blissful union seemed like a distant echo at this moment, drowned out by the dissonance of a relationship marred by violence, control, and shattered dreams. Amid the dissonance between the song's original intent and the harsh reality of her experiences, Zawadi stood at a crossroads, wrestling with the need to redefine her understanding of love, strength, and self-worth.

Zawadi, formerly a believer in the strength of her and Ruhiu's unique connection,now faced the stark reality that her marriage was dangerously veering off course at this moment. The idyllic visions of family, love, and rootedness she had longed for gave way to the harsh realisation that life had trapped her in a cycle of pain and uncertainty.

Her late period became an unexpected focal point, prompting her to open the "*Flo*" app on her phone. As Aunt Flo delayed her arrival, Zawadi stood at the crossroads, wrestling with many questions and an uncertain future. The echoes of her father's absence, the shattered dreams of a blissful marriage, and the stark realities of her present circumstance converged in a poignant moment of reflection. The strength that had sustained her through trials faced a formidable test at this moment. The questions loomed large, and the journey ahead seemed fraught with uncertainty.

Chapter Seven

A VIRTUOUS WOMAN

A wife of noble character who can find?
—Proverbs 31:10 (NIV)

Amid a tumultuous journey alongside Ruhiu, Zawadi found solace in the timeless wisdom of Proverbs 31:10–31, a passage extolling the virtues of a noble and capable wife. These verses celebrated the qualities of a woman worth far more than rubies, emphasising her industrious nature, commitment to her family, entrepreneurial spirit, wisdom, and kindness.

Upon Ruhiu losing his job, Zawadi encountered a critical juncture. She confronted a daunting decision: Should she stand by Ruhiu amidst financial struggles or return to the familiar confines of the United States to support the family through work? Drawing inspiration from the virtuous woman described in Proverbs, who worked diligently with eager hands, considered business opportunities, and brought prosperity to her family, Zawadi saw it as her turn to rise to the occasion.

Since Aunt Flo returned after a couple of months since their altercation, she deemed it the best time to set up the financial structure for the family before committing to raising a child. With determination and resolve, Zawadi embarked on a journey of entrepreneurship, exploring various business opportunities and strategising to bring prosperity to her family. Despite the challenges and uncertainties ahead, she remained steadfast in her commitment to supporting Ruhiu and building a secure future for their family.

Armed with entrepreneurial skills inherited from her mother, who had previously supported the family during her father's business setbacks, Zawadi made the difficult choice to return to the United States. Despite limited resources, she remained resolute in navigating the system and striving to raise capital for Ruhiu's business, guided by the ideals of the virtuous woman.

Yet, this decision was not without its challenges. Immigration barriers initially prevented Ruhiu from accompanying her, while her mother opposed the separation, fearing it might set a precedent for other women. Yet, Zawadi remained steadfast in honouring the promises and vows made with Ruhiu, while she concealed the abuse from her mother. The decision to go overseas offered her both space to contemplate and an opportunity to work on their relationship, yet it also reignited her separation anxiety.

FOUR MUSKETEERS:
A TALE OF UNITY AND ADVENTURE

In Zawadi's journey to America, the quartet known affectionately as the "*four musketeers*" formed an unbreakable bond that would weather the storms of change and challenge. Sharing a room with her three stalwart companions became not just a matter of convenience, but a testament to the resilience and camaraderie that defined their collective journey.

Nabby, the linchpin of their quartet, emerged as a beacon of unwavering support in the face of uncertainty. Despite grappling with her own financial limitations, Nabby's generosity knew no bounds, extending even to covering Zawadi's hair expenses—a gesture fuelled by her daily walks to work, a testament to her determination and solidarity. Their shared struggles forged a bond that transcended circumstance, weaving a tapestry of friendship and fortitude that would shape their destinies in ways they could never have imagined.

Fuelled by her determination to contribute to their shared dreams, Zawadi toiled tirelessly to send money home to Ruhiu. She also invested her inheritance from her father into Ruhiu's business, as the couple envisioned building their dream empire step by step. Zawadi's willingness to sacrifice for their shared vision epitomised her unwavering commitment to their future.

LOVE & IVF: ZAWADI AND RUHIU'S
JOURNEY AGAINST THE ODDS

Over the ensuing two years, Zawadi's routine mirrored her days in boarding school as she scrimped and saved to visit home every quarter. Her and Ruhiu's focus remained on maximising their time together to forge the life they had envisioned. Yet, the absence of the joyous cry of a newborn cast a shadow over their journey.

Amidst suspicions and intensified scrutiny, Zawadi wrestled with infertility. Pregnancy-like symptoms during IVF treatment exacerbated speculation, yet despite doctors confirming no issues, societal pressure drove the couple to undergo a series of IVFs. The strain on their relationship persisted, as did the pressure to conceive, weighing heavily on Zawadi.

The journey through fertility treatments marked a period of emotional and physical exhaustion for Zawadi. The relentless societal expectations and scrutiny became overwhelming, prompting Zawadi and Ruhiu to confront the challenges they faced. As they embarked on this arduous path, the strength of their bond and Zawadi's unwavering commitment to building a life with Ruhiu remained steadfast. The pursuit of a family became a demonstration of their enduring love and resilience.

Zawadi's journey through infertility was a harrowing battle against societal expectations, judgment, and the harsh realities of her medical condition. The ultimatum of "Get pregnant or die" underscored the weight of social pressure, overshadowing her accomplishments and her dreams of starting a family. Her body became a battleground, with five years of marriage and four failed IVF cycles leaving emotional and physical scars on both her and Ruhiu.

BEYOND THE PAIN: ZAWADI'S BOLD JOURNEY TO MOTHERHOOD

At this point , Zawadi had endured excruciating pain and humiliating bleeding for 20 years, but she persevered because she longed to create a sanctuary—a place to call her own in this unforgiving world, and to affirm her worth as a woman. Life has stripped her of many things: dreams, hopes, and aspirations. Yet, it will not rob her of her chance to start a family.

The ordeal of infertility has laid Zawadi bare, forcing her to confront her deepest vulnerabilities under the relentless scrutiny of the public eye. She has no choice but to wage this private battle in full view of a society rife with questions and prying eyes. The relentless gaze of the "womb watchers" haunts her as they would not let her breathe, demanding that she fulfill her role and pay her dues to the world as a woman.

The theories people created to explain her predicament ranged from her having damaged her womb through abortion to the spiritual theft of her children. Each judgment contributed to the mockery she faced.

The contradiction surrounding fertility issues was a poignant testament to society's skewed perceptions of illness and support. While individuals grappling with diseases like kidney failure or other ailments often receive overwhelming empathy and assistance, the narrative shifts drastically when it comes to reproductive health.

Zawadi keenly observed this dichotomy as her journey unfolded, facing a stark contrast in the reactions of those around her. Where others might receive compassion and understanding for illnesses beyond their control, the realm of reproductive health seemed shrouded in judgment and stigma. Instead of finding solace and support, individuals like Zawadi often encountered skepticism and blame, their struggles dismissed or diminished in the eyes of society.

If Zawadi has a girl, society expects her to have a boy to carry on the family name.

If she has a boy, society expects her to have a girl to complete the picture-perfect family.

If she's blessed with one of each, the pressure mounts to add another, "just in case."

And if she has no children, she might as well be dead.

For Zawadi, the prospect of pregnancy was a portal, one that led to a life imbued with deep meaning and purpose. This anticipated transformation into motherhood was envisioned as a pivotal experience, promising to enrich her existence with layers of significance previously unimagined. It was more than the biological act of carrying new life; it was a spiritual journey, a rite of passage that offered to redefine her understanding of love, strength, and connection. This journey was seen as an opportunity to nurture not just a child, but her own soul, allowing her to explore the vast depths of her capacity for care, resilience, and profound joy. Pregnancy was to be the beginning of a richer, more fulfilling chapter, where the act of creating life was intertwined with the discovery of life's true essence.

Five years into her marriage, Zawadi faced a daunting medical diagnosis that reshaped her understanding of her body and her future. She was diagnosed with stage 4 endometriosis, stage 4 adenomyosis, and fibroids, which together wrought havoc on her health and left her battling severe anemia. These conditions, which she wryly nicknamed her "three little friends"—Endo, Adeno, and Frys—posed formidable obstacles to her dreams and severely impacted her quality of life.

Despite these challenges, there was an ironic twist in her medical assessments. A doctor, upon examining her, remarked that she had a "beautiful womb." This comment, meant to be reassuring, contrasted sharply with the reality of her situation. The beauty of her womb belied the pain and dysfunction caused by her conditions, underscoring the complexity of her health challenges.

The lack of an early diagnosis had allowed her symptoms to worsen unchecked, leading to prolonged suffering. By the time the full extent of her conditions was understood, the prognosis was bleak: the doctors warned that any potential pregnancy would likely end in miscarriage. This news was a devastating blow to Zawadi, who had to reconcile her dreams of motherhood with the harsh realities of her health.

The impact of these conditions extended beyond the reproductive tract, with endometrial tissue spreading to various organs, including the kidneys, liver, ovaries, urinary tract, and anal region. The chronic nature of endometriosis and adenomyosis meant that Zawadi faced severe symptoms throughout her body, including pain, fatigue, infertility, and organ damage.

Faced with this grim reality, Zawadi decided to undergo surgery in the United States to alleviate some of the symptoms. The doctors promised high chances of conception afterwards, marking the final hurdle in her and Ruhiu's fertility journey. Their separation during this time was intended not just for her health but also to provide space for their strained relationship. Zawadi planned to pursue a second master's degree to increase her earning potential and alleviate the financial burden on her family.

Zawadi's odyssey through the annals of time unveiled the profound narratives of special children, etched both in sacred scriptures and the tapestry of history. Amidst the tumult of her own soul, she found solace and kinship in the trials and triumphs of women who had traversed similar paths before her.

The tale of Sarah, whose laughter resonated within ancient tents upon cradling her long-awaited son, Isaac, struck a chord deep within Zawadi's being. Like Sarah, she carried the burden of unfulfilled dreams, yet dared to cling to hope for a miracle beyond her reach.

Hannah's fervent prayers, rising like fragrant incense to the heavens, stirred a symphony of longing within Zawadi's spirit. She could sense the tears of barren lands mingling with her own, their collective plea for a child reverberating through the corridors of time. And in the appointed hour, just as Hannah had, Zawadi poured out her heart in prayer, trusting in the assurance of answered petitions.

The saga of Elizabeth, once barren and forsaken, resonated deeply with Zawadi's soul. The miraculous birth of John the Baptist stood as a testament to the divine ability to breathe life into the darkest shadows of despair. In Elizabeth's jubilant embrace of her long-awaited son, Zawadi discovered a renewed sense of hope for her own journey through infertility.

As Zawadi navigated the labyrinth of her struggles, she clung to these narratives as lifelines amidst the tempest. Each word, each verse, served as a guiding light through the darkest nights of her soul.

Drawing inspiration from the pages of scripture, Zawadi found resonance in the story of Joseph, born to Rachel after years of longing and anticipation. Joseph's arrival brought boundless joy to his parents and propelled him to become a prominent figure in Egyptian history, a beacon of hope amid famine-stricken lands.

In the annals of history, Zawadi discovered solace in the example of Helen Keller, a remarkable soul who surmounted the challenges of deafness and blindness to become a beacon of light and inspiration. Adopted as a child, Helen's life epitomised the transformative power of love and resilience, instilling within Zawadi a newfound determination to persevere in her own journey.

As Zawadi whispered prayers of surrender in the hushed moments of solitude, she entrusted her deepest longings to the One who holds the cosmos in His grasp. For she knew that her narrative, intertwined with those of Sarah, Hannah, Elizabeth, Joseph, and Helen Keller, bore the promise of redemption and the legacy of special children destined to shape the course of history.

Amidst the uncertainty and pain, Zawadi engaged with unanswered questions. The strain on her marriage vows, the impact of societal expectations, and the relentless pursuit of a dream family created a turbulent emotional landscape. As she faced the final hurdle of surgery, the couple stood at the cusp of realising the family they had envisioned, yet the journey ahead remained fraught with uncertainties.

Chapter Eight

LEAVE THE PAST WHERE IT BELONGS

Wash, rinse, don't repeat.
—Unknown

Zawadi's heart raced as she darted through the crowded streets, her breaths coming in ragged gasps. She could feel her legs weakening beneath her, the strain of her frantic sprint evident in every step. Suddenly, a familiar voice called out to her, and she felt a pang of dread as she recognised the speaker.

"Zawadi, wait up!" Chege's voice echoed behind her, his footsteps quickening as he closed the gap between them.

For a moment, Zawadi considered ignoring him and continuing her desperate flight. But as he drew nearer, she slowed to a stop, her chest heaving with exertion.

"Why are you running?" Chege asked concern etched in his features as he reached her side.

Zawadi struggled to catch her breath, her lungs burning with each inhale. "I-I'm sorry," she managed to gasp out between breaths. "I was... just trying to... clear my head."

Chege's eyes softened as he took in her dishevelled appearance. "You look like you've been through a storm," he remarked, gesturing to her worn-out clothes and tired demeanour.

Zawadi felt a flush of embarrassment rise to her cheeks as she glanced down at herself. Her clothes were rumpled and stained, her hair a tangled mess atop her head. She must have looked like a beggar, she realised with a sinking feeling.

A few years earlier, their paths crossed in what seemed like a farewell dinner before Zawadi departed from the US to Kenya. Despite her commitment to transparency in her marriage, sharing both the comfortable and uncomfortable truths, that innocent dinner shattered Ruhiu, sending tremors through their relationship.

CRACKS BENEATH THE SURFACE: ZAWADI'S JOURNEY THROUGH TURBULENCE AND TRUST

Yet, the turbulence didn't end there. During the trip, a medical emergency unfolded as Zawadi faced a ruptured appendix, leading to an emergency operation. She was unconscious for a while under anaesthesia, adding another layer of complexity and concern to the already stressful situation.

Invigorated by suspicion, Ruhiu sent inappropriate messages to Chege from Zawadi's phone, sparking a tumultuous confrontation between the two men. Anger and wounded pride drove Ruhiu to confront Zawadi with accusations of infidelity, resulting in a chaotic altercation in the hospital ward. The scene turned violent as Ruhiu forcefully ripped the IV out of Zawadi's hand, leaving blood splattered across the hospital walls, floor, and beds. Left alone in the chaos, Zawadi grappled with a profound sense of disappointment and embarrassment.

The hospital staff, alarmed by the intensity of the altercation, rushed to intervene. Concerned for Zawadi's safety, the doctors swiftly demanded Ruhiu's departure, barring him from returning until Zawadi had fully recovered. During this tumultuous period, the family pastor visited to pray with Zawadi for a speedy recovery. He expressed deep concern for Zawadi's well-being, stressing to her mother that had she witnessed the state of her daughter's health and the deplorable treatment Ruhiu provided, she would have hastily returned to take her daughter home.

Unfortunately, at this critical time, Zawadi's family was away on a Christmas holiday in the US, leaving her to rely on Ruhiu for support through her healing journey. This situation highlighted the community's awareness and disapproval of the unhealthy dynamics in Zawadi and Ruhiu's relationship, further validating the hospital's decision to prioritise Zawadi's safety and well-being. The pastor's remarks served as a poignant reminder of the need for vigilant care and support for Zawadi, especially in the absence of her immediate family.

Zawadi's life became a tapestry woven with threads of joy and pain, all intricately influenced by Chege's presence. Suspicions brewed in Ruhiu's mind, insinuating that Zawadi might seek closure through an affair with Chege—an offer she vehemently rejected.

GIFT IS NOT GIVING

Zawadi's inherent belief in being a blessing to all she encountered fundamentally shaped her interactions and deeply informed her self-perception. Her life philosophy, which earned her numerous friendships and occasional enmities, was a testament to her deep-seated generosity and compassion. Whether assisting colleagues, covering someone's bill, or merely offering support, these acts of kindness were essential expressions of her identity. However, these same gestures of goodwill became sources of significant discord within her marriage to Ruhiu, whose rigid and confining expectations created sharp conflicts with her naturally open-hearted demeanour.

Ruhiu's often negative and sexually tinted interpretations of Zawadi's interactions, regardless of the recipient's gender, deeply wounded her and highlighted a profound misinterpretation of her character. His doubt and jealousy starkly contrasted with her Scorpio traits of loyalty and justice, adding layers of complexity to their relationship dynamics. This continual misreading of her intentions not only perplexed Zawadi but also threatened the foundation of their marriage. Her intrinsic desire to live as a "Gift" to others was persistently undermined by Ruhiu's fear-driven accusations, starkly illustrating the intense conflict between her inherent openness and his restrictive boundaries.

The Nigerian parable, "*Ogbụ mma anaghi ekwe ka éwèlụ mma ga ya n'ázụ,*" meaning "A person who kills with a knife does not allow someone with a knife to stand behind them," profoundly resonates in this context. It mirrors Ruhiu's insecurities, which likely led him to misinterpret Zawadi's acts of kindness as potential threats. This cycle of mistrust and fear proved both damaging and revealing, exposing how deeply Ruhiu's vulnerabilities affected their union.

Zawadi's commitment to her Scorpio characteristics—intensity, emotional depth, loyalty, and a firm sense of justice—empowered her to adeptly navigate these turbulent waters with a clear sense of purpose. She recognised the necessity to safeguard her emotional health by establishing firm boundaries, yet she remained committed to addressing the deep-seated issues within their relationship. Her efforts to shift suspicion towards trust were aimed at restoring the trust and unity essential to the foundation of their partnership.

In addition to these existing strains, Ruhiu also harboured reservations about Zawadi's contributions to the church and other charities, adding another layer of tension. A notable incident was when Zawadi donated a significant sum to her local church to purchase a new pulpit, as the existing one was no longer fit for purpose. Despite this being money she had earned and earmarked in her budget for such charitable acts, Ruhiu's reaction was vehemently negative. This decision ignited endless arguments and fights, deepening the rift in their relationship.

Zawadi's mother supported her decision, affirming that the act of giving to the church was not only a fulfilment of Zawadi's spiritual commitments but also something that would bring her personal blessings. She believed that Zawadi would benefit from the prayers offered in the sanctuary, which would be amplified by her generosity. However, this perspective did little to sway Ruhiu, whose discomfort with Zawadi's financial generosity extended beyond personal expenditure to include her charitable acts, underscoring a significant clash in their values and priorities.

In a desperate attempt to salvage their marriage, Zawadi severed all ties with Chege, resigned from her job, and relocated to Kenya to be with Ruhiu. But beneath the surface, doubts lingered, hinting at deeper cracks in their relationship that mere geographical proximity couldn't mend.

SHADOWS OF SUPPORT: ZAWADI'S JOURNEY THROUGH TURBULENCE

"It's been a rough day," she admitted, her voice barely above a whisper.

Chege nodded sympathetically, his gaze filled with understanding. "I'm sorry to hear that. Is there anything I can do to help?"

Zawadi hesitated, her pride warring with her desperation. She knew she couldn't afford to turn down any offers of assistance, no matter the size.

"Do you have a few minutes to talk?" she asked tentatively, her voice trembling slightly.

Chege nodded, his eyes filled with empathy. "Absolutely. Let's find a quiet spot where we can talk openly."

Zawadi's mind buzzed with apprehension as they navigated the bustling streets to a nearby restaurant. She hadn't crossed paths with Chege in years, not since their friendship had faded into distant memories after university. Faced with confiding in him at this point, she grappled with a mix of hope, uncertainty, and nostalgia for simpler times.

With a determined stride, Chege swiftly approached the nearby ATM. Zawadi assumed he needed cash to settle their bill at the restaurant, but she couldn't shake the feeling that there was more to his actions than met the eye.

Seated in a secluded restaurant corner, Zawadi steeled herself for the conversation ahead. The aroma of grilled fish, plantain, and pepper sauce enveloped them, serving as a bittersweet reminder of happier days.

As she recounted the challenges she'd faced—the financial struggles, the heart-wrenching disappointment of failed IVF treatments, and the looming surgery—Zawadi watched Chege's expression soften with compassion.

"I am sorry for all you've endured," Chege said, his voice laced with sincerity. "Maybe you shouldn't have felt compelled to drop everything and return. Please take this. It should alleviate some of the burden," he added, passing her an envelope containing eight hundred dollars. "And know that I'm here for you, whether you need a ride to the hospital or someone to talk to."

Touched by his gesture of kindness, Zawadi accepted the envelope with a grateful nod. "Thank you, Chege. Your support means the world to me," she said, trembling.

Chege offered to order her favourite meal to take home to lighten the heavy atmosphere—a comforting reminder of the happier times they had shared.

Despite the risk of judgment, Zawadi decided to confide in her sister, Kioni, about her encounter with Chege.She prepared herself for possible examination, recognising that Kioni was familiar with their shared history and the nuances of their relationship.

As Kioni delved into Chege's background, uncovering rumours of a past marriage and why Zawadi should never trust his intentions, she felt a surge of unease. Despite Chege's vehement denial, she couldn't shake the lingering doubts that clouded her mind.By confiding in her sister, Zawadi sought solace and understanding in the middle of uncertainty. Their shared meal became a sanctuary—a fleeting moment of respite amidst life's tumultuous storms.

Zawadi felt a spark of possibility ignite within her. Despite the challenges ahead, she found comfort in the unwavering support of Chege and Kioni, knowing that they would stand by her side through thick and thin.

Chapter Nine

FIVE GOOD YEARS

> *Time is but an illusion created by beings*
> *with limited perception.*
> —**Ken Poirot**

In the aftermath of a challenging surgery, Zawadi endured not just the physical pain but also grappled with the emotional distress that followed. The surgery, initially expected to last two hours, stretched into a gruelling five-hour ordeal as surgeons navigated the complexities of her endometriosis, adenomyosis, and fibroids. Zawadi's family was in panic, fearing she may not make it out alive. The news of her low egg reserve exacerbated her mounting struggles, and it was precisely at this critical juncture that Ruhiu chose to abandon her for another woman.

Ruhiu's departure couldn't have been more devastating, leaving Zawadi to navigate her recovery alone. She had uprooted her life and made countless sacrifices, including sacrificing her career, all hoping to nurture their relationship. Yet, despite crossing the significant milestone of five years together, the marriage counselling sessions they underwent had failed to prepare her for the heart-wrenching betrayal she faced at this moment. Losing her family, a cornerstone of her identity, felt like an unimaginable cruelty.

Before the surgery, Zawadi stumbled upon social media evidence of Ruhiu's infidelity, a devastating revelation that shattered the illusion of their once-solid union. Confronting him unveiled the extent of his deception, as he callously admitted to starting a new family, leaving Zawadi with nothing but shattered dreams.

As Zawadi watched their shared life collapse like a house of cards, she couldn't help but ruefully reflect on her past decisions. She wished she had heeded her aunt Nadia's warnings, perhaps altering the course of her reality. But at this point, she was left to confront the consequences of her misplaced trust, clinging to the memories of their shared promises and dreams.

Despite enduring years of physical and emotional abuse, Zawadi remained steadfast, refusing to succumb to despair. The sting of the injection site brought her back to the present, while the African woven bracelet on her wrist he had given her invoked bittersweet memories of their shared past.

Nostalgia gripped Zawadi as she scrolled through their old photos, reminiscing about their aspirations as a young, ambitious couple. Nevertheless, life had thrown unforeseen obstacles in their path, disrupting their carefully laid plans.

Contemplating her next move, Zawadi confronted the harsh reality of financial constraints and dietary restrictions. Each bite of banana, once a simple pleasure, carried the weight of her circumstances presently. With resolve hardening, she understood the stark choice before her—get pregnant or die! Despite the bitterness of her situation, she knew she had to nourish her body for the strength to rebuild her shattered life.

In spite of her turmoil, a call from Doctor Mark offered a brief respite. Nonetheless, the title of "Mrs." was a cruel reminder of the absence of her estranged husband, Ruhiu. Despite the doctors' assurances of conception possibilities post-recovery, the strained communication and physical distance with Ruhiu left the situation feeling surreal. He had been her everything—family, best friend, lover, confidant—but at this moment, the foundation of their once-solid bond had crumbled, leaving her adrift in a sea of uncertainty.

As she hung up the phone, Zawadi pondered the path that led her to this point. The strategy of marrying her best friend had failed spectacularly despite a decade of fighting against all odds. At this moment, she stood at the precipice of an uncertain future, contending with the weight of her shattered dreams and the daunting task of rebuilding her life alone.

"I am sorry that some of the news we shared with you after your surgery was not what you were expecting," he said. "You still have a good chance of starting the family you desire. Looking at your records, I see that you are turning thirty in a few months, which

*means you have **five good years** to try with your husband. I suggest you take full advantage of it once you feel strong enough. I have also sent a referral to the fertility department allowing you to speak to them about how best they can support you through your journey. You already had four rounds of IVF; this means you wouldn't qualify for the free round offered by the government. Also, your chances of success with IVF or egg freezing may be meagre because of your low AMH [anti-Müllerian hormone] levels and raised FSH [follicle-stimulating hormone] levels, which would produce fewer eggs during stimulation. It would be advisable that you try naturally."*

Doctor Mark's words echoed in Zawadi's mind like a haunting refrain,a bitter reminder of the shattered dreams and dashed hopes that consumed her existence at this point. His well-meaning reassurances offered little solace confronting her stark reality—a reality marred by infertility, betrayal, and abandonment. The path ahead seemed daunting, a maze of uncertainty and heartache, with no clear answers or easy solutions in sight.

As she lay on her bed, engulfed by a suffocating wave of despair, Zawadi felt utterly abandoned by her so-called "ride-or-die." The tears flowed freely, mingling with the echoes of her shattered dreams. The fatigue of a relentless battle, fought with every ounce of strength she possessed, had finally taken its toll. She stood alone in the wreckage of her life, with no one left to lean on at this point.

SHATTERED DREAMS:
ZAWADI'S MELANCHOLIC ODYSSEY

The thought of navigating the daunting journey of pregnancy without a partner felt like an impossible challenge, a cruel fortuitous twist that added to her overwhelming sense of despair. The mere idea of another man touching her was unbearable, shrouded in moral dilemmas and fears of compromising her health.

Desperate for answers, Zawadi turned to her faith, seeking solace in the guidance of her pastors. Yet, Zawadi brushed aside their platitudes about patience and divine timing, considering them a painful reminder of their privileged position with their own families.

"I want Ruhiu back," Zawadi whispered, her voice trembling with sorrow and desperation. The woman who had stolen him had not just robbed her of her husband but also of her sense of self-worth. Despite the absence of a formal divorce, Zawadi clung to the remnants of their shattered union, grasping at legal claims that felt increasingly futile confronting Ruhiu's betrayal.

Hailing negativity cast its long, lingering tendrils in the shadowy corners of Zawadi's melancholic temperament. Her meticulous nature, meant to bring order and structure, morphed into an unforgiving demand for perfection, a relentless pursuit that left little room for the imperfections inherent in the human experience. The love for certainty, once a comforting ally, evolved into a paralysing fear of the unknown, fostering anxiety confronting uncertainty.

As the intricate plans Zawadi had meticulously crafted crumbled, the negative side of her melancholic temperament emerged with a vengeance. The collapse of her carefully constructed world triggered a cascade of self-doubt and a harsh internal critique as the weight of unrealised expectations bore down heavily on her shoulders. Rather than offering solace, her introversion became a breeding ground for isolation, trapping her in a cycle of deep thought and rumination that fed the melancholy nestled within.

This negative facet of her temperament wove a tapestry of gloom, tinting her perception with a persistent shade of despair. The depths she spiralled into seemed bottomless, and the struggle to emerge from the melancholic undertow became arduous, fraught with the complications of battling her temperament.

THE GIFT OF SIGHT

"Once upon a time, there was a blind girl who lived a lonely life. She had a boyfriend who was her rock and took care of her, but she hated everyone else, feeling that the world was against her because of her blindness. However, her love for her boyfriend was so strong that she would often say, "If I wasn't blind, I would marry you."

One day, a miracle happened and a kind soul donated a pair of eyes to the girl, giving her the gift of sight. She was overjoyed and eagerly awaited to see her boyfriend for the first time with her new eyes. However, when she finally saw him, she was devastated to discover that he was blind too.

Her boyfriend, still deeply in love with her, proposed to her and asked, "Now that you can see, will you marry me?" But the girl was so caught up in her newfound sight and what she saw as her boyfriend's imperfection that she refused.

The boy was heartbroken and left the girl, leaving her alone once again. She regretted her decision and the love she once had for her boyfriend was replaced with sadness and regret.

One day, she received a letter from her boyfriend with a simple message: "Take care of my eyes, my dear." The girl was struck with emotion as she realised the true love and selflessness her boyfriend had for her. He had given her the gift of sight, but at the cost of his own vision.

The girl realised that love is not about what you can see, but about what you feel in your heart. She learned to appreciate the people in her life for who they are, not for what they look like. She went on to live a happy life, taking care of her boyfriend's eyes and cherishing the love that she had for him."
- Unknown

Zawadi's heart weighed heavy with the shards of shattered dreams, each fragment a painful reminder of lost hopes and broken promises. As she sat in solitude, the tale of the blind girl and her devoted boyfriend echoed in her mind, a poignant reflection of love's complexities. The saying "Love is blind, but marriage is an eye-opener" took on new meaning as she pondered the girl's journey from darkness to light.

The memory of the blind girl's struggle resonated deeply with Zawadi, stirring a mixture of empathy and reflection. She wished Ruhiu well, hoping he found solace in the sight he possessed at this point.

This realisation that relationships could end, despite the presence of true love, was a bitter pill to swallow. Despite her profound love for Ruhiu, Zawadi acknowledged that some connections were temporary, meant to serve a purpose for a specific moment.

Seeking solace and understanding, Zawadi visited Aunt Afaafa, a beacon of unwavering support amidst life's storm. The warmth of Aunt Afaafa's embrace, the soothing cadence of her voice, and the resilience she embodied were a balm for Zawadi's wounded spirit. In the haven of Aunt Afaafa's love, Zawadi found refuge from the storm that had ravaged her life.

The reunion with Aunt Afaafa was more than just a physical meeting; it reaffirmed the enduring power of familial bonds. Zawadi pledged to nurture this rekindled connection, recognising it as a vital lifeline in the turbulent sea of her existence.

Zawadi reached out to Chege with a newfound resolve, embracing the lifeline he offered. This gesture symbolised a shift in Zawadi's journey, a pivot from the isolation of her past towards a network of caring souls willing to share her burdens. The chase through the streets, Chege catching up to her, became a symbolic pursuit of closure—a step towards healing and renewal.

SANCTUARY AND SOLACE

As Chege promised to drop Zawadi off at Aunt Afaafa's home, the car ride became a bridge between past and future, a physical journey mirroring Zawadi's emotional quest for healing. The familiar sights of the city blurred through tear-filled eyes, the car becoming a vessel for the weight of Zawadi's emotions.

Arriving at Aunt Afaafa's home, Zawadi felt anticipation mingled with apprehension. The warmth of Aunt Afaafa's welcome and the aroma of home-cooked dishes enveloped her in a comforting embrace. As they gathered around the dining table, Zawadi shared her deepest fears and struggles, laying bare the scars of her past.

Her aunt's words of wisdom offered a glimpse of a brighter future amid uncertainty. With each piece of advice, Zawadi felt a renewed sense of strength. Taking things one step at a time and focusing on her health and well-being became her guiding principle as she navigated the uncharted waters ahead. And in the embrace of Aunt Afaafa's love, Zawadi found the courage to face whatever the future held, one moment at a time.

Aunt Afaafa leaned forward, her eyes sharp with concern as she probed Ruhiu's sudden outburst. Zawadi's voice trembled as she recounted the accusation of infidelity once again hurled at her by Ruhiu. Memories flooded Aunt Afaafa's mind of past incidents when Ruhiu's insecurities had wreaked havoc on their family, leaving Zawadi vulnerable and hurt.

Expressing her disbelief at Ruhiu's behaviour, Aunt Afaafa condemned his actions, especially after the taboo encounters with their relative. She asserted that Ruhiu needed to grow up and realise that pushing Zawadi away by making baseless accusations would not lead to any resolution. The fact that he had abandoned her in her vulnerable state displayed a cruel and wicked nature.

As the conversation unfolded, Zawadi shared the issues she faced in her marriage, including Ruhiu's jealousy, which prevented her from reconnecting with a friend, Lowe, who eventually took his own life. Zawadi had offered to undergo a lie detector test to prove her innocence, but Ruhiu's insecurities seemed insurmountable.

UNRAVELING BONDS

Aunt Afaafa expressed her sadness for Zawadi's past experiences and speculated that Ruhiu might have been looking for an exit strategy. Yet, Kioni, who had her back turned, revealed that she and her husband had warned Ruhiu about Chege and Zawadi's reconnection, fearing that Chege might lure Zawadi into a compromising situation.

Zawadi felt a surge of anger upon realising that Kioni had recklessly shared mere assumptions with Ruhiu about the nature of Zawadi and Chege's relationship, thereby painting an inaccurate picture of her life. The fact that Kioni had intervened without fully understanding the situation made it painfully clear to Zawadi that her older sister prioritised her agency over Zawadi's marriage and well-being. What stung more was Kioni's persistent belief in her wisdom due to their age gap, as if it granted her the authority to dictate Zawadi's choices.

The disruption caused by Kioni's interference intensified Zawadi's resolve to distance herself from Chege once she was stable, further straining her fragile marriage. It stood as a harsh reminder of the precarious balance Zawadi struggled to maintain between her autonomy and the expectations imposed upon her by her family and society.

At that moment, Zawadi understood that she had to relinquish not just the hope of salvaging her connection with Ruhiu but also the fish and plantain with a pepper sauce that, just days before, had symbolised a momentary respite from her tumultuous life.

Overwhelmed by a surge of emotions, Zawadi unleashed her pent-up frustrations in a fiery rant.

"You wanted to save what? Save what? How dare you?! Who do you think you are? At what point have I ever initiated a call to any husband in this family? You do not respect me or anything I stand for! And here you were, empathising with me. You are two-faced! With a sister like you, who needs enemies?

"With all I have been dealing with," Zawadi continued, still speaking to Kioni, "you showed no sympathy. I came to you crying and revealing my most vulnerable parts, yet you showed no mercy and continued tearing me down secretly. What did I ever do to you to deserve such treatment?

"I planned your wedding, raised your son when you couldn't as a single mom, and sacrificed for you and your husband to the point of even ironing your husband's briefs! What on earth else could I do to show you I love you?

"And this is how you repay me? Is this a personal vendetta? Have you never heard of a code between sisters or family?

"You never saw me kiss another man or engage in inappropriate behaviour, but you still needed to call Ruhiu? If you had caught me on top of a man, as a sister, could you not call me to order on the side?

"Who behaves like this?"

"You are making me look crazy up in here! You are not my family! You are a poor excuse for a sister, and I hope you rot in hell! I never want to see you again!"

At that point, Zawadi's hands and legs started to shake uncontrollably. Kioni's actions exacerbated her mild *essential tremor*, causing her to suffer more. Abandoning her rational mind and blacking out, with no consideration for her health, Zawadi grabbed a kitchen chair and swung it at her sister. Kioni ducked, the chair barely missing her.

"Grab hold of her!" Kioni said. "She is demon-possessed! She has a lion spirit!"

Zawadi hollered back, "You are the one who is demon-possessed with behaviour like yours!"

FRACTURED HARMONY

The dynamics of Zawadi and Kioni's relationship painted a vivid tableau of deep-seated affection intertwined with fiery rivalry, a blend that shaped their interactions from childhood into adulthood. During a seemingly innocent family spelling game, their complex bond came sharply into focus. Their adopted brother, Jaali, hoped to foster a light-hearted moment among the siblings by asking Zawadi to spell a word. However, before Zawadi could even process the challenge, Kioni, ever impulsive, blurted out the answer. This premature interruption not only infuriated Zawadi but also dredged up painful memories from their shared past.In a moment of heated anger, Zawadi had pushed Kioni towards a glass sliding door.The glass shattered dramatically, and by sheer providence, Kioni moved just in time, narrowly avoiding a large, deadly shard that crashed to the ground mere seconds later. This harrowing incident etched itself deeply into Zawadi's memory, serving as a stark and haunting reminder of the simmering tensions that could so quickly escalate into genuine peril. The fragility of the glass, like the fragile balance of their relationship, underscored the constant vigilance needed to prevent a disastrous outcome.

These strains continued to manifest as they grew older. On one occasion, when Zawadi returned home late from a date with her partner Ruhiu, she was met not with sisterly concern but with Kioni's stern scolding. The situation quickly escalated beyond mere words, culminating in a physical altercation where Zawadi, consumed by rage, pulled hair from Kioni's scalp. Episodes like this highlighted Kioni's continual meddling in Zawadi's personal affairs, starkly illustrating her failure to respect boundaries, epitomising the proverbial pot calling the kettle black.

Throughout their lives, Kioni's well-intentioned but often overbearing actions clashed dramatically with Zawadi's strong desire for independence. This ongoing conflict painted a complex portrait of their sibling relationship—a rich tapestry woven with moments of protective love and intense rivalry. Each event in their shared history left profound marks, illustrating the intricate dance of closeness and conflict inherent in their interactions, shaping their bond in indelible ways.

"A broken clock is right twice a day, but that doesn't mean it should be relied upon for accurate timing." - Unknown

BREAKING POINTS AND NEW BEGINNINGS

Aunt Afaafa moved Kioni into the next room to prevent matters from escalating, then returned to calm Zawadi down. Zawadi was holding her stomach and crying. Her aunt recognised her pain, knowing that Zawadi was not supposed to exert herself physically or emotionally, not in this way and not this soon. Auntie Afaafa began to cry as she looked at Zawadi, her heart wrenching with empathy, which broke Zawadi's heart. Auntie Afaafa was like her mother, and Zawadi had sworn never to do anything to make her mum cry.

Auntie Afaafa said, "I think you should move here with me. I am troubled about you, Zawadi, and seeing you swing a chair at your sister, with stitches and your being barely able to walk, gives me great concern. You can stay as long as you like until this blows over."

Zawadi took a deep breath, with tears streaming down her face.

"It's sweet of you to be concerned, Auntie," she said, "but I don't feel safe being around here with what she did to me. And she lied after I called her on it three times, completely denying it. I need to be alone to gather my thoughts and get back on the straight and narrow. I don't have a family; unfortunately, I don't know if I can build one with everything going on with my health. I hoped to rely on the immediate family, but the orgy between Ruhiu and our relative and now a backstab? I have nothing and no one."

Auntie Afaafa asked, "Including me? You discount me, too?"

Zawadi answered, "Auntie, you know I love you dearly, but please let me go. I can't tell whose side anyone is on anymore. I do not feel safe. These happenings are not what family should be like."

Auntie Afaafa said, "Let you go where? I think you should stay with me," uttering this in an endearing voice as she reached out and embraced Zawadi. "Some women at forty-five years old haven't experienced these things. Please let me help you. You don't have money, and it's a harsh world. I will drive down tomorrow and help you pack your items."

Zawadi remained adamant and refused her auntie's offer. She called Chege and asked him to take her to Kioni's house to get her things. She no longer felt she was doing anything wrong with Chege by accepting his offer to help. The end of her marriage was already a done deal.

Zawadi left for the United States with just a couple of summer shirts, trousers, and shoes. Her trip was supposed to be short, three months. With winter on the horizon, she was starting life from scratch as she didn't have any winter-appropriate clothing. Upon her arrival at Kioni's house, she called a friend from university who was seeking a roommate. Luckily, the space was still available. Zawadi told her friend she would take the room and drive there immediately.

Zawadi knew she had enough money for one month of rent, but she believed she would be able to work things out somehow once she recovered and could get a proper job to earn enough to cover her bills.

As eloquently expressed in the movie "Babyteeth," "Some people run by packing their bags, while others run by standing still." This sentiment captures the essence of how people cope differently with life's challenges. Unlike those who might choose inaction, Zawadi refused to stand still.

Zawadi threw out her SIM card to ensure no one could reach her unless she decided to contact them. She needed a clean slate.

Chapter Ten

UNHINGED

> *Some people believe holding on and hanging in there is a sign of strength. However, there are times when it takes much more strength to know when to let go and then do it.*
> **—Ann Landers**

Due to her experiences with Ruhiu, Zawadi's concept of a soulmate underwent a profound transformation. Initially, she believed a soulmate had to be a romantic partner, but at this point, her perspective has shifted. She understood that a soulmate was not limited to a romantic relationship but could also be someone who reflected her truths and highlighted areas for growth and self-reflection. Ruhiu had served as one of these catalysts, and Zawadi acknowledged that he, too, had his connections with others.

Despite her fears and anxieties about Ruhiu moving on and his impending social media posts with his new partner, seeing those images wasn't as daunting as anticipated. Zawadi experienced a moment of acceptance, finding the courage to wish Ruhiu and his new partner well in her heart. She refused updates and messages about his life, choosing to close that chapter for her peace of mind. Blocking those who were persistent in sharing such things with her, augmented her determination to move on.

Her marriage with Ruhiu, though not formally dissolved, had reached its end in Zawadi's heart. She adopted her mum's analogy about carrying the weight of marriage—not on her head, but on her shoulders.It remained a poignant lesson, intended to cultivate the profound understanding that should the burden ever become overwhelming, she possessed the inner strength to relinquish it with graceful ease. This mindset guided her as she prepared to take control of closing this chapter in her life.

DIVORCE COURT

Zawadi's voice trembled as she spoke into the phone, seeking refuge in the familiar voice of the barrister who had helped her in the past. A figure of legal wisdom and an old acquaintance, the barrister greeted her warmly. Their conversation, initially rooted in pleasantries, soon took an unexpected turn. While expressing his concern for her well-being, the barrister questioned the necessity of a divorce, noting the youthful allure of Zawadi's marriage. Yet, Zawadi's plea for legal intervention reflected a profound truth—a reality marred by complexities beyond the surface.

The curious and caring barrister sought answers from the remnants of her family, who still provided her with some scant degree of support. He probed about Ruhiu's parents, Zawadi's mother, and the involvement of pastors alike in their tale of marital discord. Nonetheless, in response, Zawadi painted a desolate picture by mentioning Ruhiu's poor familial prowess, disrespect, and past financial strife.

The absence of in-laws and Ruhiu's refusal to engage in counselling closed the door on traditional avenues for resolution. Zawadi bared her soul, recounting the emotional burden she carried—the abuse, the betrayal with a relative, and the subsequent indifference from Ruhiu.The family's warm embrace and acceptance of him as one of their own stood in stark contrast to the current reality.

With a heavy heart, Zawadi declared divorce as her sole recourse, emphasising the unbearable weight of continuing the marriage. Acknowledging the gravity of her decision, the barrister offered understanding and support, recognising the inherent difficulty of navigating such a tumultuous journey.

In the chapters of Zawadi's unravelling life, the barrister becomes a pivotal character, a guide through the legal complexities that await her. Their exchanges set the stage for a narrative of resilience, self-discovery, and pursuing a life untethered from the ties of an oppressive past.

Zawadi's desperate plea for legal emancipation unfolded as she faced the barrister, whom she saw as a beacon of hope in her tumultuous journey. The barrister, ever committed to aiding her, requested essential documents to initiate the divorce process. Yet, Zawadi's revelation of the missing marriage certificate overshadowed her prospects. Ruhiu, in an act of cruelty, had purged the house of all personal effects, leaving her with nothing but emotional scars and abandoned belongings in a home tainted by decay and black soot.

Confronting her estranged husband, given his penchant for insults, filled her with dread. Silently acknowledging the bureaucratic hurdles, the barrister suggested an alternative. Since there were no electronic records of the marriage in the registry, the sole way to obtain the marriage certificate needed to proceed with the divorce was through a manual search of paper records filed at the registry, using the wedding date as a reference point.

Despite the complexities involved in this process, the absence of joint property or shared assets simplified Zawadi's case. The barrister provided hope in the heat of the chaos, offering a potential silver lining in an otherwise challenging situation.

The barrister, expressing empathy for Zawadi's predicament, invoked a traditional adage: "The cane a husband uses to flog the first wife with is waiting for his second wife." This proverbial expression cautioned that if a husband mistreated his initial spouse, the likelihood of his doing the same to subsequent wives was high. In sharing this saying, the barrister conveyed a poignant message about recognising patterns of behaviour and being mindful of potential recurrent patterns, urging Zawadi to learn from her past experiences.

Meanwhile, Ruhiu's callous response exposed the depth of his resentment and his unwillingness to cooperate. Acknowledging the obstacles ahead, the barrister urged Zawadi to tread carefully in her interactions with him.

INVISIBLE SCARS

Ruhiu's venomous words reverberated through the phone, leaving Zawadi reeling from the emotional onslaught. The quest for her marriage certificate had opened up a battleground marked by insults and rejection. The barrister's attempts to intervene unveiled Ruhiu's obstinate hostility, setting the stage for a challenging legal journey.

As Zawadi began the process of getting a divorce, she carried deep emotional scars from her abusive marriage with Ruhiu. Though these wounds weren't physical, they profoundly affected her self-esteem and inner well-being.

Ruhiu's verbal and emotional abuse had taken a toll on Zawadi, leaving her feeling worthless and broken inside. The barrister handling her case acknowledged the tough road ahead, recognising the legal complexities of divorce and the emotional healing Zawadi needed.

In simpler terms, Zawadi's journey to divorce wasn't just about legal paperwork; it was also about overcoming the emotional damage caused by her abusive marriage. Despite the challenges, Zawadi showed bravery as she took steps toward reclaiming her life and happiness. Ruhiu, having moved on, chose to retain possession of Zawadi's late father's bed and car, a move she deemed shameless and contrary to cultural norms.The familial support she had expected crumbled with just a brief call from one of Ruhiu's brothers. The abruptness of the dissolution, without the customary African rituals, shocked her, but she embraced her father's adage, "Good riddance to bad rubbish."

RECLAIMING IDENTITY AND LEGACY

With the support of her empathetic flatmates, Zawadi found solace in her chosen family. They created a warm, nurturing environment, sharing meals, laughter, and emotional support. She highlighted the strength of these new-found bonds during the festive season, marked by a collective effort to cook a Christmas turkey.

Despite Ruhiu's resistance, the legal system eventually granted Zawadi the *Decree Absolute* after six years. Her village elders, recognising her need for closure, performed the traditional rites, freeing her to move forward and remarry. The visible and invisible scars became markers of her resilience, strength, and transformative journey towards a new beginning.

Zawadi poured her heart into a letter addressed to her late father, seeking solace in the memories of his guidance and love.

"Dear Daddy,

I miss you deeply in this moment of despair. No man stands by me at present, and the void left by your absence is painfully evident. Losing you robbed me of witnessing your pride at my graduation and the joy of your walking me down the aisle.

In your absence, I sought a male figure to nurture me, guide me, protect me, and provide for me—a partner to build a home, shielding us from the pain of parental loss. My brothers were preoccupied with their battles, and I turned to a male friend, the two of us bonding over shared grief. We dreamed big, envisioning a future akin to the empire you and Mum built from a single room. I wished for your discerning eyes to scrutinise him.

Ruhiu, formerly a friend, visited during my teenage years, and I vividly remember your stern disapproval. You warned him not to wait as you were retrieving your double-barrel guns. Ruhiu vanished in an instant. I should have seen that interaction as a warning not to marry him.

I asked for a separation because of the strain of fertility treatments and the lack of financial security, along with my needing space to think and re-strategise. Ruhiu failed to comprehend the necessity of a break for my mental health. He viewed it as a cue to abandon the relationship, leaving me broken.

I am truly sorry for letting you down, Daddy. I've become a laughing stock, but I refuse to accept defeat. Your heroism inspires me to persevere.

The pain and abuse have eroded my confidence, compromising the identity you instilled in me and contradicting the way you raised me.

Though I lack strength at the moment, your spirit guides me to emerge stronger. "Train up a child in the way they should go, and when they grow old, they will not depart from it"—your cherished scripture. I may have strayed, but I feel the tugging in my spirit to find my way back home.

I am a true daughter of the soil, the daughter of a lion. Dead or alive, I am still a lioness.

I made a promise to you on your deathbed to make you proud and contribute to the great name you established. Ruhiu leaves me no choice. Our relationship has changed, and I must persevere. I will uphold your honour and glory, so help me, God."

Motivated by her new-found determination, Zawadi took a significant step toward reclaiming her identity.She changed her name on social media to her maiden one, liberating herself from the burdensome weight of Ruhiu's surname. Although she never legally changed her name due to the affluence and opportunities it afforded her—both at home and abroad, thanks to her father's impactful and positive influence on many people—this symbolic act marked a pivotal moment in her journey of self-discovery and empowerment.

At the poignant ten-year remembrance ceremony beside her father's graveside, Zawadi clutched the heartfelt letter she had once written. Before the ceremony began, she meticulously swept the graveside and lit candles, casting a gentle glow over the area. As she stood there, the haunting melody of Master KG's "Skeleton Move" wove through her consciousness, resonating with her heartbeat in a persistent echo. These lyrics guided her as she navigated the diverse landscapes of her life—from moments of joy and passages of struggle to the quiet spaces in between.

No matter the distance she traveled or the paths she chose to explore, the chorus of the song whispered a profound truth: there was always a way back to the origins of her heart, to the place she called home. It seemed as if the melody, with its eerie yet comforting cadence, had woven itself into her being, becoming an integral part of her soul's journey. It reminded her that every road, no matter its twists and turns, inevitably led her back to where love and memories awaited.

Surrounded by memories of her beloved father at this solemn ceremony, Zawadi reaffirmed her commitment to uphold her promise to him. The elders observed her cleaning the graveside and lighting candles, remarking that her actions were symbolic and attracted blessings. This moment became a poignant testament to her resilience and a declaration of her intent to honour her father's enduring legacy. As the lyrics of "Skeleton Move" by Master KG echoed in her mind, she was reminded that no matter where life took her, she knew the road that would always lead her back home.

Chapter Eleven

BACK TO BASICS

> *Every end is a new beginning.*
> **—Unknown**

Zawadi faced formidable forces in securing a decent job in the United States, primarily because her CV had a significant gap between jobs resulting from frequent relocations for Ruhiu. Despite her exceptional professional achievements in Kenya, her experience went unnoticed in the competitive US job market, compelling her to take up menial jobs, enduring long hours selling fragrances or washing dishes at upscale hotels.

Financially strained, she could not open a bank account and therefore deposited her earnings into a flatmate's account.Preferring self-reliance over seeking assistance, Zawadi embraced a frugal lifestyle, opting for a fruitarian/vegan diet to cut costs. The drastic reduction in her living space forced her to grapple with the stark disparity between her roles as an employer in Kenya and her present circumstances.

Frequenting the supermarket's discounted section for items near their sell-by dates became a daily routine for Zawadi. Faced with limited options, she leveraged her tech skills to outsmart self-checkout systems, ensuring she wouldn't go hungry. In this season of scarcity, she felt like a prodigal daughter, dining amongst the pigs and living in conditions worse than those of a servant in her father's house. However, her financial struggles weren't her only woes. The metaphorical pearls she had cherished—representing the valuable relationships and situations she had once held dear—had been carelessly cast before swine. These relationships, once deemed precious, were treated with disdain and trampled underfoot by those she had trusted.

This realisation of betrayal and disrespect framed her current plight, deepening her narrative of loss and resilience as she navigated her way through a season of scarcity and personal reckoning.

Upon completing her master's degree, Zawadi secured a job that, while not fully tapping into her potential, marked a crucial step forward. Despite the financial sacrifice and the bold departure from convention, her joy in orchestrating events locally and abroad transformed her perspective on work, elevating it from a mere livelihood to a passionate pursuit. Driven by passion for her work, she surpassed probation and dedicated herself to proving her commitment to her boss. The job became indispensable for her livelihood and shelter, making every absence a potential risk. Nonetheless, Aunt Flo's return, accompanied by severe symptoms (i.e. her three children) just a year after extensive surgery, posed a threat to Zawadi's job stability.

Fearing excruciating pain and potential job loss, Zawadi sought medical intervention, and the doctors placed her on the waiting list for a laparoscopy. Mindful of the potential impact on her fertility, she enquired about lifestyle changes and alternative medicine options. The doctor acknowledged the potential benefits of these treatments in healing the body but stressed the individual nature of outcomes, encouraging Zawadi to explore these treatments as part of a holistic approach to her health, understanding that each person's body responds differently to various interventions.

REBRANDING

Post-laparoscopy and the subsequent period of healing, Zawadi felt it was time for a comprehensive makeover. Her body still carried weight from previous IVF treatments, and the stress of resettling in the country was visible in her appearance. She was determined to rebrand herself for the next chapter of her life and undertook a transformative journey.

For Zawadi, rebranding involved covering up the tattoos she and Ruhiu had gotten to commemorate their engagement and fifth marriage anniversary. In this gruelling twelve-hour session, filled with pain and tears, she relentlessly pursued liberation from the haunting shadows of her past. In bold defiance, she commemorated her newfound freedom by getting another tattoo and twelve ear piercings simultaneously, each marking a significant step towards reclaiming her identity.

Reflecting on her life, Zawadi viewed the delay in having a child as a blessing. Raising a child in such tumultuous circumstances would have been detrimental. Although she had previously yearned for a baby with Ruhiu, she realised that having a child with a man she couldn't be comfortable around would have been a lifelong challenge.

Beyond external changes, Zawadi felt the need for internal rebranding. Disheartened by the limitations of traditional medicine and conflicting online information, she delved into alternative medicine, exploring Chinese herbal medication and acupuncture, which echoed Kenya's conventional medicine practices. Yet, this process was not without difficulties. She grappled with the pungent odour and taste of the herbs, starkly contrasting the fragrances and scents she loved. The acupuncture sessions were unfamiliar and uncomfortable, yet she embraced them for healing. Despite the hefty expense, she prioritised her health, hoping her sacrifices would be worth it.

Further advice from a fertility nutritionist prompted Zawadi to alter her vegan diet, which she'd chosen because of its affordability rather than because it was her preference. Embracing a new diet plan tailored for fertility became the next thing she religiously adhered to as she would pursue every avenue to enhance her chances of conception.

Zawadi found solace in the physical healing her body experienced, but her heart remained a battleground. Having held on to the belief that with time, her emotional wounds would mend and forgiveness would come effortlessly, she found that, in actuality, this proved to be a complex reality.

Her heartache stemmed from the actions of Kioni and her relative, whose behaviour seemed devoid of love and logic. Their gaslighting tactics created chaos, and both appeared oblivious to the havoc wrought by their words and actions. To Zawadi, forgiveness felt like surrendering, like a concession, with the other person escaping the punishment they deserved. Yet, Zawadi recognised that forgiveness wasn't about winning or losing, as no tangible prize was at stake.

THE F-WORD: EMBRACING FORGIVENESS AND FAMILY

Acknowledging the inevitability of offences, Zawadi decided to make peace with the *F-word*—forgiveness. Contemplating the biblical story of Joseph in Genesis, she drew lessons on forgiveness and applied them to her own life. Joseph's journey from being sold into slavery by his brothers at seventeen to becoming the head of Egypt at thirty was remarkable. Despite enduring thirteen years of pain and punishment, Joseph forgave his brothers and extended kindness to them during a famine. Inspired by Joseph's extraordinary capacity for forgiveness, Zawadi aimed to emulate his example.

She contemplated Joseph's reaction following their father Jacob's demise, as his brothers harbored fears of retribution for their actions against him in his youth. Instead, Joseph wept, expressing to them that what they meant for harm, God intended for good. Joseph's ability to forgive and find purpose in his suffering became a guiding light for Zawadi as she navigated the challenging path towards healing and forgiveness.

Zawadi reflected on the wisdom shared in Hebrews 12:15, likening unforgiveness to bitter roots. Understanding that these roots could poison her heart and affect her emotional well-being, she recognised the importance of uprooting them. The verse urged her not to allow bitterness to take hold, as it could lead to trouble and affect the hearts of many.

Zawadi drew parallels between unforgiveness and the fermentation process in winemaking. Just as prolonged fermentation turns wine into vinegar, holding onto unforgiveness could sour her life. Realising the detrimental effects of bitterness, she contemplated the physical and emotional toll it had taken on her. During her ordeal of surviving extreme bleeding, Zawadi had come to understand the urgency and imperative of forgiveness. A quotation she once read comparing unforgiveness to bleeding out deeply resonated with her, highlighting the unseen but profound impact on her soul and vitality. This experience had taught her that holding onto grudges drained her strength much like physical bleeding, emphasising the need to let go and heal, both emotionally and physically.

Meditating on Matthew 5:23–24, Zawadi grasped the counterintuitive responsibility placed on the offended to initiate reconciliation. She delved into the constructs of forgiveness and unforgiveness, recognising forgiveness as a daily practice, a decision to free the spirit and mind and a gift to oneself. In contrast, unforgiveness is a self-imposed prison, akin to drinking poison and expecting the other person to suffer.

Despite the pain caused by Kioni and Firyali endorsement of Ruhiu and his social media posts, Zawadi courageously decided to uproot those bitter roots. She resolved to forge a truce with her sisters, her other relatives, and Ruhiu, understanding the value of unity among siblings. Inspired by the scripture, "Oh how good and pleasant it is for brothers to live together in unity" (Psalm 133:1), she recognised the profound importance of familial harmony. Reconnecting with her family, Zawadi embraced their support and love, determined to break free from the victim role and build a brighter future. This biblical wisdom reinforced her resolve, guiding her toward a path of reconciliation and collective strength.

"Ed," Zawadi's older brother, remained unaware of her pain until he discovered the details. Once enlightened, he stepped into father, husband, and friend roles, becoming a dependable rock for Zawadi. In him, she found safety and support. He was a comforting presence to lean on.

Firyali, Zawadi's role model, proved instrumental in guiding her through the challenging phases. Despite occasional disagreements, their bond remained grounded in love. Firyali offered a different perspective, hoping that Zawadi would find her way.

Kioni, providing companionship during lonely times, played a vital role by offering Zawadi a softer landing wherever possible. Together, the two worked on healing the fractures in their relationship, initiating the rebuilding of their sisterhood.

Zawadi's friend Sherrie emerged as a steadfast presence. She patiently listened to Zawadi for hours as she cried and told her stories of being brokenhearted. Sherrie, embodying true empathy, cried as Zawadi's tears ran dry and prayed during Zawadi's moments of depletion. In contrast to friends who appeared with self-serving motives and departed once their needs were met, Sherrie remained, offering support without anticipating anything in return.

With her heart steadily traversing the path of healing, her professional life stabilised, her fertility plan set in motion, her familial bonds on the mend, and her successful rebranding achieved, Zawadi paused to reflect on her accomplishments for the year. As she geared up to chart new horizons and set fresh resolutions, she placed connecting with a compatible partner and lover at the pinnacle of her aspirations. The journey of self-discovery and reconstruction equipped her with the resilience and fortitude to embrace new beginnings and explore boundless possibilities.

Zawadi's journey through the labyrinth of life post-divorce and a decade-long relationship was a gripping odyssey. The intricacies of rediscovering herself amidst the chaotic tides of societal expectations and newfound freedom left her grappling with uncertainty, a quest for identity overshadowed by societal norms.

Having weathered the storms of nearly two decades entangled in the complexities of relationships, Zawadi realised the dire need for a paradigm shift. She embarked on a transformative journey of self-discovery and empowerment, shedding the shackles of societal conventions and embracing her true essence as a free spirit. With newfound wisdom gleaned from myriad sources, including books, online content, and a burgeoning spiritual connection, Zawadi forged her path with unwavering determination.

Prioritising her physical well-being, she rekindled her commitment to rigorous exercise and embraced a healthier lifestyle, culminating in a remarkable transformation that transcended mere physical appearance.Empowered by her metamorphosis, Zawadi immortalised the moment with a professional photoshoot.She radiated newfound confidence and self-assurance as she transitioned from a conservative facade to adopting a bold and edgy style.. As she shared her journey with the world through social media, inadvertently attracting the attention of modelling agencies, Zawadi's story became a showcase of resilience and courage facing adversity.

Year 2

Chapter Twelve

EAT, PRAY, LOVE

> *To lose balance sometimes for love is part*
> *of living a balanced life."*
> — **Elizabeth Gilbert, Eat, Pray, Love**

Amidst the triumphs and transformations, Zawadi found her path leading into the dating realm, navigating the murky waters of online platforms with a blend of trepidation and curiosity.From unexpected compliments to surreal encounters with ageless individuals, each rendezvous offered a glimpse into the unpredictable tapestry of human connections.

Lost in the temporal folds of her hiatus from the dating scene, Zawadi stumbled back into the game, unwittingly thrown into the fray.A face on Tinder appraised her profile, declaring that she was too decent for such a platform dominated by those seeking fleeting connections. Grateful for the unexpected compliment, she promptly bid adieu to Tinder, deactivating her profile without a second thought.

While navigating the ebb and flow of her daily routine, Zawadi's eye was caught by an advertisement for a different dating site, promising eternal connection. Succumbing to her spontaneous nature, she downloaded the app, encouraged by its premium features that deterred undesirable encounters.

Her foray into online dating resembled a plunge into murky waters, encountering married men seeking extramarital excitement , a scenario all too familiar. Zawadi, savvy in virtual courtship, imposed a one-hour time limit on each physical date. This strategic move allowed her to gracefully bow out if the chemistry failed to spark while successfully whetting her appetite for the next potential rendezvous.

One peculiar encounter stood out amidst the sea of digital misadventures. A forty-five-year-old man proudly displayed a photo of himself from his buff twenties, contrasting the older gentleman awaiting her arrival. Perplexed, Zawadi initially dismissed the older man, assuming he had mistaken her for someone else. But upon pinging her supposed date, she realised the uncanny resemblance between the waving stranger and the young man in the photograph. Astonishingly, this was her date—just the forty-five-year-old edition. Confused but composed, she approached him, but was met with his surreal revelation.

He asserted that the twenty-year-old version and the current iteration were the same, urging her to embrace the evolution. Perplexed by the bizarre twist, Zawadi struggled to maintain her composure as the evening unfolded.

Yet, the situation drastically worsened as her date showcased his legal prowess by engaging in a heated argument with the waitress over the beverages served. It became abundantly clear that this would be his and Zawadi's first and final encounter, marking the abrupt end to the idea of any future exchanges.

SCHOOL OF MEN

Playfully dubbed the curator of the *"School of Men"* by a friend, Zawadi encountered a colourful array of characters along her dating journey, each belonging to a distinct class. From those rushing to achieve marriage before forty to the enigmatic polygamists seeking excitement, Zawadi's encounters were as diverse as they were illuminating. Yet, amidst the sea of superficiality and societal pressures, Zawadi remained steadfast in her pursuit of genuine connections and shared values, emerging from each encounter with invaluable lessons and unwavering resilience.

Some classes she encountered includes:

Class A—Individuals rushing to achieve marriage before turning forty.

Class B—Those seeking legal documents to settle down overseas with openness to genuine connections.

Class C—Sugar daddies in search of a trophy partner to highlight their opulence.

Class D—Younger men interested in dating a decade younger than Zawadi.

Class E—Individuals with confused sexuality, emphasising emotional connection and the need for caution.

Class F—Traditionalists who yearned for the amalgamation of a quintessential African woman with a flourishing career.

Class G—"Mummy's boys" seek partners who can fulfil a maternal role, often embodying a "fine boy" persona."

Class H—Polygamists considering mistresses or second wives for excitement.

Class I—Gold diggers seeking financial gains in relationships.

Class J—Scammers projecting a façade of luxury without substance.

Class K—Insecure individuals defining themselves by their material possessions.

Class L— Caucasians with a black fetish seeking to date a black woman as influenced by societal trends.

THREE DATES, THREE DIFFERENT MEN, SAME DAY: CALL HER CRAZY

Zawadi vehemently disagreed with the prevailing notion that her city was lonely. Her flatmates, hailing from diverse backgrounds, exposed her to a tapestry of new experiences, foods, and cultures but, more importantly, introduced her to an array of love interests.

Drowning in a sea of date offers, Zawadi abandoned the ritual of grocery shopping and eating at home. One whimsical day, she decided to orchestrate a daring feat: three dates in a single day—breakfast, lunch, and dinner, each with its unique charm.

The beauty of this approach lies in its efficiency—one hairstyle, one outfit, one-time grooming.It epitomised the art of romantic multitasking. The whirlwind experience of three dates in a single day showcased Zawadi's adventurous spirit.

The first rendezvous unfolded under the morning sun with a Caucasian companion. Opting for a light breakfast with an unconventional touch of red wine (justifying it by saying it was five o'clock in the evening somewhere in the world), he surprised her with a shoulder rub, regaling her with tales of coaching luminaries such as Richard Branson in tennis. With the clock ticking, she gracefully excused herself, citing a shopping expedition with friends. Upon being questioned for prioritising shopping over getting to know a potential life partner, she assured him of a future meeting.

The lunch date in a Nigerian restaurant showcased her favourite whole fish with plantains and yams. On top of the two-hour delay, her date, a taciturn medical doctor, played the marriage card. Politely declining his offer to escort her home, she concealed her intentions as she prepared for her next date, keeping her strategy under wraps while her unsuspecting companion remained unaware of her plans for the day.

The dinner date unfolded at the train station, amidst her companion's pleasant demeanour, Zawadi sensed it wouldn't blossom into something more. They dined at a vegan restaurant, indulging in a vegan burger, fries, and cocktails. Their laughter echoed through the evening as her date shared amusing tales of past relationships, highlighting the theatrics of his former African flame and the typical drama that coloured their time together.

Further unravelling the tapestry of his romantic history, he recounted the saga of an Asian woman he had been seeing. According to him, she spun a convoluted tale about returning to her homeland, but he discovered on Facebook that she had been centre stage at a lavish Asian wedding, resplendent in bridal attire. Zawadi, incredulous, inquired, "Onstage? Doing what? Is she an artist?"

The animated response came swiftly: "No! She was onstage at a flamboyant Asian wedding, all dressed up and getting married!"

Amidst fits of laughter, Zawadi became thoroughly entertained by his vivid storytelling.Despite the amusement, she eventually recognised the transient nature of their connection.

Despite the laughter and connections forged, the romance with each of her dates reached a dead end. The breakfast suitor claimed she had made a grave mistake by rejecting him, asserting they were a perfect match. The lunch companion received a UN posting in Switzerland, dissuading her from pursuing him in a long-distance relationship. As for the dinner date, the promising beginning had led to an inevitable fizzle.

Ultimately, Zawadi navigated the highs and lows of her day-long dating spree, realising that despite the variety of experiences, finding genuine connection remained an elusive pursuit in the tumultuous world of modern romance.

LIFE IN THE FAST LANE

As a consequence of her social media presence, Zawadi's life took a delightful turn upon reconnecting with an old family friend and former love interest, Leon. Their reunion sparked a renewed enthusiasm for travel. Zawadi eagerly planned to explore the world with Leon, looking forward to creating lasting memories together.

While Zawadi had initially envisioned touring the world with Ruhiu, their plans fell through due to Ruhiu's visa refusals. Despite this setback, Zawadi patiently awaited the opportunity to embark on her global adventures. Leon stepped in and reignited the flame of wanderlust, introducing Zawadi to a life of luxury with business-class and first-class flights becoming the norm. From enjoying breakfast in Paris to savouring lunch in Switzerland and relishing dinner in London, Zawadi lived a dream she had never imagined.

Accommodations also took a lavish turn, with stays at five-star and notably seven-star hotels—the latter a revelation for Zawadi, who had previously known solely of hotels with a maximum of five stars. The experience opened up a new world for her, filled with opulence and grandeur. Embracing the journey, she embarked on solo trips, forging connections with strangers and gaining a fresh perspective on travel.

Leon's attentive and caring nature further elevated Zawadi's experience of life. He upgraded her living arrangements from a single bedroom in a shared house to a penthouse in an upscale area of the town, generously covering all associated costs. Leon went above and beyond by providing funds to furnish the flat, ensuring Zawadi's comfort and well-being.

Displaying unmatched generosity, Leon handed Zawadi his American Express card and a debit card with her name linked to his details. This gesture meant she didn't need to dip into her funds for expenses, a level of financial support she had not experienced from a romantic partner. Leon also took charge of meals, preferring takeout or dining at restaurants using the bank cards he provided. His thoughtfulness extended to Zawadi's grooming, with regular changes to her hair and nails, contrasting her previous routine on a strict budget.

In this new chapter of life, Zawadi felt surrounded by abundance, care, and opportunities to explore the world in ways she had merely dreamed of.

JUST SAY YES!

Zawadi's eyes darted around the chaotic club in sheer panic. The dance floor bore evidence of spilt alcohol due to the energetic revelry. She couldn't fathom Leon's position, finding him on his knees in the centre of the dance floor with a ring box open and the lyrics to Drake's "*Controlla*" echoing in the background courtesy of the DJ. Suspicion had arisen in Zawadi as she witnessed Leon approaching the DJ and engaging in a covert conversation with him, which piqued her curiosity. His dismissive response to her enquiry had left her with more questions than answers. Still, she refrained from making a scene, unaware Leon had orchestrated for the DJ to play the song on cue.

Then came the unexpected proposal, and time seemed to freeze. "Zawadi, will you marry me?" echoed the chaotic atmosphere. She stood there, frozen, caught in a whirlwind of flashing cameras and recording devices capturing what others perceived as a romantic moment. Unable to find her voice, she shifted uneasily, yearning to escape. She locked eyes with Kioni and her husband and realised they were in on the plan. The awkwardness lingered until Leon, in embarrassment, finally rose and hugged her with forced laughter.

"Why did you do that? Why?" Zawadi whispered into Leon's ears, her romantic sensibilities clashing with the uncoordinated proposal.

Zawadi, a self-proclaimed romantic, struggled to comprehend the messy nature of the proposal. Whispering young women nearby commented on her perceived reaction, questioning, "What is wrong with her? If only she understood the difficulty of finding a man. She is fronting."

Leon, placing the ring box back in his pocket, resorted to his phone, attempting to distract himself from the awkward aftermath. Kioni, observing the situation, offered her perspective: "You should have just said yes and told him 'No' later rather than embarrassing him publicly."

The club's pulsating beats formed a backdrop to the unfolding drama, leaving Zawadi entangled in a whirlwind of emotions and unanswered questions.

Zawadi's world remained a whirlwind as she and Leon stepped into the silent Lyft, leaving behind the chaotic club scene. The tension in the air was palpable, and Zawadi's heart, still tangled with the echoes of a past love for Ruhiu, felt the weight of the unexpected proposal. The realisation that everything had escalated within a mere three months left her shaken.

"What was that? In a club?" Zawadi finally broke the silence.

"Was it the venue, or did you not want to say yes?" Leon responded.

"I don't know. Maybe a bit of both," Zawadi admitted, her mind racing with unanswered questions.

"I asked your sister to organise a romantic place, but for some reason, she didn't realise they weren't open today," Leon explained.

"But what was the rush? And what kind of ring was that? I would never have planned such a shabby proposal for Kioni," Zawadi said, expressing her confusion.

"I was nervous and forgot your ring at home, which is why I came with mine," Leon confessed.

"Wow! You have yours already?" Zawadi felt off guard.

"Of course! I will need one, won't I? Your engagement ring cost me twelve thousand US dollars. I had already bought you a lovely outfit, you had done your hair, and I had flown across the Atlantic for the special day. I didn't cancel all the plans because of the venue," Leon replied, defending himself.

The two fell into an uneasy silence yet again. Upon arriving home at the penthouse, Leon retrieved Zawadi's ring box and slammed it on the kitchen counter.

"You have two weeks to decide and wear that ring proudly on your finger. I also no longer want to hear anything about any pastor. You must attend my church every Sunday without fail, represent the family, and give offerings on our behalf, ensuring they will stand up for us on the day of need. If you refuse, the relationship ends, and I'll break up with you. I will also cut off the payment for this house and cancel the credit and debit cards," Leon declared.

Although Zawadi desired to start a family, Leon seemed to fit in in many ways, and fear and uncertainty gripped her. Leon's church friends had advised her to aim higher, igniting a familiar feeling she had experienced at the time of Ruhiu's proposal. This time, she vowed not to ignore her feelings or her counsel.

Entering the bathroom, Zawadi locked the door and called her mum in tears.

Her mother reassured her and advised her to leave the ring as is, telling Leon she needed time to think. After the call, Zawadi remained on the toilet seat, struggling to piece together the complex puzzle of her emotions. Unsettled and unable to legally remarry in the United States without the original validated Decree Nisi or Decree Absolute obtained in Kenya, Zawadi stood at a daunting crossroads.

Leon's history of three failed marriages had left Zawadi hesitant and apprehensive about taking such a risk with a man who, given their family connection, she feared might see her as a pity project. Despite making excuses for him and attempting to justify his actions based on their shared family history, Zawadi knew deep down that she wasn't ready to rush into anything with him. Content with the current state of their relationship, she longed for a connection unburdened by the conventional constraints of marriage at this juncture.

UNRAVELING: THE ROCKY ROAD WITH LEON

During a trip around America with Leon, they landed in New Jersey with just a few hours to spare that night before Zawadi's flight to Houston the next day. Despite Leon's fatigue, he decided to join her on a train ride from New Jersey to New York allowing her to enjoy the sights and sounds of the ever-vibrant city. She was blindsided by Leon's anger upon her request for some photos of herself by the Statue of Liberty. He lost his temper and began yelling at her.

"I am not your photographer!" he declared, dropping her phone on a park bench before walking away. Zawadi experienced a sinking feeling, much like the abandonment she felt as her siblings left her during a childhood swimming outing.

Strolling towards the car, struggling to put one foot in front of the other, Leon continued to yell, threatening to leave her unless she entered the Lyft. Something in him seemed to snap, transforming him into someone she no longer recognised. As they drove off, Zawadi remained silent. After a few miles, Leon tossed a few hundred-dollar bills at her demeaningly, promising money for her trip to Houston the next day.

Feeling degraded, Zawadi wanted to escape the cab and distance herself from this changed, monstrous version of Leon. She did nothing to deserve such mistreatment except ask for a few pictures.

Upon reaching the train station, the driver was confused by the few bills Leon had scattered in the Lyft. Uncertain about whom to give the money to, the driver went back and forth between Zawadi and Leon. Unwilling to compromise her self-worth, Zawadi folded her hands, shrugged her shoulders, and walked away unaware of the resolution.

With no funds for her trip, she approached the ticket machine to secure a train ticket from New Jersey to New York using Leon's credit card he had put in her name. Leon, growing increasingly frustrated, contemplated returning to New Jersey. At the top of the stairs, he began screaming at Zawadi, urging her to board the imminent train. Zawadi, bewildered by his outburst in front of strangers, remained silent. Deaf to his rant, she pretended not to recognize him, finding his loss of an American accent somewhat comical.

"Are you crazy? Get on the train!" Leon hurled at her, leaving Zawadi to wonder if he had utterly lost his mind. Notwithstanding this chaos, she clung to her determination not to diminish her self-worth for the sake of someone who had turned into a stranger.

As Zawadi walked away from the escalating confrontation with Leon at the train station, he threw the train tickets he had bought at her. Unfazed by his actions, she sought help from a man to purchase tickets to New York. Leon's frustration seemed to intensify. Her disregard for his behaviour may have pushed him over the edge.

Observing him from the corner of her eye, Zawadi watched as Leon boarded the train to New Jersey, leaving her with scant money and no cellular network for communication. Unprepared for the unexpected turn of events, she ended up on a train bound for New York, unintentionally moving in the opposite direction from Leon. The situation struck her as comical, a peculiar twist in their tumultuous journey.

Despite the dampening experience, Zawadi aimed to protect her peace. She made the most of her time in New York, exploring Times Square and visiting the Empire State Building. Her lack of awareness about train times made her barely catch the train to New Jersey. Along the way, she encountered friendly strangers who showed her around and captured memorable moments.

At Leon's apartment, Zawadi had little time to rest before heading to the airport. Despite the rocky incident, they reconciled, hoping it signalled merely a temporary setback.

On another occasion, during a dinner date with Leon, Zawadi ordered a big bowl of Chinese soup and requested a separate bowl for Leon to share with her. Leon, expressing his disinterest, lost his temper as she insisted. He called an Uber. Despite his stormy exit, they eventually rode home together. However, the pattern of abusive behaviour had become evident.

Leon's apologies and reconciliations didn't erase the scars of his erratic behaviour. Zawadi realised that staying with him meant compromising her dignity and self-worth. Leon's emotional instability had become too much to bear.

RUNAWAY BRIDE

The next chapter in Zawadi's journey of self-discovery unfolded as she grappled with the complexities and uncertainties surrounding the institution of marriage. After Leon, she received four more engagement proposals. Each engagement proposal reminded her of her experiences with Leon and Ruhiu, prompting her to question whether a marriage was on her life's path.

Despite her desire for companionship and raising a family, Zawadi couldn't ignore the red flags that emerged with each proposal. The fear of another failed relationship loomed large in her mind, urging her to tread cautiously and seek clarity before taking the next step.

Zawadi turned to trusted individuals in her community for guidance, including her pastor and a marriage counsellor at church. These mentors functioned as a sounding board, helping her navigate her uncertainties and discern whether her hesitations were rooted in external factors or internal doubts.

In the mosaic of life, a preacher likened marriage to two rough stones, each with its unique jaggedness and imperfections, brought together in a union that is both enduring and transformative. As these stones are subjected to the inevitable pressures and trials of life, they begin a process akin to an age-old natural phenomenon—gradually, through the daily rub of experiences, disagreements, and mutual support, they wear down each other's rough edges.

This metaphor speaks to the essence of marital growth, where the friction of living and growing together serves not to break them apart, but to refine and smooth their surfaces. Over time, what once caused friction becomes the catalyst for creating a polished unity, a relationship characterised by an ease and flow that only comes from years of learning, forgiving, and adapting to one another.

This enduring process highlights the beauty of commitment and the transformative power of love—how two individuals, once rough and disparate, can evolve into partners who fit together seamlessly, their once prominent edges now smoothed into complementing contours. In this divine alchemy of marriage, the preacher sees not just the smoothing of stones but the crafting of a singular masterpiece, bearing testament to the resilience, patience, and unfailing dedication that love demands.

Through introspection and candid conversations with her mentors, Zawadi confronted her misconceptions about marriage and challenged societal expectations. She realised that marriage was not a universal remedy for loneliness or individual incompleteness; instead, she realised that she could attain wholeness and fulfilment through various avenues beyond marriage.

Pastor T's insightful counsel prompted Zawadi to question the necessity of marriage in her life. She pondered the joys of parenthood and companionship, recognising that she could pursue these experiences through alternative means such as adoption or community involvement.

As Zawadi reflected on the limitations and uncertainties of marriage, she began to reshape her views on relationships and personal fulfilment. She understood that true satisfaction and happiness transcended the confines of marriage and were deeply rooted in spirituality and self-acceptance.

With a newfound perspective on life and relationships, Zawadi embraced the journey of self-discovery with an open heart and mind. She recognised the importance of prioritising her personal growth and well-being before embarking on a shared life with a partner.

As she continued to navigate the complexities of love and companionship, Zawadi remained hopeful that one day, she would find a partner who shared her values and aspirations. But until then, she was determined to live a life filled with purpose, joy, and fulfilment, regardless of her marital status.

Zawadi's journey of self-discovery and empowerment continued, guided by the lessons learned and the wisdom gained along the way. With each step forward, she embraced the beauty of life's uncertainties and the power of resilience to overcome adversity. Through it all, she remained steadfast in her pursuit of personal wholeness and fulfilment, knowing that true happiness came from within.

Chapter Thirteen

BABY BLUES

> *Tough times never last, but tough people do.*
> —Robert H. Schuller

Relieved that Aunt Flo was no longer disrupting her life, Zawadi attributed this newfound balance to the Chinese treatment. It looked like a positive sign, a beacon of hope amidst the storm. With a couple of years having passed since her diagnosis of low AMH, she decided to take a leap, entrusting her hopes as she visited the fertility clinic.

Encouraged by the Chinese herbal doctor's confidence in the treatment, Zawadi held on to the possibility of a miracle. Although her dream of starting a family with Leon had faded, and though love was yet to find its way to her, she hoped to preserve her fertility by freezing some eggs. With determination in her heart, she made the call to the fertility clinic, taking a step towards a future she hoped would include the chance to build a family.

THE WEIGHT OF TRUTH

Zawadi's heart raced as she awaited the doctor's verdict, her hopes balanced precariously on the edge of uncertainty. As the words finally escaped the doctor's lips, reality struck her with a force akin to a sledgehammer. The declining levels of Anti-Müllerian Hormone (AMH) revealed a grim truth – her chances of successful egg freezing were dwindling.

The doctor's diagnosis reverberated in her mind as she struggled to comprehend the gravity of the situation. The twenty eggs produced during previous IVF cycles felt like a distant memory, eclipsed by the harsh reality of her declining fertility. Each attempt at egg freezing would strain her already stretched financial resources, a daunting prospect she hadn't fully prepared for.

Feeling betrayed by the medical profession, Zawadi questioned the decisions that had led her here.Placing her trust in experts, she believed each procedure would bring her closer to her dream of motherhood. Currently, faced with the stark truth of her situation, doubts crept in, clouding her judgment.

According to the proverbial biological clock, she was thirty-three and had two more years to go before the dreaded decline. She had eaten whole foods and a majority plant-based diet, paid heavily for alternate treatment, exercised, prayed, and fasted to optimise her body, but it seemed that all her efforts had been in vain.

Grasping for guidance amidst the uncertainty, Zawadi explored her options. The doctor's suggestion of donor eggs and sperm, along with the possibility of surrogacy, offered a ray of optimism amidst the uncertainty. Yet, the fifty-fifty success rate loomed large, casting a shadow of doubt over her aspirations.

The hefty financial burden of nearly sixty thousand US dollars for a 50 per cent chance of success weighed heavily on her mind. With no genetic connection to her or a future partner, Zawadi couldn't shake the parallels with adoption – a path she had considered before but resonated more deeply at this point.

In a moment of clarity, Zawadi voiced her thoughts, drawing strength from her faith and belief in the power of love. She spoke of the meaningful endeavour of offering love and opportunity to a vulnerable child, inspired by the example of Jesus' adoption by Joseph in Christian faith.

The doctor's response echoed her sentiments, acknowledging the significance of love and nurture in shaping a child's life. As Zawadi contemplated her options, the idea of adoption took root, sparking a deeper evaluation of her choices.

With a heavy heart but a renewed sense of purpose, Zawadi thanked the doctor and vowed to explore the path of adoption further. Armed with newfound clarity and determination, she stepped forward, ready to embrace the journey ahead, guided by the weight of truth and the power of love.

As she left the clinic, Zawadi noticed the varied emotions of the couples in the waiting room, each grappling with their own hopes and fears. The experience of IVF, with its injections and dashed expectations, loomed over her thoughts. Yet, amidst the uncertainty, she found solace in the knowledge of her options, particularly the possibility of adoption, free from the constraints of a ticking clock.

Zawadi shared the news with her sisters, who offered unwavering support and empathy. Together, they agreed that adoption was a more viable solution than pursuing costly fertility treatments. Her male friends offered their assistance, but none of their proposals resonated with her.In contrast, her sisters, niece, and friend Sherrie offered to carry the baby if needed, showering her with an outpouring of love and support that deeply touched her.

Seeking a different perspective, Zawadi contacted one of her mentors and shared the news with him, hoping for guidance and insight.

THE POWER OF THE HERE AND NOW

After Zawadi had shared the news with her mentor, he said, "Zawadi, thank you for sharing this news with me. Can I share a story with you?"

Zawadi answered, "Yes, please."

"One day," her mentor said, "a fisherman lay on a beautiful beach with his fishing pole bolstered in the sand and his solitary line cast out into the sparkling blue surf. He was enjoying the warmth of the afternoon sun and the chance of catching a fish.

"About that time, a businessman came walking down the beach trying to relieve some of the stress from his workday. He noticed the fisherman sitting on the beach and decided to find out why this man was out fishing instead of someplace working hard to make a living for himself and his family. 'You aren't going to catch many fish that way,' the businessman said. 'You should be working rather than lying on the beach!'

"The fisherman looked up at the businessman, smiled, and replied, 'And what will my reward be?'

"'Well, you can get bigger nets and catch more fish!' was the businessman's answer.

"'And then what will my reward be?' asked the fisherman, still smiling.

"The businessman replied, 'You will make money, and you'll be able to buy a boat, which will result in larger fish catches!'

"'And then what will my reward be?' asked the fisherman again.

"The businessman was beginning to get irritated by the fisherman's questions. 'You can buy a bigger boat and hire some people to work for you!' he said.

"'And then what will my reward be?' repeated the fisherman.

"The businessman was getting angry. 'Don't you understand? You can become rich enough that work for a living becomes a choice, not a necessity! You can spend all the rest of your days on this beach, looking at the sunset. You won't have a care in the world!'

"The fisherman, still smiling, looked up and said, 'And what do you think I'm doing at the moment?'

"The story's moral is that you are where you must be presently. If you would stop fighting the waves and allow the tide to take you on the journey meant for you. Society imposes a boilerplate template on everyone, but do you know your current path isn't what God originally designed for you? You always said you were an oddball and never fit in right from your childhood.

But perhaps you're exerting too much effort to fit in when you're one of 'The Chosen', meant to stand out and blessed with the opportunity of isolation. This is something rare that few people can enjoy, seeing as life and commitments result in the hustle and bustle of life. Imagine all the lives you can touch with your story.

Some women are designed to be moms, others aunties—and others should not come within ten feet of any child. I have seen you around your nieces and nephews, and sometimes, I've had to look hard to tell who the child is and who the adult is. I have no question in my mind that you would make a fantastic mom. I know this will not be the first time you have heard this. Ex-boyfriends have told you this. Your hairdresser echoed the same thing as well.

Some lead from the front, others from behind, and others sideways," Zawadi's mentor said.

"We may all want to lead, but not necessarily in the same form and capacity. We sometimes play lead roles in life, and other times, we play supporting characters, but the beauty of life is in knowing our place in the order of life.

I genuinely believe that life can be as straightforward or as complicated as you make it. The beautiful thing is that you get to choose.

Your family and I can all empathise with you, but you must deal with the thoughts and pain alone. I may not have the answers, but I want you to look around, count your blessings, recognise the progress you've made, and open your mind to the possibilities. Remember, there is still a chance for you to get pregnant. No one said it was the end of the road for you. I assure you, many people would pray to have the life you currently have. Moreover, consider the story of your own mother, Zawadi. She had your younger brother at the age of 45, showing that all hope is not lost even later in life. Your situation is not unique, and there remains a possibility for change and new beginnings. Your mother's experience is a testament to the unexpected joys that life can still offer, and it serves as a reminder to remain hopeful and open to the opportunities that the future holds.

I've heard that people who lose one of their senses gain a heightened use of the others. What are you gaining as a result of this experience?

Women are containers full of love, always looking for something or someone to pour themselves into. I know you will find the proper expression soon.

You need to *stop*, see, and *smell* the roses.

I have to go. I'll call you tomorrow to check on you. Take care, my friend."

Zawadi answered, "Thank you. I appreciate you. You always have the right words. Speak soon."

EMBRACING WAVES: THE JOURNEY TO SELF-DISCOVERY AND PARENTHOOD

After her conversation with her mentor, Zawadi noticed a recurring pattern in her life: things hardly ever went right for her the first time around. There always seemed to be a learning curve, whether it was her education, career, friendships, or relationships. Taking her mentor's advice to heart, she decided to stop fighting against these waves of uncertainty. Through experience, she learned that the second time around often yielded better results. Finding solace in this realisation, she embraced her life's unique pattern.

Finding comfort in the outpouring of love and support, Zawadi reflected on her mentor's words, embracing the idea of the present moment. Her mentor's parable about the fisherman reminded her of the importance of surrendering to the journey meant for her, rather than fighting against the waves of life.

Embracing her unique path, Zawadi resolved to count her blessings, recognise her strengths, and open her heart to the possibilities ahead. With a newfound sense of peace, she awaited the next chapter of her life, guided by the weight of truth and the power of love.

Although she filled her mind with food for thought from her mentor, Zawadi's growling belly demanded immediate attention. She indulged in her favourite greasy Chinese takeout, a whole chocolate cake, and three bottles of red wine— a cheat day from her usual regimen of avoiding alcohol, fatty foods, and processed foods, especially during her attempts to conceive. Today, though, she allowed herself this indulgence.

Returning home, Zawadi changed into her comfortable onesie, laid her treats on her bed, and settled in to watch **"Pretty Woman"**. Simultaneously, she opened her laptop to research the adoption process in her area, a decision weighing heavily on her mind.

The following day, Zawadi reminisced about the movie "*Losing Isaiah*", a childhood favourite that had left a lasting impact on her. As an adult, the film's portrayal of selfless love between Isaiah and his adopted mother continued to evoke deep emotions within her.

As she scrolled through the adoption website, admiring the beautiful baby pictures, Zawadi reflected on the profound love she felt inside her, longing to share it with a child. She pondered the disparity between the intensity of love some women felt for their partners compared to the love they extended to adopted or fostered children.

Drawing from her own experiences with her adopted brother Jaali, Zawadi resolved not to measure her need for love and companionship solely through the lens of having children. She refused to settle for less than she deserved in a partner and recognised the importance of healing her heart and soul before opening herself up to a new relationship.

Considering her age and the life experiences of the men she attracted, Zawadi contemplated various options for building a family, including surrogacy or adoption. She remained optimistic about possibly creating the family she craved, albeit through unconventional means.

With the adoption website's requirements in mind, Zawadi prioritised meeting the criteria, focusing on securing a two-bedroom house and ensuring financial stability. Determined to provide a stable and loving environment for her future child, she committed herself to upskilling and enhancing her career prospects.

Despite the challenges and uncertainties she faced, Zawadi remained hopeful for the future, believing that she would have another chance to make things right. With a rigid study routine and proactive steps towards advancing her career, she took control of her destiny, determined to create the life she envisioned for herself and her future child.

Chapter Fourteen

STAINS OF RESILIENCE

> *Do not judge me by my success, judge me by how many times I fell down and got back up again.*
> —**Nelson Mandela**

Zawadi's journey had been determined and resilient, boosted by her unwavering commitment to building a better life for herself and her future child. With a new job and a promising salary increase, she had set out on a path toward stability and fulfilment. Little did she know, though, that a single moment would shatter her composure and set her on a course she never anticipated.

Surrounded by the chatter of her colleagues in the bustling canteen, Zawadi's world crumbled around her. Shockwaves surged through her body as she felt warmth spreading between her legs. Before she could grasp the situation, she confronted a sight that would haunt her – a massive blob of blood staining the pristine floor beneath her feet.

Frozen in disbelief, Zawadi wrestled with a flood of emotions. Panic and embarrassment threatened to overwhelm her as she struggled to make sense of the surreal scene unfolding before her. Should she cry? Should she run? Should she collapse and fake a miscarriage to escape the humiliation?

In that moment of chaos, Zawadi longed for a superpower to make herself invisible, to disappear from the prying eyes of her colleagues. With trembling hands and a racing heart, she scanned the room for any sign of recognition, desperate to escape the scrutiny of those around her.

Driven by instinct, Zawadi abandoned her lunch and fled to the safety of the women's restroom, seeking refuge from the chaos that threatened to engulf her. Despite her layers of protective clothing, the relentless bleeding persisted, leaving a trail of crimson in its wake as she sought solace in the confines of the bathroom stall.

135

As she sat in silence, overwhelmed by her predicament, Zawadi couldn't shake the questions about the choices that had led her to this moment. The countless surgeries, the endless cycle of treatments – each one had promised relief from the pain and uncertainty of her condition, yet none had delivered on their lofty assurances.

Feeling like a prisoner of her own body, Zawadi reached a breaking point. With resignation, she declared her surrender to the relentless tide of her circumstances.

"I give up," she cried out, her voice a whisper in the empty confines of the restroom.

Her frustration and despair spilt forth as she confronted Dr Mark, demanding answers for the endless cycle of surgeries and treatments that had failed to deliver on their promises. In a moment of desperation, she agreed to a contraceptive injection, an eleventh-hour action to regain control over her life amidst the chaos that threatened to consume her.

Yet, as she grasped for stability confronting uncertainty, Zawadi couldn't shake the lingering doubts that gnawed at her soul. The injection offered a sliver of promise, a temporary respite from the relentless bleeding that had plagued her for so long. But fear and apprehension loomed large beneath the surface, casting a shadow over her fragile sense of optimism.

As the weeks passed and the bleeding continued unabated, Zawadi grappled with the harsh reality of her situation. The promise of stability had eluded her again, leaving her adrift in a sea of uncertainty and doubt. Yet, amidst the chaos that threatened to engulf her, Zawadi clung to a flicker of hope –a belief in the resilience of the human spirit and the enduring power of love to conquer the darkest days.

In the quiet solitude of her home, Zawadi sought solace in the support of her mentor and Auntie Afaafa, finding strength in their unwavering belief in her ability to overcome the challenges ahead. With each passing day, she drew closer to the truth that had eluded her for so long—that while confronting uncertainty, the journey towards healing and redemption was worth taking, guided by the light of hope that burned bright within her heart.

Year 3

Chapter Fifteen

KINDNESS

> *In a world where you can be anything, be kind.*
> **—Unknown**

I stood frozen, my mind racing as I looked down at Zawadi's seemingly lifeless body on the floor, bathed in blood. The scene resembled something from a crime network show, and a mix of shock and sorrow enveloped me. Was she gone, and had the weight of her struggles finally taken its toll?

Memories of Zawadi's struggles and battles with life's complications flooded my thoughts. She had faced traumas and tribulations, yet her resilience and strength prevailed. The juxtaposition of her vibrant spirit with the current lifeless state of her body created a jarring contrast.

As I assessed the situation, the weight of responsibility pressed upon me as questions swirled in my mind; I wondered if there were signs I missed or cues I had failed to pick up on. The perplexity of Zawadi's affluent upbringing, intelligence, and support from family and church deepened the mystery surrounding this tragic moment.

Amid my swirling thoughts, I couldn't help but reflect on the fragility of life and the silent struggles that some individuals endure. With all her brilliance and vitality, Zawadi had battled demons in the shadows, and this time, it seemed that they had taken their toll.

I wished she had reached out and shared the burden that had become too heavy to bear alone. The whys echoed in my mind as I sought understanding, grappling with the harsh reality that sometimes, the most vigorous souls can be consumed by darkness.

At that moment, with Zawadi's still form before me, the urgency of the questions persisted. But at this moment, there were no easy answers, just the haunting silence of a life interrupted.

Earlier that morning, a sense of unease settled within me like a heavy shroud. I couldn't shake the worry that had gnawed at my thoughts since the previous evening when Zawadi's voice, strained and weary, reached me through the phone.

"I'm fine," she had insisted, her words a feeble attempt to mask the weight of her illness. "I appreciate your concern, but I really can't have visitors right now."

But concern, fuelled by a deep-seated sense of responsibility and faith, propelled me forward despite her protests. Ignoring the voice of doubt that whispered in the recesses of my mind, I resolved to check on her, to ensure that she wasn't facing her struggles alone.

With a determined stride, I made my way to her apartment building, the familiar path now cloaked in a surreal haze of apprehension. As I approached the entrance, a sense of urgency quickened my steps, each heartbeat a steady rhythm urging me forward.

Upon reaching the building, I found myself at a crossroads of hesitation and resolve. Zawadi's plea for solitude echoed in my ears, but the nagging sense of duty spurred me onward. With a steady hand, I retrieved the spare key she had entrusted me with, a symbol of our bond forged through years of shared joys and sorrows.

Using the key, I slipped through the security doors of the building, my presence unnoticed amidst the morning bustle of residents beginning their day. With each step, I willed myself forward, a silent prayer on my lips for strength and guidance.

Navigating the labyrinthine corridors, I traced the path to Zawadi's door, each footfall a testament to the depth of my concern. As I stood before her door, a surge of apprehension washed over me, the weight of uncertainty pressing down like a leaden cloak.

Taking a deep breath, I raised my hand to knock, but a sudden wave of doubt stayed my hand. What if my intrusion was unwelcome? What if Zawadi resented my intrusion, viewing it as a breach of her boundaries?

But in the end, it was the flicker of hope that spurred me forward, the belief that perhaps, in my presence, Zawadi might find solace and comfort amidst the storm raging within her. With a resolute resolve, I inserted the key into the lock and turned it, the metallic click echoing in the quiet of the morning.

As the door swung open, I stepped into the threshold of Zawadi's world, my heart heavy with anticipation and trepidation. Whatever lay beyond that threshold, I knew that I had crossed a boundary, both physical and emotional, driven by a bond that transcended mere friendship.

Little did I know that this simple act of checking on a friend and mentee would set in motion a series of events that would forever alter the course of our lives.

As I knocked on Zawadi's door, my worry intensified with the absence of a response. The gravity of the situation loomed over me, and the thought of just leaving crossed my mind. As a successful married man with a family, my involvement with Zawadi was purely to support her through a tough time. Yet, the potential misinterpretation by others weighed heavily on my conscience.

A RACE AGAINST TIME

Contemplating the possible consequences, I envisioned being seen as a suspect in her death if the police were involved. The uncertainty surrounding Zawadi's condition added to the turmoil. With life slipping away, I finally realised the urgency and decided to call for an ambulance. Panic set in as I reached for my phone, realising I didn't have her exact address.

Frantically searching her home, I hoped to find any document with the necessary details. The reality of the situation sank in, prompting me to do more than pray. Recollections of movie scenes flashed before me as I rushed to the kitchen and grabbed a bowl of water to pour over Zawadi. As that failed to elicit a response, desperation led me to resort to slapping her and trying to revive her, all while grappling with the unfolding crisis.

Then, a knock echoed throughout the room. To my amazement, the ambulance services had arrived in under ten minutes. Although it felt like a swift response, it carried the weight of a lifetime. It seemed as though someone up there must have heard my prayers.

The paramedics swiftly connected the ECG and other equipment to Zawadi's body, employing various techniques to resuscitate her. After about fifteen minutes, Zawadi gradually opened her eyes. She scanned the room, moving quickly to each paramedic and my side. Finally, her eyes fell on her clothing and the floor, both stained with the evidence of her struggle.

"Thank you, God!" I screamed in sheer relief and excitement.

In the softest voice, with the tiny ounce of strength left in her, Zawadi barraged me with a series of questions:

"Why are you here?"

"Why are paramedics with huge dirty boots all over my white rug?" (*"She cared more about that bloody white carpet than what was standing right before her."*)

"Why am I covered in water?"

"Can someone tell me what is going on?"

Then, tears started pouring down her face as she realised what could have happened.

As I stared into Zawadi's eyes, her whole life flashed. Losing her life amidst it all was not something I had seen coming by a long shot. "Hasn't she been through enough already?" I muttered to myself. "Who did she offend? How did her life end up here?"

Borrowing a Nigerian colloquialism, I said, "*Na only you waka come?*" which translates as "*Why do you appear to be the sole one experiencing constant misfortune?*"

Regardless, I remained thankful that I had rejected Zawadi's request not to come to visit.

FEED HER

The paramedics helped Zawadi to the sofa and asked her questions to ascertain what had happened. All she could remember was getting up from the couch to get something and, the next time, she opened her eyes, seeing that she had passed out on the floor. Before wheeling her off to A&E, the paramedics asked me to make something to give her some strength.

I brought her a tray that looked like something out of a comedic movie scene—reminiscent of Kevin in "*Home Alone*", who haphazardly made breakfast with cereal and an overflowing mug of milk. My tray was laden with hot chocolate, orange juice mixed with green energy powder, a glass of milk, oats in a bowl, the medication I had brought, biscuits, and an egg sandwich. As I hurriedly took the food to Zawadi, some of the drinks spilled on the tray, adding to the chaos. It was an absolute mess. But who cared? This young woman had to eat something. Given her current state, the presentation was the least of my concerns; the important thing was ensuring she consumed what she needed.

She had a bit of the juice before the paramedics wheeled her off.

"She has a weak pulse! Quick; we need to get her to the hospital immediately!" the paramedic holding Zawadi's hand exclaimed.-

SURVIVOR TURNED WARRIOR

Zawadi's health condition stabilised. She looked at her right hand, observing the needle and blood transfusing into her body.

On her left hand was a drip to rehydrate her. She also had multiple plasters across both hands, which were very sore from the failed attempts of the phlebotomist to find her tiny veins.

Both hands looked like pincushions.The multiple dark bruises gave Zawadi's hands the appearance of those of a drug addict who shot herself up regularly. Whenever she moved the arm with the blood going through to adjust herself or reach for her phone, the transfusion device would emit a blaring noise, sounding like a smoke alarm. It was uncomfortable for the other patients and for Zawadi, too, as it sounded like the noise she'd heard the previous night, resembling the sound from the moment one of the patients went into cardiac arrest and passed away right in front of her.

The wristband put on Zawadi as she was checked into the hospital by the medical staff terrified her. While it functioned as a means to ensure healthcare workers were dealing with the right patient, it also held the grim implication of identifying her in case of her passing.

She did her best to move as little as possible, but whenever the sound inadvertently went off, she would quickly call the nurse's attention using the buzzer beside her bed. The nurse would fiddle with the peripheral intravenous catheters (PIVC), which stopped the sound.

The nurses had wrapped Zawadi's upper arm in the blood pressure cuff connected to a standing monitor. Zawadi's index finger had an oximeter, which monitored her pulse.

The hospital's setup was reminiscent of boarding school, with everyone in their respective corners and tiny cubbyholes to store valuables.Zawadi was dressed in a collarless, ill-fitted hospital gown, exposing her backside.

She turned away whenever she noticed the other patients' backsides as they tried to get out of bed to use the restroom or go for a short walk around the ward. Despite the discomfort and vulnerability that gnawed at her, Zawadi remained determined to preserve her dignity amidst the sterile confines of the hospital ward. With each movement, each shift in position, she instinctively reached for the thin hospital gown, a feeble attempt to shield herself from the prying eyes of the world.

Whether sitting up in bed or making her way to the bathroom, she moved with a cautious grace, her hands a shield against the unwanted exposure of her most intimate self. It was a ritual born of necessity, a silent plea for privacy in a space where boundaries blurred and walls whispered secrets.

As she navigated the cramped confines of the hospital ward, Zawadi's movements were careful and deliberate, her gaze fixed on the ground as if searching for solace amidst the cold linoleum tiles. Each step was a silent protest against the indignity of her circumstances, a refusal to surrender to the dehumanising reality of illness.

She was fragile, and the nurses informed her she had contracted COVID, which meant admission to the red zone with the other aged patients who had contracted COVID. Tears streamed down her cheeks as she experienced mixed emotions, including gratitude for surviving the ordeal, the shock of catching COVID, and being relegated to an area from which people barely made it out alive.

What further traumatised Zawadi was living alone during the pandemic. If she had passed away, it might have taken weeks for anyone to find her. The finitude of life could not be any more apparent as she watched the agony that the older patients faced as they battled for their lives.

Zawadi reached out to her sisters through a video call on FaceTime, and as they connected, tears flowed freely. Life's trials had imparted a crucial lesson to Zawadi: the importance of cherishing and holding dear those closest to her heart, for the sands of time are ever-shifting, much like the ticking of her biological clock. Seeing her sisters again was a blessing, particularly after the recent scare that loomed, threatening to snatch her away from them.

Having just had a brush with death and being confined to a bed, Zawadi had a lot of time to reflect on life and its true meaning, what matters, and what persists after we are gone.

NINE LIVES

In the heart of South Africa's *Wild Wild West*, Zawadi's college camping trip promised adventure, but what unfolded was a testament to the guiding hand of fate. As the class embarked on a whitewater rafting excursion, Zawadi hesitated, her lack of swimming skills a looming barrier.But her friends assured her she wouldn't sink with a life jacket. It was called a life jacket for a reason, after all. Buoyed by assurances from classmates, she plunged into the rapids, only to meet danger head-on.

Striking her head on a rock, Zawadi's world faded into darkness, but a guardian angel appeared—a villager, a saviour in disguise, pulling her by the neck of of her life jacket into his boat. Her classmates remained oblivious to her brush with death, consumed by their own merriment. Grateful yet shaken, Zawadi retreated into herself, haunted by a sense of fragility.

Haunted by the shadows of her past, Zawadi's resilience was tested once more in the face of a failed IVF cycle and the torment of her period, compounded by her husband's prolonged absence.Unable to move her legs, desperate to use the bathroom and concerned about making a mess on the bed, she attempted to navigate the situation. In the struggle, she fell from the bed, causing further distress. Unable to move, Zawadi eventually had to bear the discomfort and slept on the floor covered in blood. This grim situation was reminiscent of her previous encounter on the night she tried escaping for a night out with her cousin Scarlet, only to be caught by her older brother. Back then, she had also ended up sleeping on cold concrete floors to be concealed from him. These harsh memories weren't new to her; the cold, unforgiving concrete had been an all too familiar bed during her troubled past, echoing a life marked by constraints and challenges.The following morning, with some relief, she reached for her phone and called her mother for assistance. Her mother, having a spare key, entered to provide much-needed help.

Reflecting on this experience, Zawadi realised that if she were still married to Ruhiu, there was no assurance he would have been there for her during that critical time. It seemed that, in unexpected ways, God orchestrated the presence of people to support Zawadi at precisely the moment she needed it the most.

Reflecting on her life's close calls—near-suffocation by a friend during a play date as a child, brushes with death in Soweto and Johannesburg, and moments of unconsciousness—Zawadi recognised a divine presence. Angels, she believed, intervened to preserve her life, a feline survivor of countless trials.

She sensed a uniqueness about her experiences, having survived afflictions despite being unable to fully comprehend their purpose. While it's often said that God assigns his toughest battles to his strongest soldiers, Zawadi found herself yearning for a path less fraught with challenges and obstacles. Despite her resilience and inner strength, she longed for a smoother, less tumultuous journey through life. Each trial she faced tested her resolve, leaving her weary and longing for respite from the relentless storms that seemed to buffet her at every turn. Yet, even in the midst of her struggles, Zawadi remained steadfast in her faith, hopeful that brighter days lay ahead despite the darkness that surrounded her.

In the wake of the COVID pandemic, Zawadi was permitted only one guest during her hospital stay. She chose her aunt Afaafa to accompany her during her stay. Despite the inherent risks of exposure to the virus and the potential repercussions for her job, aunt Afaafa embraced her role wholeheartedly. Taking unplanned extended periods off work, she navigated the delicate balance between her health and her responsibilities to be a constant source of comfort and support for Zawadi. In the face of uncertainty, aunt Afaafa's unwavering presence served as a beacon of strength and solidarity, a testament to the profound bond between family members in times of need.

Each morning, as the nurses made their rounds to deliver breakfast, Zawadi was presented with a menu for the day ahead, offering choices for both lunch and dinner. The standard breakfast offerings included a selection of tea or hot chocolate paired with toast or cereal. Despite the modest portions, Zawadi often found solace in the simplicity of toast and cereal, providing a comforting start to her day and staving off hunger until lunchtime. However, what truly warmed her heart was the inclusion of African options on the menu, offering a taste of home amidst the sterile hospital environment. These familiar flavours served as a comforting reminder of her roots and provided a much-needed sense of comfort during her prolonged stay in the hospital.

Zawadi kept her church family and prayer groups informed about her health situation. A particularly emotional Zoom call with a prayer group of women she considered sisters moved Zawadi to tears. Despite not meeting most of them in person, she found that their prayers brought a deep connection.Her church organised regular prayer calls, ensuring she received spiritual support. Upon discharge, they also promised a support package and planned a visit to lift her spirits.

Jaali, distant during Zawadi's divorce, sought redemption by leveraging his position as a pastor of one of Africa's prominent churches. Despite the security protocols, he reached the *General Overseer* (GO) during a church camp meeting, securing prayers for Zawadi. She hoped these prayers, including a personal message from the GO, would bring divine intervention in her life.

Eager to know her discharge timeline, Zawadi pressed the buzzer, seeking the attention of nurses or doctors to provide updates on her recovery and potential release.

Chapter Sixteen

MEDICAL CONUNDRUM

I'm a conundrum or an enigma. I forget which.
—James A. Owen

Zawadi's initial hospital admission marked the beginning of a relentless cycle, with six subsequent admissions to follow. Each time, she clung to the doctors' assurances that the prescribed medications would restore normalcy to her life upon discharge. However, hope clashed with the harsh reality as she found herself returning whenever her blood levels plummeted once more.

With each admission came a new doctor, each pledging that their prescribed treatment was more potent and guaranteed long-term success. Yet, after completing the specified course and dose, the relentless bleeding would inevitably resurface, casting doubt on the quality of care she received and the medical team's ability to navigate the complexities of her case.

One medication induced temporary menopause, halting her period but introducing a new set of complications. Fluctuating body temperatures, from extreme heat to sudden chills, left her exhausted, constantly explaining her condition one moment and requesting a blanket the next. It felt as though she had exchanged one problem for another in her quest for a solution.

Upon completing the course of medication and the return of her cycle, a new wave of embarrassment washed over Zawadi as she experienced fainting episodes, each accompanied by a significant loss of blood. Sensations of three distinct heartbeats — one in her head, one in her heart, and another in her belly — along with a pounding headache, served as an urgent signal to call for an ambulance.

In fleeting moments of consciousness, Zawadi summoned the strength to crawl towards the door, leaving it ajar for paramedics. Standing was impossible; she relied on this brief window to take proactive measures before succumbing to the incapacitating effects of the bleeding.

As paramedics transported her to the waiting ambulance, whether in a wheelchair or on a gurney, Zawadi couldn't escape the curious gazes of neighbours and onlookers. She shielded her face, unwilling to embrace the unintended attention, a shy and private person suddenly exposed in a way she never anticipated.

During one of Zawadi's hospital episodes, her blood clots reached a staggering size, comparable to those experienced during childbirth or a miscarriage. This prompted doctors and nurses to resort to weighing them for an accurate estimate of her blood loss. Since she was undergoing a blood transfusion, traditional blood tests wouldn't suffice to gauge her blood levels accurately. Instead, the weight of the clots became a crucial factor in determining the need for additional units of blood. As her body battled against the relentless bleeding, Zawadi felt increasingly detached from her own physical form.

Her case had evolved into a medical enigma. Despite exhaustive tests, including MRIs and a barrage of prescribed medications, the persistent bleeding remained a mystery. The doctors diagnosed her with dysmenorrhoea, menorrhagia, dyspareunia, and a significant case of adenomyosis and endometriosis, adding layers to the complexity of her condition.

Her recurrent hospital visits turned her into a recognisable figure. Upon each return, the nurses and matrons would playfully jest, saying, "I know you miss us very much. You can't help but come to visit us." Over time, Zawadi formed a camaraderie with the hospital staff, finding solace in their warmth and care. Following her father's advice to be friendly and bring laughter wherever she went, she developed a bond with her healthcare providers.

For Zawadi, the doctor's office became more than just a place of medical treatment; it evolved into a sanctuary, a haven where hope flickered amidst the shadows of her illness. Each appointment offered not only the promise of physical healing but also a lifeline of emotional support and understanding. In the comforting embrace of Dr. Mark's clinic, she found solace from the tumult of her afflictions, cherishing the compassionate care and unwavering companionship offered by her healthcare providers. Yet, beneath this facade of reassurance lay a deeper yearning, a longing for connection and validation that transcended the confines of medical intervention. Amidst the sterile walls and clinical procedures, Zawadi unearthed the essence of true healing, discovering that it blossomed not only from pills and prescriptions but also from the tender touch and empathetic presence of those who walked alongside her on this arduous journey.

While Zawadi valued the support and friendship, she couldn't shake the lingering sensation that her intimate familiarity with the hospital's every nook and cranny might be a double-edged sword.

One day, a nurse approached her, enquiring about her belief in God. The nurse wanted to pray with her, convinced that someone as young as Zawadi shouldn't face such adversity. The nurse attributed the issue to spiritual causes, a sentiment Zawadi had encountered before.

Two nights prior, Zawadi had a haunting dream in which two women on the same plane engaged in a fierce battle for spiritual power. One of the women emerged victorious, causing a mighty wind that led to the plane's crash. Miraculously, everyone perished except Zawadi. She lay lifeless on the floor. The triumphant woman approached, stomping on Zawadi's belly and shouting, "So, you think you can get pregnant?" Struggling for life, Zawadi woke up in a cold sweat. She prayed but found no clear interpretation. Perhaps the nurse's spiritual concerns held some weight.

Chaplains visited the hospital wards, offering prayers to patients, including Zawadi. Previously a giver of support, Zawadi found herself at this moment on the receiving end of the love she had previously and generously shared. This experience brought memories of her active involvement in the Society of *Saint Vincent de Paul* during high school.

Following her discharge, Zawadi found herself gaining weight as well-wishers inundated her with various foods and concoctions aimed at aiding her recovery. Among these was a peculiar blend of tomato, SuperMalt, and milk, touted as a remedy to replenish her blood and restore her vitality.

SOS

Zawadi keenly sensed the pain and fear reflected in Aunt Afaafa's eyes each time the doctors readmitted her and discharged her from the hospital. Despite her aunt's efforts to stay strong, it was evident that Zawadi was waging a daily battle, with her life and strength slipping away.Aunt Afaafa went above and beyond, driving for two hours every time to visit Zawadi, laden with groceries to cook and stock up her fridge.

Climbing a flight of stairs became an arduous mission for Zawadi. Every step was a struggle, prompting frequent stops and laboured panting. Her heart pounded fiercely, as if on the verge of escaping her chest, accompanied by searing pain. She despised being in this vulnerable state, reliant on others. Passers-by occasionally offered help, but her standard response was a resolute no.

DIGITAL DILEMMA

During this harrowing time, Zawadi's family, distant and unable to provide physical support, felt the weight of concern for her well-being. During her recovery at home, an unexpected technological mishap added another layer of stress.

Apple released a software update that, without Zawadi's knowledge, had caused her phone to crash.With the automatic update setting enabled, her phone succumbed to the "screen of death" and eventually displayed nothing but black. She exhaustively tried various troubleshooting methods she already knew, some of which she had found through online searches, but none proved effective. As hours passed and the situation became increasingly dire, she decided to visit the Apple store, taking a chance despite the lack of available appointments. The urgency stemmed from the crucial need for communication, especially to call emergency services and prevent unnecessary panic amongst her distant family.

In a race against time and technology, Zawadi resorted to her MacBook to message Firyali about her predicament. She was unable to make calls, order an Uber, or drive, which meant she relied on a forty-five-minute bus ride to reach the Apple store.

Every action was in slow motion, and the journey to the bus stop took longer than usual. Upon reaching the Apple store, the queue length was daunting. Struggling in her weakened state, she requested the woman behind her to hold her spot while she found a place to sit on a ledge near an adjacent store.

The pandemic added an extra protocol layer, elongating the wait times for customers to enter the store. An attendant approached Zawadi, informing her that the store was about to close and advising her to book an appointment for the next day. In response, Zawadi explained her health condition, emphasising the urgency given her inability to call for help in case of another episode due to the software update issue.

With kindness and understanding, the Apple store made an exception for Zawadi, prioritising her issue and fixing her phone; nonetheless, after the engineers reset the device, its functions became unusable until she restored the operating system from a previous backup via a Wi-Fi connection or laptop.

Just as she stepped outside the mall, her mentor called a timely intervention that showcased his caring nature. Unfamiliar with the caller's number because of the phone reset, Zawadi was pleasantly surprised to find her mentor online. Concerned for her safety, he promptly ordered an Uber, arranged an Uber Eats delivery, and ensured she made it home safely.

Upon her return, Zawadi found her home surrounded by police and ambulance services attempting to break down her door. Concerned family members, having not heard from her for about four hours, were in a state of panic. During Zawadi's video call with them, emotions ran high as they saw her face and realised the gravity of the situation, unsure of the resolutions timing or method.

At this point, Zawadi had received nineteen blood transfusions. Her complexion lightened, and she humorously remarked to her mum that she was multi-racial at that point, having received blood from people of various backgrounds. Unfortunately, because she had received blood transfusions, she was no longer eligible to donate blood herself. She expressed profound gratitude to all blood donors, considering them her invisible angels who had generously given her the gift of life.

Zawadi's mum, residing in Kenya, took a proactive step to support her daughter's health. She ordered premium herbs, covering the cost of treatment that Zawadi couldn't afford. The positive news of Zawadi's improved condition brought relief and joy to her mother.

FAILED SURGERIES

After Zawadi's persistent appeals, the most experienced gynaecologist agreed to review her case and recommended a laparoscopy as a potential solution. This procedure would mark the seventh operation related to her health problem. In preparation, Zawadi took time off work, and her Aunt Afaafa arranged to be with her. Zawadi tried to ease the burden on her aunt by ordering groceries and pre-cooked meals, ensuring she had enough stock whilst recovering at home.

Despite Zawadi's careful planning, both attempts at the laparoscopy were unsuccessful. The first time, after being administered anaesthesia and rolled into the operating theatre, she woke up to the news that the surgery hadn't proceeded as expected because of discrepancies between scans and the actual situation.

On the second attempt, the medical team debated the best treatment course. The female doctor believed the surgery would make minimal impact, while the male doctor vehemently defended his diagnosis. In a distressing turn of events, Zawadi faced severe dehydration during the day of the attempted laparoscopy. Because she had been fasting since eight o'clock the night before and being the last patient of the day, she suffered from dehydration. The anaesthesiologist struggled to find her tiny veins, attempting to draw blood from her foot. Upon that failing, he proposed the sole viable option was in her neck. The disagreement and lack of veins led to the cancellation of the surgery, leaving Zawadi in a state of frustration and uncertainty.

Feeling disappointed and fed up, Zawadi demanded the doctors stop everything. Despite her exposed backside, she jumped off the surgery table, stormed out of the operating theatre, grabbed her belongings, got dressed, and left for home. The medical team assured her they would reschedule the surgery for the morning, but Zawadi had lost confidence in the care provided. Upon returning home, she promptly composed a complaint letter to express her dissatisfaction with the hospital's medical team.

Chapter Seventeen

LET'S MAKE A MOVIE

> *If my life was a movie, no one would believe it.*
> **—Arnold Schwarzenegger**

Amidst the unpredictable rhythms of life, Zawadi maintained an unwavering optimism, seeing each hospital visit as an opportunity to weave a unique tale. Despite the challenges, she approached her time in the hospital with resilience, finding ways to infuse it with meaning and memorable experiences.

During her stay, Zawadi found solace in witnessing the impact of her company's products on the lives of older patients, which reaffirmed her sense of purpose and direction, reminding her of the importance of her work in positively influencing the lives of the vulnerable. Taking cues from her mentor, she learned to pause and savour the moments that unfolded during her hospital stay, recognising the beauty amidst life's complexities.

Zawadi diligently chronicled these moments in her diary, finding solace and therapy in the written word as she navigated the challenges and triumphs of each unique chapter of her life. Through her diary, she hoped to one day reflect on the strength that carried her through the ups and downs of her journey.

EPISODE 1: HARMONIES OF HOPE

In the confined space of the rickety lift, the potter, a nurse, and Zawadi sought solace and inspiration in the uplifting tunes of gospel songs rendered by the potter and nurse, filling the air with messages of strength, faith, and unwavering resilience. The potter, who was Jamaican, added depth and authenticity to the music, his voice echoing the rich tones of the original singers. The first song, "I Am Under the Rock" by Donnie McClurkin, resonated with the assurance of finding refuge and protection. His rendition brought a comforting familiarity that felt almost protective. The second, "The Blood Will Never Lose Its Power" by Andraé Crouch, felt like a musical balm concocted to soothe Zawadi's spirit, with the potter's authentic delivery enhancing the healing power of the lyrics. This musical interlude in the lift provided a profound sense of peace and reassurance, momentarily lifting Zawadi's spirits amid her challenges.

EPISODE 2: BEDSIDE SYMPHONY

Amidst the shifting dynamics of the ward, with beds seemingly engaged in a dance of musical chairs, Zawadi couldn't ignore the playful demeanour of the nurses. The constant relocation of patients and rearrangement of the ward became a light-hearted routine, almost like a game of musical beds orchestrated by the nursing staff.It was as if the nurses had found a way to infuse humour into the hospital's otherwise serious and challenging atmosphere.

Perhaps, in their way, they aimed to bring joy and lightness to the patients' lives. The ward's transformation, rather than a pragmatic adjustment for new patients, took on a whimsical quality—a unique and unexpected source of amusement during a health-related journey.

EPISODE 3: MIDNIGHT SERENADE

At the stroke of midnight, an unexpected spectacle surrounded Zawadi in the shared ward. An older woman, a fellow patient, seemed to have an ongoing feud with another occupant, who was engrossed in a lengthy phone conversation. The continuous chatter from the phone call disrupted the tranquillity of the night, and the older woman was having none of it. With unwavering determination, the older woman became the self-appointed advocate for a peaceful night's sleep.

Her persistent and amusing refrain echoed through the ward: "Get off the phone! Get off the phone!" Despite the plea, the phone-bound culprit either remained oblivious to the protest or ignored it altogether. The clash of wills between the two patients added an unexpected layer of humour to the otherwise sombre hospital ward environment. In this nocturnal comedy of manners, the pursuit of a good night's sleep clashed with the unyielding persistence of a sleep-deprived crusader.

EPISODE 4: GLAMOUR AMIDST GLOOM

A striking exception was in the hospital ward's subdued atmosphere—a graceful older woman who seemed to defy the sad surroundings. With an air of elegance, she diligently engaged in a daily self-care routine, transforming her hospital bed into a makeshift beauty salon.

Adorned with impeccable red lipstick, matching nail polish on her hands and feet, and meticulously brushed blonde hair, this radiant soul stood out like a Hollywood star among the ward's ordinary residents.

While others may have overlooked their outward appearances in the clinical environment, this glamorous woman carried a pocket mirror. She ensured that she presented herself with a touch of timeless charm every day.In a space often associated with healing and recovery, her commitment to maintaining beauty and poise added a touch of glamour to the hospital routine.

EPISODE 5: NOCTURNAL LAMENT

Amidst the symphony of sounds that echoed through the hospital ward at night, there was a distinctive and poignant melody—an older woman, a guardian of the night, releasing heartfelt wails that filled the air. Her cries echoed through the corridors, reaching the ears of patients and nurses alike. Despite her apparent distress, her reality was less dire.

The nurses, familiar with her nightly serenades, understood that her needs were not physical but emotional. She sought solace in the reassurance of the nurses' presence, crying out like a nocturnal troubadour longing for the comfort of a caregiver. The nurses, with a blend of patience and understanding, would approach her bedside, urging her to desist. Nevertheless, the night's lullaby continued a poignant reminder of the unspoken yearnings that often accompany the solitude of the hospital's nocturnal hours.

EPISODE 6: CULINARY THEATRICS

A culinary battleground emerged in the form of endless complaints about the food quality, a relentless symphony of discontent. The communal fridge became a battlefield, with skirmishes breaking out over what items were deemed fit for residents. Prohibited ingredients, akin to elusive contraband, led to heated debates.

Despite these daily theatrics, Zawadi chose a different script. She found contentment in the simple blessings of being alive, appreciating whatever the kitchen staff served. Her perspective was a quiet rebellion against the tumult, affirming the notion that life was a profound gift in all its simplicity.

While some sought to outsmart others—whether in culinary matters or fan heists—Zawadi observed the spectacle with a certain detachment. The allure of being entertained by the theatrics outweighed the urge to participate.

Amidst the chaos, a dash of charm arrived with some male doctors, injecting a bit of colour into Zawadi's days. Amidst the complaints, they emerged as unintentional comic relief, momentarily diverting attention from the mundane grievances that echoed through the hospital halls.

EPISODE 7: LITERARY DRAMA UNVEILED

Amidst the hospital saga, a fellow patient stood out—an avid book lover surrounded by at least a dozen books on the windowsill beside her bed. As a kindred spirit with a love for literature, she piqued Zawadi's interest. However, this patient was not just a book enthusiast but also a drama queen of epic proportions.

Every service rendered and every piece of aged furniture became a stage for her discontent. She wielded threats like a seasoned litigator, promising to call her influential son to unleash retribution upon the hospital. Zawadi couldn't shake the thought of someone with such apparent clout finding herself in this hospital drama.

The anticipated arrival of the hunky son was a moment of excitement, but it took an unexpected turn. Instead of championing his mother's cause to the medical team, he unleashed a barrage of accusations, branding her a liar and a handful.

The unfolding argument involved property disputes and a lift to take her upstairs. As the tension escalated, they drew the curtains for privacy, although the other patients, including Zawadi, could still catch every word.

In a rage, the son departed, Burger King meal in hand, leaving behind a trail of entertaining chaos. While Zawadi didn't condone the disrespectful tone he had used with his mother, the spectacle offered a momentary diversion from the hospital routine.

EPISODE 8: CONFRONTATION IN CUFFS

In an unexpected twist, one hospital scene unfolded and ended up in a confrontation with law enforcement. A girl in police custody, handcuffed to an officer, found a target for her frustration in Zawadi. Convinced that Zawadi had locked eyes with her, the girl began cussing at Zawadi, prompting the police to intervene and calm the situation. Yet in the relative privacy of the restroom, the commotion persisted.

Inside the restroom presently, the girl continued her attempts to break free. She pleaded with the police to uncuff her, claiming she was on her period and needed both hands. As the officer reluctantly allowed her into the restroom, the girl resumed her verbal assault on Zawadi. In a desperate attempt to escape, she tried to run but was caught and restrained again by the police. The hospital drama currently featured an unexpected cameo from the legal system.

EPISODE 9: CROCS BARTER BANTER

Amidst the pressures and tension that often envelop the hospital environment, an unexpected and light-hearted moment unfolded. A man keenly observed that Zawadi shared the same name as his wife, spelt out on her Crocs, and initiated a playful barter for the footwear. The Crocs, a subject of discussion over time, evolved into a delightful source of humour within the hospital walls.

Despite Zawadi being manoeuvred in a wheelchair because she had lost the use of her legs, the man skilfully injected a dose of fun by offering fifty dollars for the Crocs. In response, Zawadi, with a playful twinkle in her eye, countered with a request for five hundred dollars. This amusing exchange provided a welcome and brief reprieve, casting a light-hearted atmosphere as they awaited their MRI scans.

EPISODE 10: TRANSFUSIONS AND LAUGHTER

In one of Zawadi's hospital visits, her dehydration was evident to such an extent that her mum, in her ever-endearing way, made a light-hearted jest, playfully suggesting that after multiple visits emphasising the need to transfuse her daughter with blood, the medical staff had progressed to saturating her with several pints of water. The analogy parallels Jesus and his association with water and blood, conveying reassurance for Zawadi's well-being.

Amused by her mother's wit, Zawadi couldn't help but appreciate the creative comparison. This whimsical remark injected fun into the challenging situation, illuminating the resilience and positive spirit that persisted in adversity.

With each episode, Zawadi's hospital journey unfolded like a series of unpredictable scenes in a captivating drama, each moment imbued with its unique blend of humour, tension, and humanity.

MOVIE OVER

Zawadi's condition was not just painful; it was debilitating—her womb was glued to her bowels, impacting her everyday activities and causing severe discomfort. Facing the recommendation for surgery, she learned of the stark consequences: the procedure might necessitate a permanent colostomy bag. This possibility weighed heavily on her, complicating her decision further.

During a particularly fraught discussion, she confronted her doctor, her voice thick with emotion.

"Take it out? You sound like you are asking me to take out my braid and get another one put in. It's effortless for you to say. Do you know the weight of what you have just said to me? Taking out my womb is not an option. You might as well classify me as dead. What kind of life would I have? I want a family. What else can be worth living for? I haven't had much luck thus far, but I am still hopeful that the right man and the right day will come."

The doctor replied, "You'd rather have a baby or die trying? See, there is no cure for endometriosis and adenomyosis, but at least we can preserve your life, eliminate the monthly bleeds and reduce the pain."

Zawadi said, "You are asking me to take such a drastic action and live with Endo? It doesn't make any sense. Please make it make sense."

"Do you realise an average woman should have a blood level of one hundred and fifty grams per litre?" the doctor asked. "You were brought in here with twenty grams per litre. You were a few hours from a stroke or potentially a heart attack, considering you were still bleeding. You are a miracle lying in front of me. Are you telling me that a baby is worth putting your life on the line? You realise that the world is changing. People are opting out of procreating, and others are adopting or fostering. Have you ever considered these options?"

"Doctor, you don't seem to get the point. I am Kenyan. Do you know what that means?" Zawadi asked him.

"I have some Kenyan friends, but please enlighten me," the doctor responded.

"We girls," Zawadi answered, "are raised to be mothers and build families. I know that the mindset has progressed as I have witnessed a few bold women standing in their truth of being single past thirty-five or pursuing a career rather than a family. But how many examples do I see in my day-to-day life? I'll tell you, few or next to none. I often have to look to celebrities to find someone."

The doctor said, "Hmm. It's not the baby then. It is your life versus standing up for your cultural norms and traditions. That is a fascinating perspective. You are a Christian, correct?"

"Yes, I am."

"Well, you will need another miracle because you live on borrowed time. I can't promise anything. I will speak to my colleagues at the other hospital. But if we can get the bleeding under control, there remains no guarantee that it will be a permanent solution. Do you have a partner?"

Zawadi replied, "No, I don't. The paramedics asked the same question. Why does everyone keep asking the same question?"

The doctor answered, "Well, for two reasons. The main reason is that having a baby will resolve most of the issues we diagnosed. The second reason is that I am concerned about your well-being, as you might not be alive today had your friend not arrived in the nick of time."

"This is like déjà vu," Zawadi confessed. "What have I been trying to do for the past ten years? Doctor, how long do I have to decide?"

"Not very long," the doctor answered. "The earlier, the better. You have been to the A & E six times at this point with very critical low blood levels. Unfortunately, none of the scans or tests reveal the root cause of your nonstop bleed. We have to keep you alive. It's time for your next pint of blood. I suggest you rest. We can pick up this conversation once I speak to the other doctors."

"Why? Why? Why?" Zawadi asked.

All Zawadi had were questions and few or no answers. Just like Job in the Bible, the thing she feared the most had come upon her.

Zawadi's mind often wandered to her memories of a young couple she observed while growing up in a residential camp. Their life seemed like a picturesque dream—two children, a boy and a girl, residing in a beautiful, unassuming bungalow surrounded by two classy luxury cars parked outside. The aroma of warm, delectable food wafting from their kitchen, the scent of fresh pastries filling the air, and the comforting fragrance of diffusers created an atmosphere that made everyone feel immediately at home. Zawadi couldn't help but admire the seemingly perfect life this family led. That instance represented a poignant expression of love, a gesture that transcended her usual reserve, and marked a unique and memorable moment in their wedding celebration.

NEW NORMAL

Zawadi's journey with chronic pain had been a relentless challenge, shaping her daily life into a continuous battle for balance and comfort. Determined not to let her conditions define her, she embarked on a comprehensive pain management routine designed to reclaim her independence and vitality.

Each morning, Zawadi began her day not at the break of dawn as she once did, but at a time that allowed her body to wake naturally, reducing the strain on her system. Her bedroom was equipped with a small station containing scheduled medications and a logbook for tracking dosages and symptoms, a routine meticulously overseen by her caring physician. The iron supplements were crucial, yet they came with their drawbacks. Accompanying them were stool softeners, a necessary addition to combat the constipating side effects that made her days challenging.

Physical activity, once centred around high intensity and competition, now took a gentler form. Zawadi embraced yoga, finding the slow stretches and controlled breathing not only eased her physical pain but also brought tranquility to her mind. On warmer days, she found solace in the rhythmic strokes of swimming, her body supported and soothed by the cool water.

Her kitchen underwent a transformation as well. Where once processed snacks filled the pantry, now shelves were stocked with anti-inflammatory foods like leafy greens, nuts, and berries. Her morning routine included preparing a smoothie, rich with spinach and flaxseeds, designed to reduce inflammation and nourish her body gently.

Pain relief also came in the form of heat and cold therapies. A heating pad was always within reach, providing comfort during flare-ups of muscle pain or abdominal cramps. For acute pain, especially after her physical therapy sessions, ice packs were her refuge, reducing inflammation and numbing the sharper pains.

Mindfulness became a cornerstone of her daily life. Each evening, Zawadi dedicated time to meditation, sitting quietly in her living room, a space adorned with soft pillows and calming, neutral colours. The practice of mindfulness extended beyond meditation; it was part of her breathing exercises and even cognitive behavioural therapy sessions, which she attended weekly. These sessions equipped her with coping strategies, transforming her approach to pain from one of endurance to one of management and recovery.

Regular check-ups with her doctor were marked clearly on her calendar, a regular reminder of the importance of monitoring her progress and adapting her treatment plan. These visits were as much about medical reviews as they were about reassurance and adjustments to her strategies to cope with her conditions.

Zawadi's story was one of adaptation and resilience, a testament to the power of comprehensive care tailored to one's unique needs and challenges. Her life, once dictated by the limitations imposed by her conditions, was now a narrative of empowerment, woven through with practices and routines that affirmed her strength and her refusal to be defined by her pain.

BOUNCING BACK

After her discharge, Zawadi continued her journey towards healing through counselling at her church. As she engaged in sessions to navigate the intricacies of her experiences, her counsellor, recognising the need for additional support, conveyed a special invitation. The church's lead pastor desired to have a counselling session with Zawadi. This unexpected and significant gesture made her feel seen, loved, and valued.

Her counsellor promptly arranged an appointment, bringing Zawadi face to face with the esteemed pastor. The fact that such a sought-after and respected figure within the community would take the time to counsel her left an indelible impression. That moment stood as evidence of the community's commitment to supporting its members, and for Zawadi, it reinforced worthiness and importance that her past experiences had obscured. This encounter marked a pivotal moment in her healing journey as she embraced the opportunity for guidance and understanding offered by someone she held in high regard.

Chapter Eighteen

CONVERSATION WITH PASTOR T

> *Mentoring is a brain to pick, an ear to listen, and a push in the right direction.*
> **—John C. Crosby**

Pastor T's response to Zawadi's heartfelt narration was pro-found empathy, her voice a soothing balm amidst the tur-moil gripping Zawadi's soul. "Thank you for entrusting me with your story, Zawadi. Your courage in opening up is admirable, and I want you to know you're not alone in this journey. Togeth-er, we'll navigate through the storm one step at a time. Can you share with me more about the profoundness of the pain you're experiencing?"

Zawadi took a moment, savouring the warmth of Pastor T's understanding and the sanctuary of her presence. "It's more than just physical pain, Pastor," she began tentatively, her words unravelling the intricate layers of her anguish. "It's a relentless ache that transcends the boundaries of the physical realm. It's like a heavy burden weighing down my spirit, settling deep within my chest and refusing to dissipate." As she spoke, Zawadi delved into the labyrinth of her emotional turmoil.

This unseen weight doesn't confine itself to physical illness; it shadows me in moments of tranquillity as well. It permeates my thoughts, colours my emotions, and distorts my world percep-tion. As the pain ebbs, it leaves an unsettling void, a disconcert-ing emptiness that feels foreign and unnatural.

Pastor T nodded in silent acknowledgement, her eyes reflect-ing a deep understanding of Zawadi's suffering. "Tell me more about the ways this anguish manifests in different facets of your life, Zawadi," she gently prodded. The more we unravel its com-plexities, the closer we come to finding solace and healing."

With Pastor T's gentle encouragement, Zawadi traversed the labyrinth of her emotions, each word a poignant brushstroke on the canvas of her pain. "It's a constant presence, Pastor," she confessed, her voice trembling with the weight of her emotional burden. "It feels as though someone is squeezing my very essence, suffocating me from within. And while painkillers offer fleeting respite, they are but temporary reprieves. I've grappled with this for decades, and it casts a pervasive shadow over every facet of my existence."

Her vulnerability laid bare the relentless grip of her suffering, its tendrils intertwined with every aspect of her being. Zawadi continued her voice, a haunting melody of despair and resilience.

As she shared her struggles, she dared to hope that Pastor T, with her wisdom and compassion, could offer a glimmer of solace amidst the darkness that threatened to consume her. That moment marked a pivotal turn in her odyssey, a courageous step towards unraveling the enigma of her pain.

Pastor T's response was genuine concern, her words a lifeline amidst the storm raging within Zawadi's soul. "I'm deeply sorry to hear of your suffering, Zawadi," she murmured, her voice a gentle caress. "From what you've shared, it appears you've explored every avenue of conventional medicine available to you."

Zawadi's sigh held the weight of a thousand battles fought and lost. "I've consulted countless doctors, Pastor," she admitted wearily. "I've undergone surgeries and tried medications, but it feels like I'm fighting a losing battle. Their relief is fleeting, and the root of my affliction remains elusive. It's a constant uphill battle, with no end in sight."

Her words hung heavy in the air, bearing witness to the frustration and despair that had become her constant companions. Pastor T listened intently, her heart heavy with the knowledge of Zawadi's endless struggle.

"While we continue to seek answers within the realm of medicine, let us also explore the emotional and spiritual dimensions of your affliction," Pastor T suggested gently. "Sometimes, healing emanates from the most unexpected of sources. Know that I am here to accompany you on this journey every step of the way."

Pastor T's words promised unwavering support, a beacon of hope amidst the storm within Zawadi's soul. At that moment, a bond was forged between them, a silent vow to confront the darkness and emerge into the light of healing.

As the conversation unfolded, Pastor T delved into the intricate web of Zawadi's coping mechanisms, her questions probing Zawadi's psyche with surgical precision. "What do you believe triggers these cravings for alcohol and talcum powder?" she inquired softly, her eyes alight with empathy.

Zawadi hesitated briefly, grappling with the vulnerability of her confession. "I believe it's my way of coping, Pastor," she admitted hesitantly. "Whenever the pain becomes unbearable or if I feel overwhelmed by life's burdens, I turn to alcohol. It offers a temporary respite, a fleeting escape from the torment within. I've read that my talcum powder and clay cravings are a symptom of my low iron levels. It's as though my body is desperately seeking something it lacks."

Pastor T nodded in understanding, her gaze unwavering in its compassion. "Thank you for your honesty, Zawadi. We must address these issues holistically, exploring healthier coping mechanisms together. Additionally, I will connect you with members of our congregation who have walked similar paths. Their shared experiences may offer invaluable support and understanding."

Zawadi's gratitude was palpable, a flicker of hope amidst the darkness that threatened to engulf her. "I appreciate that, Pastor," she murmured, her voice tinged with relief. "I've felt incredibly alone in this journey, and the possibility of finding understanding within our community is heartbreaking."

In that moment, Pastor T became more than a mere confidante; she was a beacon of hope amidst the darkness, a guiding light illuminating Zawadi's path to healing and wholeness.

Pastor T's wisdom cut through the fog of uncertainty that shrouded Zawadi's heart, her words a beacon of clarity in the tumult of conflicting emotions. "It is not your responsibility to nurture a man into maturity, Zawadi," she affirmed gently. "From what I've gathered, this gentleman, I'm sorry to say, falls short of the mark. Your determination to see the good in him is admirable, but it's imperative to recognise if a relationship is toxic and detrimental to your well-being."

Zawadi recoiled slightly, her heart torn between the desire for redemption and the sting of reality. "But, Pastor," she protested weakly, "as a woman of the cloth, surely you've encountered stories of redemption, of transformation? Is it not our duty to extend grace, to believe in the potential for change?"

Pastor T's gaze softened with understanding yet remained resolute. "Indeed, redemption is a cornerstone of our faith," she acknowledged. "But there comes a point when extending grace becomes enabling destructive behaviour. Your safety, both physical and emotional, must take precedence. From all indications, this man is not ready for the journey of growth and healing that lies ahead."

Zawadi's heart ached with the weight of Pastor T's words, the truth of her assessment echoing in the chambers of her soul. "But I love him and we are engaged to be married?" she whispered, her voice trembling with uncertainty. "We grew up together. Our mothers are like sisters. Doesn't that count for something?"

Pastor T's response was unwavering in its conviction. "The desire for marriage is indeed an honourable one, Zawadi," she affirmed gently. "But it does not justify subjecting oneself to abuse or neglect. Your well-being matters, and sometimes, the most courageous act of love is to walk away from what no longer serves your highest good."

Zawadi's heart swelled with a tumult of conflicting emotions, torn between the echoes of her engagement and the imperative of self-preservation. "But how do I find the strength to let go, Pastor?" she implored, her voice raw with vulnerability. "How do I untangle myself from the expectations and obligations that bind me to this union?"

Pastor T's response was a wellspring of wisdom, her words a lifeline in the storm of doubt and fear. "Strength lies not in holding on but in letting go," she counselled gently. "It's about recognising your inherent worth and mustering the courage to choose yourself, particularly when it feels agonisingly difficult". You are worthy of affection and respect, Zawadi, and it's time to reclaim your power."

Zawadi's heart trembled with the weight of Pastor T's words, the seed of liberation taking root in the fertile soil of her soul. "But what of the future, Pastor?" she murmured, her voice a fragile whisper. "How do I navigate the uncertain waters that lie ahead?"

Pastor T's response infused hope, her eyes alight with the promise of new beginnings. "The future is a blank canvas, Zawadi," she declared, her voice resonating with quiet confidence. "It's an opportunity to rediscover yourself, to embark on a journey of self-discovery and renewal. Trust in the process, and know that you are not alone. I'll walk this path with you every step of the way."

Zawadi's heart swelled with a newfound sense of courage, the shackles of fear and doubt falling away like dust in the wind. "Thank you, Pastor," she whispered, her voice choked with emotion. "Thank you for believing in me, for guiding me through the darkness. I'm ready to embrace the light, to step into the unknown with courage and grace."

At that moment, amidst the hallowed sanctuary of Pastor T's guidance, Zawadi found the strength to embrace her truth and embark on a journey of healing and self-discovery. The journey was fraught with challenges and uncertainties, yet it shimmered with the radiant light of hope and possibility.

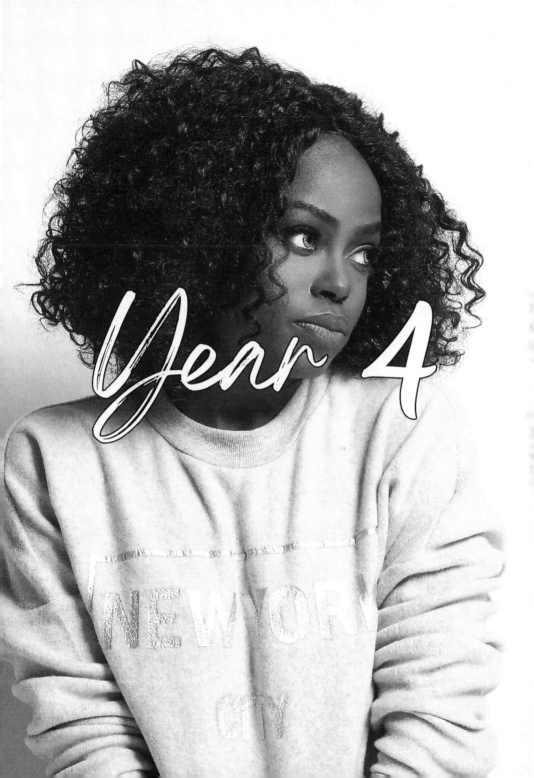

Year 4

Chapter Nineteen

GOD ON MUTE

> *Silence sometimes speaks volumes.*
> **—Unknown**

At a crossroads, Zawadi contended with profound life decisions that carried immense weight. The choice between proceeding with a hysterectomy or holding onto faith for healing weighed heavily on her shoulders. Divorced and facing infertility, she felt a deep sense of vulnerability that amplified the gravity of the decision before her.

Upon deep reflection, she realised that her dilemma transcended the mere desire for motherhood. It was about finding peace and assurance in walking the right path in life—living with purpose and intention. She sought a life that, at her time's end, she could look upon with pride, knowing she had lived intentionally. Refusing to engage in meaningless activities to pass the time, she grappled with societal norms ingrained that starting a family was the ultimate benchmark of a successful life, serving as her reference point for fulfilment.

Amidst her physical suffering and the threat to her life, Zawadi was engulfed in a deafening silence. Feeling pressed on every side, she underwent a Gethsemane-like experience—a profound period of pressure and anguish. Biblical scholars challenged her belief that God communicates through audible voices, guiding her to perceive God's presence in life's little and mundane aspects. To find solace and connection to her Source amidst the noise, she turned to meditation and breath work, making these practices her form of prayer.

ECHOES OF SILENCE: ZAWADI'S CRISIS OF FAITH

Initially, prayer had been her sanctuary, providing solace in times of distress. Nonetheless, as she returned repeatedly without receiving the much-desired beacon of possibility, it became a place tinged with despair. Her earnest petitions seemed unheard, leaving her knees sore from the weight of her supplications. Her prayers felt like echoes bouncing off the ceiling, leaving her feeling unheard and her faith seemingly impotent. The sacred space of prayer, formerly revered, turned into a frightening place she dreaded.

Zawadi joined multiple prayer groups to intensify her spiritual efforts and religiously adhered to prayer times. She delved into scripture, devotionals, and church services, seeking answers and divine intervention. Joining a Bible school became another avenue to deepen her understanding of God, including undergoing tests and exams to bridge any perceived gap in her relationship with the divine. These efforts stemmed from her desperation to connect with a higher power and find solace amidst her turmoil.

Despite her fervent prayers and religious activities, Zawadi remained in perpetual motion yet saw no noticeable progress or change in her situation.Despite daily moments of stillness, both physically and in spirit, she felt an unsettling void—a life devoid of God's voice and direction, especially regarding her pressing issue. In a time she most desired divine intervention, God, in her perception, remained silent. Prefacing her prayers with a disclaimer of "Thy will be done," she attempted to cover for God and explain the apparent divine silence.

Recalling the biblical account of Hannah, a woman who struggled with infertility, Zawadi found solace in the parallels with her own life. Hannah's fervent prayers at the entrance of the tabernacle, initially mistaken for drunkenness, eventually led to the birth of her son after years of supplication. Inspired by Hannah and other women in the Bible who faced infertility, such as Sarah, Rebekah, and Rachel, Zawadi followed their template, hoping for a similar resolution to her struggles.

In contrast, unlike Hannah, Zawadi's prayers transformed from prolonged hours of fervent supplication to a mere few words, eventually culminating in silence, mirroring what she perceived as God's silence. This shift prompted her to question the validity of what the leaders taught within the Christian faith. She wondered if her life teachers sold a false narrative about life, prayer, faith, and God.

Seeking answers from fellow church members and leaders, Zawadi encountered explanations that seemed more concerned with maintaining the validity of their beliefs than addressing the intricacy of her circumstances. Everyone appeared to have an answer designed to uphold existing doctrines rather than entertain the possibility that some aspects of their faith might be flawed, requiring reassessment and reframing to alleviate undue suffering. Zawadi wrestled with a crisis of faith, torn between the teachings she had received and the stark reality of her silent and seemingly unanswered prayers.

CHURCH CULT

Zawadi's encounter with the street evangelist and subsequent immersion into the weekly Bible classes led by the enigmatic figure marked a pivotal chapter in her spiritual journey. Despite the physical discomforts she endured during the sessions, including cramps during mandatory camera-on sessions, the gatherings became a refuge of kindness and connection for her.

As the intensity of the Bible study increased and the frequency of the classes escalated, Zawadi reached a pivotal juncture. The organisation's teachings clashed with those of her regular church, whose leaders explicitly instructed her to avoid teachings from other congregations. This directive and the prohibition on exchanging numbers or interacting with other group members outside of the leader raised concerns within Zawadi.

Delving into the organisation's online presence revealed troubling revelations. The followers hailed the leader as the sole true prophet, proclaiming salvation to lie exclusively in following him—a stark contradiction to the teachings of Jesus and traditional Christian beliefs.

In her determination to seek truth and transparency, Zawadi requested that the curriculum be shared with her pastor for feedback. Nonetheless, her inquiry met with resistance, and the course leaders swiftly expelled her, branding her a troublemaker. The abrupt severance of ties with church group turned family left her heartbroken and adrift, grappling with isolation and betrayal.

Recognising the insidious tactics employed by the cult to isolate her, Zawadi felt herself spiralling into a disorienting abyss. The complex landscape of denominations and their varying beliefs overwhelmed her, prompting a strategic withdrawal from active engagement with the church.

In pursuit of a profound connection with her soul, Zawadi undertook a fast—more than just a spiritual practice, but a journey of quiet reflection for her soul and spirit. Commencing on a fateful Monday morning, the fast symbolised a period of introspection and self-discovery as Zawadi navigated her beliefs' labyrinth and reconsidered the enigmatic cult's captivating allure.

Chapter Twenty

DIVINE DIALOGUES

> *Questions are the echoes that lead us to the profound, and answers are the whispers guiding us through the complexities of faith.*
> **—Unknown**

In the sacred realm of faith, Zawadi initiated a profound conversation with friends, where the threads of suffering and spirituality intricately wove a tapestry of introspection and resilience. Much like the biblical Job, she faced a series of trials, each challenging an elaborate pattern in the fabric of her life.

THE NARRATIVE OF JOB

The biblical account of Job portrays him as a righteous and faithful man who loved God deeply. Satan confronts God, suggesting that Job's goodness is contingent upon his happy life. In response, God allows Satan to test Job's faith by subjecting him to a series of trials.

Job's ordeal begins with the loss of his livestock, his servants, and all his children. Subsequently, he is afflicted with painful sores all over his body. Despite the devastating circumstances, Job remains steadfast in his faith and praises God. Despite his wife urging him to reject God and accept his impending death, Job refuses to waver.

Three friends come to support Job in his grief, sitting silently with him for seven days. On the seventh day, Job breaks his silence, and the four dialogues are about the reasons behind Job's suffering. The friends offer their perspectives, attempting to make sense of Job's afflictions.

At the story's culmination, God appears to Job, presenting impossible questions highlighting human understanding's limitations in grasping God's ultimate plan. This divine encounter humbles Job, leading him to appreciate God's incomprehensible power. Job never receives a direct explanation for his suffering, but in the end, God restores his health and blesses him with twice as much property, more children, and a long and prosperous life.

Job's narrative profoundly explores faith, suffering, and God's mysterious ways, highlighting the importance of trusting God's wisdom in the face of adversity.

ZAWADI'S NARRATIVE UNFOLDS

Zawadi's narrative unfolded, recounting her experiences traversing the realms of faith, prayer, and the uncharted territories of her soul. Like Job's companions, friends offered varied perspectives, attempting to decipher the enigma of her afflictions.

Zawadi became consumed by the weight of the discourse with her friends. Each point dissected, every layer of their conversation mulled over with a newfound thirst for understanding. Despite her knack for argumentation and quick wit honed by her legal background, she realised that these discussions transcended the realm of mere debate. They delved into matters of wisdom and understanding that surpassed her current level of comprehension.

With each new insight gained and every perspective considered, Zawadi felt herself evolving. She embraced the challenge of grappling with complex ideas, knowing that pursuing wisdom was a lifelong journey. As she continued engaging in meaningful discourse with her friends and others, she sharpened her intellect and cultivated a more profound sense of empathy and compassion.

FAITH IN FLUX

The exploration commenced with the theme of faith—a delicate dance between belief and doubt. Group member Mo's call for more faith met with Zawadi's poignant reflection on the nature of her faith. Mo's response to Zawadi's plight was a straightforward call for more faith. Yet, wrestling with the stark contrast between her faith and the concrete results of her prayers, Zawadi challenged this perspective. She reminded her companions of the scriptural teaching that every individual possesses a measure of faith, highlighting the biblical assertion that faith as small as a mustard seed can move mountains.

To illustrate her point, Zawadi shared a personal anecdote from her high school days in the mountainous terrain of Kenya. Reflecting on her youthful innocence, she recounted moments of closing her eyes and praying for one of the mountains to move during the journey to school. Despite her unwavering prayers spanning six years and more than one hundred trips, the mountains stood resolute, prompting her to question the effectiveness of her faith and the realisation of the promises found in scripture.

Continuing her introspection, Zawadi narrated a pivotal shift in her church affiliation, orchestrated by her father, from a denomination akin to the Jehovah's Witnesses to the Pentecostal Church. In the new church, she observed a zealous emphasis on faith and miracles, with believers confidently anticipating the fulfilment of their prayers. Nevertheless, the miracles expected often eluded Zawadi, leading her to question the essence of her faith and whether she had the "wrong type" of faith.

Zawadi's reflections uncovered a nuanced comprehension of faith that transcended mere belief in miracles to encompass a broader acceptance of life's uncertainties. Her journey delved into the potentiality of unanswered prayers and the profound act of aligning one's will with the divine amidst adversity. In questioning the nature of her faith, Zawadi prompted deep inquiries into the intricacies of faith, its manifold complexities, and the myriad ways individuals navigate their unique spiritual paths.

SIN: A FAMILIAR NOTE

Sin, a familiar note in religious discourse, played its part in the dialogue. Group member Clara's suggestion that sins might hinder prayers prompted Zawadi to counter the cleansing power of Christ's sacrifice. Clara's input regarding Zawadi's situation introduced a common perspective within certain religious circles—that the presence of sin might impede the effectiveness of prayers. Clara posited that sins could be the obstacle if the issue weren't related to faith.

In response, Zawadi delved into Christian theology, emphasising the belief that Jesus's blood serves as a cleansing force capable of washing away sins. This concept aligns with a fundamental tenet of the Christian faith, in which the sacrificial death of Jesus atones for the sins of believers.

Zawadi's response suggested a reliance on the redemptive power of Christ's sacrifice to address any potential hindrance caused by sin in her prayers. It underscored her profound understanding of forgiveness and cleansing as integral components of her faith, challenging the notion that sins might pose a barrier to effective prayer. The conversation delved into the theological intricacies of Christianity, shedding light on the diverse interpretations that believers may hold regarding the interplay of belief and sin in their spiritual journeys.

PRIDE: HUMILITY'S COUNTERPART

Pride, humility's counterpart, entered the stage as group member Timi urged Zawadi to humble herself for divine favour. Timi offered counsel to Zawadi based on the biblical principle that God extends grace to the humble while resisting the proud. Timi's suggestion centred on the idea that Zawadi must cultivate humility to receive God's grace.

In response, Zawadi, seemingly wearied by the trials endured for nearly eighteen months, passionately expressed the profound depths of her humility. She painted a vivid picture of a life predominantly spent at home, in hospitals, and in prayer. She also illuminated the deep losses she had weathered in her career and marriage. The battles with her health had brought her to the lowest points, drawing parallels to the woman with the issue of blood in the biblical narrative.

Zawadi, noting a profound shift in her perspective that had emerged from confronting death multiple times, articulated the way this experience had reshaped her worldview, rendering previously important things seemingly insignificant. She detailed her daily plea for forgiveness, underscoring her conscious effort to maintain humility in prayer and acknowledge any sins, whether by omission or commission. She poignantly conveyed the emptiness she felt and the transformative impact of confronting mortality.

Zawadi's response reflected profound spiritual introspection. It delved into the nuances of faith, humility, and the quest for meaning amidst deep struggles. It touched on themes of loss, humility, and the reassessment of priorities within her spiritual journey.

FASTING: A SPIRITUAL DISCIPLINE

Fasting, a spiritual discipline, presented itself as a potential path. Group member Lamel proposed fasting to Zawadi, drawing inspiration from a Bible story whereJesus instructed his disciples that certain miracles could occur solely through prayer and fasting.

In response, Zawadi pointed out a practical limitation, explaining that her health condition rendered her sick and unable to fast. Despite this constraint, she acknowledged the support she had received, noting that others, including strangers, had taken on the responsibility of fasting and praying on her behalf.

Furthermore, Zawadi introduced another biblical reference, citing the instruction that, in the case of a sick person amongst believers, the believers should call upon the elders to pray over the sick person and anoint them with oil in the name of the Lord. This reference emphasised the communal aspect of prayer and the belief in the effectiveness of collective intercession for healing.

Zawadi's response underscored the hurdles of implementing certain spiritual practices while facing health issues.. It also stressed the communal nature of faith, illustrating the manner in which believers come together to support and intercede for one another in times of need.

WORDS: AFFIRMING AND CHALLENGING

Words, both affirming and challenging, were exchanged. Timi proposed a shift in Zawadi's language, suggesting that instead of saying she was sick, she should declare, "It is well." This recommendation aligned with a common practice in certain Christian circles, encouraging believers to speak positive declarations over their lives as an expression of faith.

In response, Zawadi added a touch of sarcasm, introducing the term *Christianese* to describe Christian phrases or language that often involves affirmations of positivity and well-being, regardless of one's current reality. She humorously highlighted the expectation to use optimistic language in the face of challenging circumstances.

Zawadi's response delved into the intricacies of expressing faith and positivity amidst adversity, prompting questions about the authenticity of language used in religious contexts. It sparked a broader conversation about the interplay between faith and language and the acknowledgement of one's reality within the framework of spiritual teachings.

ANOINTED ITEMS: TANGIBLE EXPRESSIONS OF FAITH

Anointed items, blessed water, and elders' prayers emerged as tangible expressions of faith. Mo inquired about using anointing oil, a common practice in certain Christian traditions, and Zawadi responded by recounting her experiences. She shared instances of being prayed over and receiving anointing oil and handkerchiefs from prominent ministers and general overseers of churches. Despite these practices, she expressed that her situation remained unchanged.

In a poignant recounting of her father's illness, Zawadi narrated a story that unfolded at the border, encountering complications due to new liquid volume restrictions. A pastor had given her a bottle of anointing oil, ensuring its potency for her father's healing. Faced with the challenge of adhering to the liquid restrictions, Zawadi encountered a desperate situation.

To preserve the supposed potency of the anointing oil, Zawadi made a drastic decision—she drank as much of the oil as she could. Additionally, she applied the oil to her body, hoping to transfer the anointing to her father upon her arrival home. The outcome of this extraordinary effort was left unspoken, creating ambiguity and inviting interpretation.

This narrative captured the lengths individuals may go to in desperation, navigating through faith, uncertainty, and a deep desire for healing. The unspoken resolution added an extra dimension, leaving interpretation open to the reader's imagination and emotions.

In response to Mo's inquiry about blessed water, Zawadi confirmed that she had received multiple bottles of holy water from her Catholic friends. She then delved into a poignant memory from her Catholic boarding high school, recalling mandatory morning Mass. She shared an experience involving a blind Reverend Father who relied on her and a classmate to guide him to his seat.

The Reverend Father showed care and concern for Zawadi's well-being in adversity. On days her painful periods prevented her from assisting him to the morning Mass, he would provide her with holy water from Rome, believing it could bring about healing. Zawadi expressed that the anticipated resolution never materialised, and the reverend died.

This narrative captured a blend of compassion, religious rituals, and the nuances of seeking healing within the context of faith. The unfulfilled hope and eventual passing of the reverend added emotion and reflection to Zawadi's journey, shedding light on the intersection of personal struggles and religious practices.

PRAYER OF ELDERS

In the sacred space of shared belief, Lamel discussed Zawadi's interactions with spiritual leaders, particularly her pastor. Lamel inquired whether Zawadi's pastor had prayed over her, to which Zawadi responded with a solemn affirmation, recounting both in-person and virtual prayers she had received. She then shared a poignant anecdote involving the General Overseer (GO) of a prominent denomination who had prayed over her father. Despite the initial surge of hope accompanying the prayer, Zawadi expressed her profound shock and disappointment upon her father's eventual passing.

This encounter left an indelible mark on Zawadi, leading her to describe it as a "God crisis" and confess her faith struggle. The unanswered questions and the loss of her father shook her to the core, causing her to question the very foundation of her beliefs. This sentiment echoed her earlier mention of a shaken faith, suggesting an ongoing internal conflict.

Zawadi's candid admission of her internal turmoil and the impact of unanswered prayers provided a window into the complexity of faith facing adversity.It reflected the internal struggles individuals may grapple with upon being confronted by the limitations of human understanding and the unpredictability of life's outcomes.

THE NAME AND THE BLOOD OF JESUS

The conversation shifted towards spiritual practices, specifically invoking the name of Jesus and pleading his blood. Mo queried whether Zawadi incorporated these elements into her prayers, and Zawadi confirmed that she consistently did. She then recounted a compelling experience related to sleep paralysis.

During episodes of sleep paralysis, Zawadi had sought guidance from church leaders, who advised her to invoke the name of Jesus and plead the blood of Jesus, attributing the experience to spiritual attacks. Despite her diligent adherence to this advice, she found it ineffective. However, a turning point occurred after a prayer session with her pastor. During one particular episode of sleep paralysis, Zawadi, feeling a familiar sense of dread, asserted that she had recently prayed with her pastor and proclaimed that the negative presence had no authority in her space. To her surprise, this declaration caused the presence to retreat immediately and it never resurfaced.

This incident introduced a layer of mystery and confusion to her experiences. Zawadi wondered why the invocation of her pastor's involvement had an effect, whereas her previous calls in the name of Jesus, which she expected to be more powerful, did not yield the same result. The unexpected resolution brought both relief and a set of new, perplexing questions about the nature of her spiritual encounters and the specific elements that contributed to her deliverance.

This account delved into the intersection of spirituality and personal experiences, exploring the diverse ways individuals turn to their faith in moments of distress. It also highlighted the intricacies of spiritual practices and the unpredictability of outcomes encountered in situations that defy straightforward explanations.

DIVINE DISSONANCE

The topic shifted to incorrect requests, which Timi gently suggested might be a factor in Zawadi's situation. Timi raised the possibility that Zawadi's requests might not align with God's will, leading Zawadi to ponder the goodness concealed within her plight. Zawadi believed in God's benevolence but questioned whether any good could emerge from her misfortunes.

In a vulnerable moment, Zawadi revealed that she had started avoiding church because she felt out of place amidst others' testimonies of miraculous experiences. Despite desiring personal miracles, she felt they were elusive and questioned whether her expectations of God were limiting His power.

This reflection exposed individuals' emotional and existential struggles while grappling with adversity and questioning their relationship with the divine. Zawadi's honesty about her feelings of isolation within her faith community added depth to the narrative, shedding light on the complex dynamics of faith amidst personal afflictions.

GIVING

The discussion turned towards acts of generosity as Lamel proposed that Zawadi might find favour with God through charitable deeds, such as supporting an orphanage and engaging in selfless acts.

Zawadi's name, meaning "**gift**," perfectly encapsulated the essence of her life from a very young age. Her journey of generosity began in the sunlit halls of her community church, where she not only absorbed the stained-glass stories of faith and hope but also learned to live them out. From the tender age of seven, Zawadi was deeply involved in her church's youth activities, where her early encounters with scripture memorisation and recitation were not just about winning contests but nurturing a profound connection to her faith.

As she grew, so did her acts of kindness. By age twelve, Zawadi was already a little philanthropist within her church community, leading projects that ranged from Sunday school picnics to charity drives. Each Christmas, she organised the assembly of gift baskets for less fortunate families, pouring her heart into every detail, ensuring that each gift was a token of love and hope.

With a vivid memory of the profound impact that church activities had on her in her formative years, Zawadi recognised the youth assembly as a golden opportunity to foster a similar spirit of encouragement and camaraderie among the younger generation. This assembly was more than just a gathering; it was a vibrant festival of faith and fellowship, featuring not only races and other sporting competitions but also Bible recitation contests that mirrored her own cherished experiences.

Determined to infuse the event with an extraordinary sense of occasion, Zawadi undertook a gesture of profound generosity. She invested in gold medals, each elegantly inscribed with motivational scriptures. These medals were not mere awards; they symbolised achievement, perseverance, and the shared values of the community. Zawadi envisioned these medals as beacons of inspiration, designed to honour and celebrate the hard work and dedication of the recipients. Through this thoughtful gesture, she aimed to foster a culture of excellence and unity, encouraging ongoing personal and communal growth.

Her father, moved by her thoughtfulness and selflessness, offered to reimburse her for the expense. However, Zawadi graciously declined. This act of giving was deeply personal and sacrificial. She believed strongly in the biblical principle of sowing seeds of generosity, confident that these seeds would grow into a harvest of goodwill and strengthened community ties. Her refusal to accept repayment was her commitment to this belief, marking a pivotal moment in her journey of faith and giving.

These early experiences of organising and giving, from simple Sunday school activities to the impactful gesture at the youth assembly, were not just acts of charity. They were the foundation of Zawadi's character, weaving a continuous thread of generosity and faith through the fabric of her life. As she faced health challenges in later years, the joy and pride from these moments served as a beacon of strength, reminding her of the impact of her actions and the enduring power of community support.

Each reflection on these moments bolstered her resolve and reminded her that her contributions, however small they might have seemed at the time, had lasting impacts. Her life, rich with acts of kindness, stood as a testament to the belief that giving, in all its forms, is both a gift received and a gift given.

MERCY

Mo: "Zawadi, I know how much your faith means to you, especially in these tough times. But isn't there a danger in expecting too much from... well, from praying for mercy? Isn't that a bit like waiting for a rescue that might never come?"

Zawadi looked thoughtful, considering her friend's concern, and her mind drifted to a story that had always given her comfort.

Zawadi: "Mo, let me share something with you. In the Bible, there's a story about two men who went to the temple to pray. One was a Pharisee and the other a tax collector. The Pharisee stood and prayed about himself, boasting about his righteous acts, essentially thanking God that he was not like other men, including the tax collector. But the tax collector stood at a distance, wouldn't even look up to heaven, but beat his breast and said, *'God, have mercy on me, a sinner.'*"

She paused, her voice soft but clear.

Zawadi: "This story, found in the Gospel of Luke, chapter 18, verses 10 to 14, shows us that the tax collector, not the Pharisee, went home justified before God. It's a lesson about humility and the power of seeking mercy—not as a passive act, but as a profound, humble acknowledgment of our own limitations and the need for grace."

Mo: "So, you see your prayers as... what, exactly? A way to admit your own limits?"

Zawadi: "Exactly, Mo. It's not about resignation. It's about recognising that some things are beyond my control, and that's okay. It's about knowing that it's okay to not be okay and asking for strength to endure. The tax collector's prayer is short, but it's deep—it's about throwing yourself on the mercy of a higher power, trusting that this plea doesn't go unheard."

Mo listened, the emotional depth of her words stirring empathy within him.

Mo: "I never thought of it that way. I guess I've always seen asking for mercy as a kind of defeat, but you're talking about it as a form of strength."

Zawadi: "It is, Mo. It's perhaps the strongest thing I do. Each day, when the pain is more than I can bear, I remind myself of the tax collector. His humility isn't weakness; it's a powerful surrender to something greater than himself, and that gives him—and me—dignity in our most vulnerable moments."

Tears welled up in Mo's eyes as he grasped the depth of Zawadi's faith and her perspective on mercy.

Mo: "Zawadi, thank you for sharing that. I think I've misunderstood your strength all this time. Your faith, your prayers for mercy, they're part of how you fight, aren't they?"

Zawadi: "They are, Mo. And every day that I can face the world, despite the pain, is a testament to that strength. Mercy doesn't just mean deliverance; it often means the courage to continue."

As they sat together, the sun began to set, casting long shadows across the path. The conversation had opened a new door to understanding between them, bridging Mo's rationality with Zawadi's spirituality, deepening their friendship in the shared silence that followed.

PSYCHICS

The mention of consulting a psychic evoked a strong reaction from Zawadi, revealing her boundaries regarding exploring alternative beliefs. She firmly rejected the idea, citing her reluctance to delve into spiritual territories she didn't understand. Upon Timi sharing a perspective implying skepticism towards modern-day prophets within Christianity and suggesting a return to what she called the original African religion, Zawadi reacted strongly, defending her faith and firmly rejecting the idea of abandoning Christianity.

Zawadi's response underscored her emotional intensity and the personal significance attached to matters pertaining to belief and spirituality. She vehemently opposed the suggestion, questioning whether it aimed to provide clarity or confusion. Her metaphorical mention of drinking poison to quench her thirst emphasised her deep discomfort with the proposed course of action. Additionally, she challenged the notion of abandoning the faith she had held for many years, highlighting the emotional intensity and personal significance attached to matters pertaining to belief and spirituality.

SCRIPTURAL COMFORT

Zawadi found solace in scripture, explicitly citing Isaiah 43:2 to illustrate her reliance on biblical verses during challenging times. The passage emphasises that God promises to be present and protective in the midst of adversity. Zawadi drew strength from these verses, highlighting the significance of biblical texts in shaping her understanding of faith and resilience facing difficulties.

> *"When you go through deep waters, I will be with you. When you go through rivers of difficulty, you will not drown. When you walk through the fire of oppression, you will not be burned up; the flames will not consume you."*
> **—Isaiah 43:2 (NIV)**

This use of scripture reflected a common practice among believers who turn to religious texts for guidance and solace in times of hardship.

BELIEF SYSTEMS

Mo introduced a thought-provoking perspective on the situation, urging consideration of the broader context beyond mere answers to prayers. By questioning whether the focus should solely be on the response to pain and suffering rather than specific answers, Mo presented a nuanced view. Lamel's acknowledgment of Mo's point underscored the importance of understanding the peculiarities of human experiences facing adversity. This exchange signified a profound exploration of the role of belief and the significance of one's attitude and response during difficult times.

GRACE

Grace, the unseen hand shaping difficulties into spiritual growth, echoed through Lamel's words and in Zawadi's spiritual journey. The idea that God's refusals could add depth to the conversation by being seen as answers to prayers in the long run was underpinned by the reference to Peter Forsyth's quotation suggesting a higher purpose or understanding behind apparent refusals or hindrances.

Mo's contribution expanded the discussion by addressing a broader issue within religious communities—specifically, the pressure placed on individuals regarding marriage and children.

Mo encouraged a more flexible and personalised understanding of life paths and purpose, suggesting that pastors must reconsider their approach and that God might have different individual plans. This highlighted the diversity of aspirations and experiences within a religious community.

The Scripture, "My grace is sufficient for you, for my power is made perfect in weakness" (2 Corinthians 12:9), along with the wisdom from Proverbs 24:10, "If you falter in a time of trouble, how small is your strength!" resonates deeply here, emphasising that God's grace is not only a buffer but a transformative force in the face of life's challenges, urging a reassessment of personal faith and resilience.

ACCEPTANCE

Acceptance marked a profound shift in Zawadi's journey. The acknowledgement of the five stages of grief hinted at a healing process, an emotional alchemy turning pain into acceptance. Zawadi's acknowledgement of moving towards acceptance reflected a significant step in her emotional and psychological journey. The reference to the five stages of grief, commonly associated with the Kübler-Ross model (denial, anger, bargaining, depression, and acceptance), suggested a process of coming to terms with losses. Zawadi's statement indicated a growing understanding and willingness to embrace her circumstances, which can be crucial to coping and finding resilience facing adversity. Drawing on the Scripture, Mo reminded the group of Jesus' words in John 16:33, "In this world you will have trouble. But take heart! I have overcome the world." This verse reinforced the inevitability of trials for Christians, emphasising resilience and hope in the face of difficulties.

Zawadi's reflections formed the backdrop for existential questions, challenging the assumptions of causation and correlation. Her poignant plea to refrain from rationalising and to embrace

humility echoed the universal quest for understanding confronting life's mysteries.

As Zawadi confronted life's adversities, including health issues
and divorce, she refused to let these challenges rob her of hope,
love, memories, or spirit. Pondering the intricacies of Christianity, she explored the idea that Christians might partake in
Christ's suffering and challenged the notion that life is meant to
be a straight line of positives.

BELIEF SYSTEMS AND THE MYSTERY OF PRAYER

The discussion delved deeper into the intricacies of belief systems and the mysterious nature of prayer. Mo's perspective
challenged the notion of seeking immediate answers in prayer,
urging a broader understanding of faith beyond mere outcomes.
This prompted a reflective exploration of faith's role in navigating life's uncertainties. Throughout the discourse, the group
referenced James 1:2-4, which urges believers to *"consider
it pure joy, my brothers and sisters, whenever you face trials of
many kinds, because you know that the testing of your faith pro-
duces perseverance. Let perseverance finish its work so that you
may be mature and complete, not lacking anything."* This scripture provided a vital lens through which to view the challenges
discussed, emphasising the value of trials in fostering spiritual
growth and resilience.

COLLECTIVE PRAYER AND HOPE

As the discussion unfolded, collective prayer emerged as a beacon of hope amidst the shadows of uncertainty. Mo's gesture of
seeking forgiveness and proposing prayer for a miracle resonated with the group's collective sentiments. Lamel's suggestion to
cast out perceived demons echoed a shared belief in the power
of communal intercession for divine intervention.

Zawadi found solace amidst the tumultuous seas of doubt and uncertainty in the hallowed space of shared prayer, as voices intertwined in a chorus of belief and supplication. The collective prayer became a demonstration of the enduring power of faith to transcend individual struggles and usher in moments of collective hope and resilience. This unity in prayer aligns with Matthew 18:19-20, where Jesus says, "Again, I tell you that if two of you on earth agree about anything you ask for, it will be done for you by my Father in heaven. For where two or three gather in my name, there am I with them." This passage highlights the profound impact of collective prayer, affirming the presence and support of the divine in communal faith actions.

As the evening drew close, the sacred realm of faith embraced Zawadi and her friends, weaving a tapestry of shared experiences and collective resilience. In the gentle embrace of faith, they found the strength to navigate the winding paths of life's uncertainties, united by the timeless threads of belief and hope.

Chapter Twenty One

JOURNEY THROUGH DARKNESS

> *The best way out is always through.*
> **—Robert Frost**

A HAUNTING NARRATIVE

Zawadi's life seemed scripted like a horror film—fraught with fear and uncertainty, holding her in its chilling clutches. Her longing for an escape and guidance was palpable as she navigated the complex emotional turmoil. Facing her trauma required a holistic approach, often involving professional help to explore the depths of her psychological distress.

Addressing her deep-seated emotional wounds was daunting. It required revisiting painful memories and unraveling the complex ties of her past traumas. Seeking comfort in mental health professionals and trusted friends became crucial in her healing process, providing a safe space to express and gradually ease her burdens.

Her whispered confession, "The world would be a better place without me," laid bare her intense emotional pain. The losses of her father, husband, and brother deepened her sense of isolation. Listening to Asa's song "Bibanke" offered her a cathartic outlet, helping her channel her emotions through its haunting melodies.

In this shadowed valley of her life, Zawadi found a somber resonance in the Psalmist's words, "Even though I walk through the valley of the shadow of death, I will fear no evil, for you are with me" (Psalm 23:4). This scripture became a beacon in her darkest moments, reminding her of divine presence and protection despite the encroaching evils that life presented. Her journey was a testament to the dual nature of existence—where the promise of God's companionship in darkness did not preclude the reality of facing evil, but provided the courage to confront and move through it.

DAMAGED GOODS

Zawadi's recent ordeal fractured her self-esteem, casting her as *"damaged goods."* This label, laden with shame and a sense of irreparability, weighed heavily on her. She bore emotional scars that made her feel diminished and unworthy, a common aftermath for survivors of trauma.

She wrestled with deep-seated guilt and emotional scars, a fate many assault survivors know too well. Her trust, once freely given, now seemed a regrettable lapse, amplifying the chaos within her. The biblical image of an impure spirit that returns with seven worse spirits to an empty, swept house poignantly reflected her attempts to heal, only to be besieged by a resurgence of pain that dredged up both known and hidden wounds from her past.

The manipulative acts of the perpetrator planted seeds of despair in Zawadi, convincing her that he had irrevocably marred her self-worth. She doubted her capacity to recover, questioning her own resilience. Despite the comforting biblical message that one is never burdened beyond what they can bear, Zawadi felt overwhelmed and ill-prepared to handle the aftermath of her trauma.

NEWS AND SOCIAL MEDIA

In her profound vulnerability, Zawadi saw her path to recovery strewn with hurdles. The contrast with her sister Kioni, who could consume crime dramas unfazed, highlighted the personal nature of trauma. For Zawadi, such content triggered severe anxiety, pushing her towards lighter, educational material to manage her stress. Zawadi made a deliberate choice to avoid the news and social media, even at the risk of seeming uninformed during conversations. This decision was part of her broader strategy to protect her inner peace. She understood that while staying updated on current events was important, the constant stream of negative headlines could trigger anxiety and disrupt the mental and emotional stability she had worked hard to achieve.

Her friends and acquaintances sometimes expressed surprise or disbelief at her lack of awareness about the latest happenings, but Zawadi prioritised her wellbeing over societal expectations. She found other ways to engage in meaningful discussions without needing to immerse herself in potentially distressing news cycles. Instead, she focused on topics that were uplifting, educational, and contributed to personal growth and understanding.

Zawadi's approach was a careful balancing act. She cultivated a selectivity in her consumption of information, choosing sources and topics that added value to her life and aligned with her goals of healing and self-discovery. She encouraged her circle to share insights and summaries of important events in ways that were thoughtful and considerate, thus remaining informed without overwhelming herself.

This intentional distancing from the news was not without its challenges. There were moments when Zawadi questioned if she was too disconnected from the world. However, she consistently reminded herself that her mental health was paramount, and that staying healthy emotionally was as important as being knowledgeable.

By creating and maintaining boundaries around her media consumption, Zawadi not only safeguarded her peace but also fostered a deeper understanding of her own limits and needs. This practice helped her to maintain her focus on recovery and personal development, proving that sometimes, stepping back from the world's noise is necessary to hear one's own voice more clearly.

> *"Finally, brethren, whatsoever things are true, whatsoever things are honest, whatsoever things are just, whatsoever things are pure, whatsoever things are lovely, whatsoever things are of good report; if there be any virtue, and if there be any praise, think on these things."*
> — **Philippians 4:8(KJV)**

VALLEY OF PAIN

For eighteen months, Zawadi battled non-stop bleeding—a harsh reminder of her body's relentless rebellion against endometriosis, adenomyosis, fibroids, and anaemia. These weren't just medical terms but vicious invaders tearing at her life's fabric.

The pain she endured was akin to being stabbed repeatedly with jagged knives, each twist intensifying her agony. It was as debilitating as gunshot wounds, each flare-up a bullet tearing through her. The constant pain clouded her senses, rendered her immobile, and fuelled her anger and frustration.

Zawadi's dependence on painkillers had become as crucial as air, a necessary staple in every handbag, stashed in her office drawer, and abundantly stocked in her medicine cabinet, now more akin to a pharmacy poised for endless emergencies. Simultaneously, her wardrobe evolved into an array of black attire, each outfit carefully chosen not just to mask her suffering but to discreetly handle any unexpected bleed-outs. This return to practical, tomboyish garments helped her cope with her physical condition. Once a vibrant presence in social circles, Zawadi found herself increasingly isolated. Friends, unable to grasp the extent of her enduring pain, slowly drifted away, leaving her to navigate her challenges in solitude.

She woke up every morning to a battle that no one sees, a war waged within the walls of her own body. For twenty long years, she had been a prisoner in her own flesh, shackled by pain so fierce it steals the breath straight from her lungs. Endometriosis, adenomyosis, fibroids, anaemia—these aren't just words. They are constant, uninvited companions that have gnawed at the fabric of my life, leaving it threadbare in places once vibrant and whole.

Every cramp, every sharp, unexpected stab is a reminder of the turmoil hidden beneath the surface. The treatments, the medications... none of them brought real relief. They're just brief pauses in a never-ending storm.

Zawadi's Voice :

"And now, they want to take my womb—my hope for a child, to tear it from me as if it's nothing more than a troublesome appendix. This... this is not just a surgery; it's a surrender, a white flag raised against my dreams of motherhood.

I stand here, on the precipice of a decision that is no choice at all. Without my womb, maybe the pain will lessen, maybe it will give me moments of peace. But what is peace when it costs you a part of your soul? The very thought of it is a new kind of agony—it's an ache that no scalpel can cure and no therapy can soothe.

Why continue? Why endure another day when the essence of what I hoped to be—a mother, a creator of life—is being stripped away from me? The future feels like an empty corridor, echoing with the laughter of children I will never know, the soft murmurs of love to little ears that will never hear my voice. It's a barrenness that goes beyond the physical, a desolation of the spirit."

THE THRILL OF FALLING IN LOVE

Internally, Zawadi's struggles transformed her views on love into a complex narrative, making love both a villain and a saviour in her relational dynamics. She confessed to being addicted to the thrill of falling in love, unable to differentiate genuine happiness from emotional highs. Peeling back these layers, she recognised their physiological roots.

Her childhood craving for approval, a simple "Well done, Zawadi," had extended into her adulthood, revealing a deep-seated emotional need. She sought comfort in the company of men, which felt as soothing as a baby in a mother's arms, highlighting her longing for acceptance and security.

Zawadi's inability to refuse others and her repetitive cycles of tumultuous relationships had eroded her self-esteem. Using relationships as a temporary salve for rejection became a harmful coping mechanism. The realisation that she was re-enacting her initial traumas through these romantic entanglements added complexity to her behaviour patterns.

Her narrative illustrated the intricate interplay between her past traumas, coping strategies, and the relentless quest for emotional satisfaction. Recognising these patterns was crucial in addressing the root causes of her distress.

Zawadi often seemed externally composed, like a broken thermal flask—intact on the outside but shattered within. This duality was evident as she maintained physical boundaries in her relationships while leaving her emotional self unguarded, forming deep soul ties that compounded her struggles.

Her tendency to quickly move on after relationships gave others the impression of a hard-hearted demeanour, yet internally, she grappled with profound pain. Caught in a web of authenticity and deception, she pushed away genuine connections out of a fear that they would eventually end, leaving her even more isolated.

This internal conflict pulled her in opposing directions, highlighting the dichotomy between her desire for true intimacy and her defensive behaviors. This conflict influenced her tumultuous journey in love and emotional security.

THORN IN THE FLESH

As Zawadi delved deeper into her values and the daunting task of embodying them, her path of self-discovery and alignment sharpened into focus. Her narrative, rich with biblical allusions, drew parallels to Paul's discourse on human frailty and his metaphorical "thorn in the flesh," a poignant reflection of her own trials. Like Paul, who articulated his internal conflicts and spiritual burdens in Romans 7:15–20 and 2 Corinthians 12:7, Zawadi found her personal struggles similarly underscored by themes of enduring hardship and seeking divine grace.

These biblical narratives added a layer of depth to Zawadi's experiences, framing her struggles within a larger, almost cosmic battle between personal aspirations and the harsh realities of life. Her story, woven with these ancient threads, painted a vivid and complex portrait of her inner world—one marked by contradictions, spiritual seeking, and the quest for meaning amid suffering.

Her identification with these scriptural heroes not only enriched her understanding of her own trials but also offered a lens through which others could view and perhaps comprehend the intricacies of her journey through suffering and resilience.

CHURCH

Zawadi's experiences in church as a divorced woman often left her feeling marginalised, underscoring a palpable lack of support within traditional religious communities. Each Sunday, as she listened to the stream of testimonies about the miraculous interventions in others' lives, her isolation deepened. It felt as though God Himself was sidelining her, favouring others with blessings and breakthroughs while she continued to struggle with her personal and health crises. This stark contrast between her experiences and those shared during services only intensified her distress, reinforcing her feelings of exclusion.

Despite these challenges, Zawadi found some solace in the shift towards online church services, a change brought about by the COVID-19 pandemic. The transition from in-person gatherings to virtual worship allowed her to continue participating in her faith community without the discomfort and judgment she often felt in physical settings.

The pastor, embracing the change, referred to the online attendees as his *"onesie family."* This affectionate term reflected a sense of unity and inclusivity that was sometimes missing from the brick-and-mortar services. It helped Zawadi feel somewhat connected, despite her reservations and the pain that often kept her physically isolated from the world.

This virtual connection, however, was a double-edged sword. While it offered a sense of belonging and allowed her to maintain her spiritual practices, it also served as a constant reminder of the challenges she faced in finding her place within the traditional church community. As she navigated her faith journey from the confines of her home, Zawadi continued to wrestle with the complex feelings of being part of a community that had not always felt welcoming or supportive. Yet, she held onto her faith, seeking comfort in the words and music that streamed into her home every Sunday, hoping for a deeper understanding and acceptance both from above and from those she worshipped with, even if only digitally.

ROMANTIC RENDEZVOUS

Zawadi's attempts at dating often unfolded like pages from a book she wished she could rewrite. Each new chapter began with hope but quickly darkened with the recurring themes of misunderstanding and retreat. As she ventured into the world of relationships again, her past and her present — marked by constant bleeding, relentless pain, and the echoes of a marriage that had not yielded children — became stumbling blocks too significant for many to overcome.

Her disclosures about her health, necessary for honesty and transparency, often led to chilling silences or abrupt departures. Online conversations that once buzzed with the potential of something meaningful would vanish into the void, leaving her with a screen as empty as her hopes. In person, the moment her past or her pain became the topic, the interest in her companions' eyes would dim, replaced by a retreat that was sometimes polite, sometimes abrupt, but always painful.

The question about why her first marriage had not produced children seemed to linger in the air, a silent spectre that haunted her interactions. It was a question loaded with judgment and assumptions in a society that often viewed fertility as a measure of a woman's value. Her honesty about her struggles with infertility and health issues, rather than eliciting support or understanding, often triggered a retreat — a ghosting from individuals who had no desire to navigate the complexities of her life.

Each disappearance was a blow not just to her hopes for companionship but to her sense of self-worth. She found herself grappling with a profound loneliness, compounded by the fear that her body and her past were too much for anyone to accept. It wasn't just the physical symptoms of her condition that caused her pain; it was the emotional isolation that came from being repeatedly left behind.

Zawadi's heart ached for acceptance and understanding, for someone who would see beyond the surface complications and recognise the depth of her resilience and the purity of her intentions. Yet, as each potential relationship dissolved before her eyes, she was left wondering if her search for love was a futile one, destined to be overshadowed by the reality of her health and the scars of her past.

This cycle of hope and heartbreak tested her resolve, but it also deepened her understanding of her own needs and boundaries. Each painful experience taught her more about the importance of finding someone not merely willing to endure the complexities of her condition but capable of embracing them as part of the beautiful, intricate tapestry that made up her life.

EATING AND EXERCISE

Zawadi's health was impacted by four debilitating conditions that severely affected her daily life, especially her fitness aspirations and dietary habits. She had always dreamed of competing in gym and fitness competitions, pushing her body to its limits in a display of strength and endurance. However, her health conditions presented significant barriers, making rigorous training sessions almost impossible.

Her love for dining was equally compromised. During her menstrual cycle, an adhesion of her bowel to her womb made eating an excruciating ordeal. The pain and discomfort during these periods discouraged her from enjoying meals, which otherwise offered her great pleasure. When she was not on her cycle, although she could eat somewhat better, the relief was short-lived as using the bathroom became a new challenge due to obstructions in her bowel. At one point, Zawadi went two months without being able to relieve herself, a situation so severe that it necessitated emergency visits to the hospital for relief.

The prescribed painkillers and iron tablets she needed to maintain her sanity and manage her iron levels further exacerbated her constipation, placing her in a relentless catch-22. While these medications were critical for managing her pain and preventing anaemia, they contributed to her severe digestive issues, complicating her ability to maintain any semblance of normalcy in her eating and exercise routines. This intricate web of health issues not only hindered her physical activities but also deeply affected her psychological well-being and quality of life.

DATA DILEMMA

As Zawadi grappled with her health challenges, she found her-self confronting not only the physical symptoms but also the looming spectre of technology and privacy concerns in the dig-ital age. In a world where personal information is increasingly stored online, she couldn't help but worry about the confidenti-ality of her medical condition, particularly in the realm of digital health records and social media.

The thought of her health data being accessible online with-out her consent sent shivers down her spine. Would her medical history be secure from prying eyes, or would it become fodder for targeted advertisements or even discrimination? Zawadi un-derstood all too well the potential consequences of her health information falling into the wrong hands.

Social media, once a platform for connecting with friends and sharing life updates, now felt like a double-edged sword. While it offered a space for support and solidarity with others facing similar health challenges, it also posed a risk of exposure. Would her struggles with chronic illness be met with empathy and un-derstanding, or would they become the subject of gossip and judgment?

Navigating the intersection of technology and privacy in the digital age added another layer of complexity to Zawadi's already challenging journey. As she sought to safeguard her health and maintain her dignity, she grappled with the paradox of needing to share personal information for medical care while also fear-ing the potential repercussions of that very disclosure.

In a world where data breaches and privacy violations were all too common, Zawadi couldn't afford to be complacent. She had to weigh the benefits of technology-enabled healthcare against the risks to her privacy, making careful decisions about which information to share and with whom. For Zawadi, protecting her health also meant safeguarding her privacy in an increasingly digital world.

WORK

Zawadi's health struggles profoundly impacted her professional life, particularly her role as a consultant at one of the Big Four law firms. Her inability to work regularly or aim for higher achievements due to her conditions left her feeling stagnant and isolated, a painful reality given her core value of fostering quality relationships—a goal that seemed elusive both personally and professionally.

WORK SOCIALS

Unable to commit to work-related social gatherings—critical for networking and growing a client list in the highly competitive consultancy environment—each missed event wasn't just a lost evening but a missed opportunity to connect with potential clients and colleagues, essential for advancing her career and expanding the business. Her absences, often perceived not as a necessity due to health but as antisocial behaviour, further alienated her from her peers.

This misunderstanding compounded her sense of isolation, making her feel as though she was on the outskirts of the vibrant professional community she once thrived in. Despite her best efforts to explain her situation, the fast-paced nature of her industry left little room for colleagues to truly understand the extent of her struggles. The professional world, often unyielding and unsympathetic to personal challenges, moved forward swiftly without her.

Zawadi's inability to engage fully in her work and social functions meant not only missing out on immediate networking opportunities but potentially jeopardising her future career growth. This reality hit hard, reinforcing her feelings of being sidelined, not just by her physical condition but also in her career aspirations. It became increasingly clear that her journey to maintain her professional standing and personal well-being was fraught with challenges, highlighting the delicate balance she struggled to maintain between managing her health and sustaining her career in a demanding and often unforgiving corporate landscape.

Zawadi's decision to pursue a career in the sciences and project planning role, was not merely a professional choice but a reflection of her inner need for control and perfection. Her meticulous nature, initially an asset in the precise field of data analysis, began to blur the lines between her professional and personal life, revealing the complexities of her inner world. This obsession with order and precision eventually morphed into a nuanced dance with chaos, a paradoxical craving for the unpredictability she so diligently sought to control. Curiously, Zawadi sometimes found herself orchestrating chaos, creating disorder only she could resolve—a dual-purpose endeavour that not only satisfied her craving for complexity but also showcased her unmatched skill in restoring order. With just a handful of variables, she could generate a myriad of impeccable solutions, each arrangement a testament to her ingenuity and relentless pursuit of perfection.

LUXURY OR NOTHING - OCD

Zawadi's quest for quality and external excellence was not just a pursuit of aesthetic perfection; it mirrored her inner struggle, manifesting as a compulsive need to control her surroundings. This need arose from a deep-seated wound that sought perfection as a soothing balm. Her incessant organizing and reorganizing, her creation and resolution of chaos, served as a shield against the vulnerabilities and imperfections she feared might reveal her true self.

This obsession, while outwardly appearing as a high standard for excellence, was fundamentally a navigation tool for the unpredictable seas of life. It was her strategy to feel secure in the vast, often tumultuous expanse of human existence. Yet, beneath the surface of this seemingly flawless pursuit, Zawadi's heart yearned for something deeper—not just for impeccable arrangements but for acceptance and peace within the beautifully flawed tapestry of life.

Deep down, Zawadi knew that her obsession was more than just an inclination towards order; it was a lifeline, a way to manage the overwhelming sense of being adrift in a world where chaos lurked around every corner. Her craving for luxury and perfection was not about the luxury itself but about what it represented: a world where everything has its place, where unpredictability is mastered and tamed, where she could feel a semblance of control.

Yet, as she pursued this external excellence, she increasingly recognised the exhausting nature of her quest. The compulsive behaviours that once seemed protective began to feel constrictive. Zawadi found herself questioning whether the peace she sought could truly be found in this relentless pursuit of order or if real tranquility lay in embracing the imperfection and uncertainty of life. In a transformative shift, Zawadi began to replace her OCD compulsions with art projects, channeling her need for control into creative expressions that not only benefited herself but also brought joy and beauty to others. Her journey through the realms of obsessive-compulsive behaviour gradually evolved into a deeper exploration of her vulnerabilities and a quest for genuine self-acceptance within the beautifully complex human experience. This newfound outlet in art became a powerful means for her to explore and accept the unpredictable nature of life, fostering a true sense of peace that had eluded her in her earlier compulsions.

5AM CLUB

Before her health took a severe toll, Zawadi was a dedicated member of the "5am Club"—a concept popularised by leadership expert Robin Sharma, involving rising at 5am to dedicate the first hour of the day to exercise, reflection, and personal growth. This rigorous morning routine, which she had maintained since high school, set a disciplined tone for her day, fostering productivity and a sense of achievement.

The 5am Club required Zawadi to engage in vigorous physical activities such as running or gym workouts, followed by a period of meditation and planning her day. This early start not only energised her but also allowed her to cultivate a mindset geared towards personal and professional success. Her mornings were meticulously structured, involving a blend of physical exertion and mental preparation that propelled her through the day with clarity and focus.

However, as her health conditions became more intrusive, adhering to such an early and demanding routine became untenable. The pain and physical limitations imposed by her conditions meant that waking up at 5am often left her exhausted rather than energised, with the early morning workouts becoming sources of dread rather than empowerment.

Recognising the need to prioritise her health, Zawadi adapted her routine to accommodate slower mornings. Now, instead of the 5am start, she allows herself to wake naturally and spends the first part of her day gauging her pain levels and managing her symptoms. This slower start helps her to better understand what her body can handle each day and adjust her activities accordingly. The focus has shifted from external achievements to internal balance and wellness, aiming to equip her with the strength and stability needed to face the world each day.

This change, while necessary, was a significant shift from the lifestyle that had once given her a sense of control and momentum. Now, her mornings are less about pushing her limits and more about listening to her body, reflecting a deeper understanding of her needs and the complexities of her health conditions.

FRIENDS

When she mustered the strength to engage with her friends, to laugh and converse as if all was well, it was like a fleeting moment of respite—a temporary reprieve from the darkness that loomed on the horizon. But for Zawadi, these moments of strength were often followed by periods of withdrawal, when she retreated into herself like an animal seeking shelter in its cave. In these moments of solitude, she wrestled with her demons, struggling to find the light amidst the shadows that threatened to consume her.

The loneliness of Zawadi's journey was magnified as people drifted away, unable to grasp the length and complexity of her healing process. Her once vibrant social life had dwindled to a distant memory. Despite valuing quality friendships deeply, they had become virtually non-existent. Her inability to commit to any social engagement left people feeling disappointed, and even when she explained her situation, her reasons were often perceived as mere excuses.

Many overlooked the profound weight of Zawadi's struggles, as silent obstacles continuously eroded her progress. Infertility emerged as a poignant battleground, enveloped in both emotional and physical turmoil. Despite her relentless efforts to press forward, she often felt overshadowed and overlooked, her accomplishments fading into the backdrop. This lack of acknowledgment only deepened her internal uncertainties and amplified her struggle against formidable external barriers.

Navigating a labyrinth of societal expectations and judgments, Zawadi frequently stumbled over hurdles others placed in her path. Those who viewed her through rose-tinted glasses unwittingly distorted their perceptions, dazed by their preconceived notions. The phrase *"Thank God that God is not man"* resonated within her community, serving as a gentle reminder that humans do not hold sway over fate. This belief provided a soothing balm against the harsh scrutiny of critics who dared to judge her life too hastily.

The premature judgments cast upon her felt akin to sipping unfermented grape juice—too raw and unsophisticated, blatantly revealing society's shortsightedness towards the fluidity of individual growth. Amidst this turmoil, Zawadi grappled with overwhelming emotional responses. These were not merely triggered by current events but stemmed from deeply buried traumas and suppressed feelings. In her desperation to fill an inner void, she pursued relationships, material possessions, and fleeting pleasures, hoping to replace the lost familial ties, inadvertently setting herself on a path to further turmoil.

For someone who once found solace in the fragrant embrace of diffusers and perfume candles, the acrid smell of her own blood would become an unbearable assault on her senses. The once comforting scents would be replaced by the metallic tang of iron, an unwelcome intrusion into her olfactory sanctuary. Alone in her suffering, she would long for the familiar embrace of fragrances, now lost in the void of her isolation.

Her journey also mirrored the tribulations of Job, particularly in how he was perceived and treated by his peers. This comparison shed light on Zawadi's feelings of alienation amidst her prolonged challenges, highlighting the profound loneliness that can accompany intense personal adversity.

Just as Job faced judgment and a lack of understanding from those closest to him, Zawadi encountered similar trials. The biblical notion that "an enemy can be found within one's own household" resonated deeply with her, capturing the pain of facing judgment and scant empathy from those she had expected to be her support network.

Her experience underscored the complexity of navigating personal hardships in a world that often fails to recognise the silent battles individuals face, challenging her to redefine her sense of self and purpose against a backdrop of societal misconceptions.

WORKFLOW OF LIFE

True healing had long eluded Zawadi, who found herself charting an unknown course devoid of the comforting presence of family guidance or the well-trodden paths set by societal norms. The allure of external validation often veered her away from a much-needed introspection. She chased a sense of completeness through traditional symbols of success—a marriage symbolised by a ring, the joy of motherhood, a dream career, global travel, and an envisioned idyllic life—each venture ending in disillusionment. It wasn't until she released her grip on these external identities that she began to unearth the answers to the existential questions that plagued her.

As Zawadi commenced the arduous process of peeling back the layers of her conditioned identity, she was confronted with the daunting challenge of redefining her self-worth. Slowly, painstakingly, she learned to detach her value from the societal milestones of success that had long dictated her worth. This transformation, though liberating, came with its share of anguish; each step away from her previous self involved a profound mourning for what she once believed was essential for her completeness.

Standing at a pivotal crossroads, stripped of her familiar coping mechanisms, Zawadi plunged into the depths of her psyche, seeking new forms of resilience. In moments of intense vulnerability, she found herself praying for divine mercy and strength, fully embracing her flaws and fervently seeking a pathway through her tangled web of struggles.

DIAPER DIVAS CLUB

In Zawadi's world, the term "*diapers*" took on a whole new meaning, referring to the hefty pads she had to wear during her menstrual cycle. Despite the challenges they posed, Zawadi found a glimmer of humor in her situation. Embracing the playful spirit of her journey, she joked that during that time, these pads gave her the appearance of a *"BBL"* (Big Booty Look), bringing a lighthearted touch to her struggles. And when she had to buy them, she approached the aisle with all the discretion of a teenager buying condoms, pretending the huge diapers were for her granny at home, even though nobody asked. As a proud member of the *"Diaper Divas Club,"* Zawadi found camaraderie and resilience in embracing the quirks of her experience, turning even the most mundane aspects of her journey into moments of laughter and solidarity.

JAGGED EDGES

Zawadi's journey through her complex emotional landscape was marked by a profound lack of expression of internal feelings, shaped by her cultural background where expressing emotions was often stifled. Her struggle was further complicated by her limited proficiency in English, which deepened her sense of isolation in an environment that required her to articulate feelings she was barely allowed to acknowledge.

BLACK-AND-WHITE

Her thought patterns were distinctly black-and-white, a mindset that served her well in achieving goals and meeting deadlines but now contributed to her mounting frustrations. This all-or-nothing approach led her to view any imperfections as catastrophic failures, fuelling procrastination and severely hampering her ability to maintain balance in her life.

ADDICTION

Taking her prescribed painkillers usually plunged Zawadi into a deep, immediate sleep, offering a fleeting escape from her tormented reality. This routine of suppression had led her down a destructive path, where pent-up emotions erupted in bursts of anger, overeating, chasing misguided ambitions, and engaging in inappropriate sexual advances. These behaviours were now culminating in the most perilous impulse yet—suicidal ideation.

In this critical moment, the accumulation of suppressed emotions and unresolved pain threatened to overwhelm Zawadi's resolve to find a healthier path through her suffering. Her story poignantly underscores the urgent need for robust support systems and mental health resources, particularly for those grappling with the dual challenges of cultural constraints and personal turmoil. It highlights the dire consequences of neglecting mental well-being and the essential role of compassionate, culturally sensitive interventions in preventing such devastating outcomes.

PERMANENT PAINKILLERS:
A DESPERATE SEARCH FOR SOLACE

As Zawadi grappled with feelings of insignificance, these thoughts evolved into a formidable adversary. In her darkest moments, she envisioned dramatic gestures of despair, such as ending her life in public. However, the potential trauma such actions might inflict on innocent bystanders held her back. Instead, she considered a more solitary escape, retreating into the shadows of her pain without a public spectacle.

Drawing on the tragic knowledge gleaned from her father's battle with cancer, inadvertently had provided her with knowledge about consuming large number of pills all at once.

DARK CLOUD

The dark cloud of despair had been her constant companion, an ominous presence lurking at the edges of her consciousness, casting shadows over every aspect of her existence. It followed her everywhere, a relentless specter that haunted her even in the supposed safety of her own home. She found herself paralyzed with fear, unable to even use the bathroom in her ensuite without feeling its oppressive weight bearing down upon her.

On the train, surrounded by the hustle and bustle of the city, the dark cloud would descend upon her with an almost palpable intensity. Terrifying thoughts would creep into her mind, whispering of sinister possibilities lurking behind every face. She would glance at the person seated next to her and be assailed by visions of violence, imagining them as a potential murderer or a harbinger of death. The darkness seemed to seep into her very bones, filling her with an overwhelming sense of dread and unease.

Winter was the darkest time of all, both metaphorically and literally. As the days grew shorter and the nights stretched on endlessly, Zawadi found herself consumed by a profound sense of hopelessness. The darkness seemed to envelop her, suffocating her with its icy embrace. She tried to stave off the encroaching gloom with an array of remedies—bright lights, cheerful art, mirrors to reflect the light, and SAD lamps to mimic the sun's rays—but none could dispel the darkness that clung to her like a second skin.

ME TOO!

Zawadi endured thirteen gruelling days without food, clinging desperately to water for survival. Each day melded into the next, marked by dramatic weight loss, ominous signs of illness, and the symbolic act of shaving her head—a ritualistic shedding echoing the turmoil within. Financial strain compounded her woes; having left her job due to mental anguish, she reluctantly turned to government aid programs, concealing her distress behind a veil of isolation and procrastination.

As eighteen arduous months elapsed, Zawadi's life became etched with relentless tests, unyielding pain, and an inexplicable illness. This baffling ailment stood in stark contrast to her previous state of health, marred solely by bouts of malaria and typhoid upon her return to Kenya for love.

On the other hand, the distressing chapter in Zawadi's life reached its climax one fateful night. A cancelled train, the late hour, and a trusted date's accommodation offer at his Airbnb property converged into a harrowing violation. The beacon of faith and safety she had perceived in her date had morphed into a predator, stripping Zawadi of her autonomy. The assault triggered a trauma response rooted in past wounds, rendering her defenceless and frozen, unable to fend off the assailant or flee the assault.

In the aftermath of the assault, Zawadi was engulfed in emotional turmoil, rendering her voiceless and detached from reality. Numbness enveloped her, and at home, she sought solace in cleansing rituals, endlessly showering to scrub away the unseen residue of violation. Yet, her solitude offered little respite, underscoring her struggle to find equilibrium amidst relentless turmoil.

This stark exploration led Zawadi to delve into trauma and resilience on her quest for self-redemption.

Seeking solace, Zawadi made a desperate call to her mentor, underscoring the depth of their bond. His immediate response to her distress solidified their connection, highlighting his unwavering commitment to her well-being. Witnessing her inconsolable state, he comprehended the gravity of her pain, recognizing that her aversion to physical contact was proof of her shattered sense of trust and safety.

The mentor's impassioned reaction mirrored his protective instinct as he yearned for retribution against the assailant. His offer to confront the perpetrator showcased his dedication to her healing and protection.

Zawadi's decisive actions—blocking the assailant and severing all connections—signalled a definitive step towards self-preservation. They marked her reclaiming of autonomy and her resolute stance against further harm, an empowering declaration of boundaries.

As her mentor departed, leaving her to confront the trauma, his promise of continued support echoed, assuring her that she was not alone in her healing journey.

SWEET MOTHER, I WILL NEVER FORGET YOU

In the depths of her despair, Zawadi felt as though she was drowning in an abyss of darkness, her very soul entangled in the tendrils of her anguish. Like the woman with the issue of blood, she stood at the edge of a precipice, her spirit bleeding out in silent agony, craving even the faintest glimmer of hope to penetrate the shroud of despair.Laid out before her were fifty painkiller tablets and her favourite flavoured vodka, a grim tableau set for a final act of despair.

"Mummy." Zawadi's voice quivered, barely audible through the phone's receiver. She reached out to her mother, seeking solace in the comforting embrace of maternal understanding. Her mother, attuned to Zawadi's emotional frequencies, could sense the turmoil brewing beneath her daughter's fragile facade.

"Zawadi? Zawadi? What's wrong?" her mother's voice crackled with concern and urgency, a lifeline thrown to her daughter in the darkness.

"Mummy, I... I don't want to die, but... but I don't know how to live!" Zawadi's words spilled out in a raw, desperate outpouring of emotion, each syllable a testament to the depth of her anguish.

Her mother's heart clenched with worry, her own maternal instincts kicking into overdrive. She longed to reach through the phone, to envelop her daughter in a cocoon of love and protection. "What do you mean, Zawadi?" she implored, her voice trembling with emotion, mirroring the turmoil raging within her daughter's soul.

LAMENTATIONS OF ZAWADI

Zawadi poured out her heart, her words tumbling out in emotion. "Mummy, I've never understood how this world works. Everything feels immensely complex and overwhelming. I barely made it through school and didn't have any unique talents. I hoped if I could at least carve out my small piece of heaven with Ruhiu, I could at least do something right, but I messed that up, too.

"Like the incident during whitewater rafting in South Africa, I closed my eyes and jumped into marriage and other significant life decisions, sometimes hitting my head on the proverbial rock, and other times rescued by an angel. There was always a big life decision, such as choosing a career, picking a life partner, or getting a job. I had to fly out of the nest, ready or not.

"Life has no pause button, and I've been groping in the dark as I stumbled through life. Dad afforded me the luxury of pausing whenever the pressures of life came at me, but that space he held has become a thing of the past. I know you would always support me if I reached out, but at this stage of my life, I should be giving to you, not depending on you, thus I've done my best over the years to keep my life up.

"I did my best to follow the life steps to rebuild a better life, but everything fell apart.

"God has broken me and won, but he refuses to stop. Blow after blow, it's relentless. Such strong blows on a little person like me. I can't take any more. What kind of Father is he? I prefer my earthly father. He would never let me suffer continuously like this. Every month, I drain my pockets, buying medications and various supplements. All my resources are devoted to health, money that could have been invested or used for better causes.

"God planned to end me all the while. Well, he finally got his wish, and I'm going to help him get there faster by doing it myself."

"Doing what yourself?" Mum asked urgently.

"But I had to hear your voice."

"Zawadi, where are you?"

"I'm at home, Mum."

Using her second phone, Zawadi's mum swiftly sent an SOS message to her sister, Aunty Afafa, requesting her to go to Zawadi's house ASAP. Without receiving any details, Aunt Afaafa immediately headed to Zawadi's house, assuming it was another one of Zawadi's bleeding episodes.

Zawadi's voice cracked with emotion as she continued, "Mummy, what did I do wrong? I know the Bible says God chastises those whom he loves. But this is too much for one person to handle. Was he going to chasten me until he killed me? I could barely sleep last night and joined a church prayer call this morning before I was going to pull the plug on my life. Upon joining, the woman leading the call was praying quite fervently. She said God had woken her at three in the morning and asked her to pray for someone who was about to take their life. She said she could not sleep the whole night. I broke down at my desk and typed in the comment, 'It is me.' I didn't anticipate anyone recognising me at the time I typed those words.. But someone did. My church leaders went full swing, from saying prayers to making calls.

"But what was the point of saving me if God plans to continue to use me as his punching bag?"

ZAWADI'S MUM'S RESPONSE

Mum's voice softened, filled with an undying well of love and compassion that transcended her words. "Zawadi, please, I implore you to listen to me, if this is the last thing you do," she began, her tone carrying a weight of urgency and heartfelt sincerity. "I, your grandma, and the entire family have steadfastly rooted for you, though perhaps we haven't always made it abundantly clear. Traditionally speaking, a parent should never have to bury their child, and the thought of bidding you farewell in such a manner is a pain too unbearable to fathom. Those who decide to take their own lives are not just robbing themselves of a future. Still, they're leaving a chasm of sorrow and questions that can never be filled or answered, especially considering the unnatural manner of their passing. Know this, Zawadi—we love you unconditionally, regardless of the trials you face or the paths you choose."

"Have you ever stopped to think of your dad or me before considering such a drastic step?" Mum's voice carried a poignant mixture of affection and pride. "Zawadi, my dear daughter, please understand this unequivocally—I love you and am endlessly proud of you. No matter what you do or don't achieve, no accomplishment or misstep could ever diminish the depth of my love for you. And let me tell you, God feels the same way about you. Your father, may he rest in peace. He cherished you beyond measure and was brimming with pride at the mere thought of you. I know he didn't vocalise it as often as he should have, but the truth of his love for you remains as steadfast as ever."

"At the time you entered this world, Zawadi, it was amidst a whirlwind of joy and celebration," Mum continued, her voice carrying the weight of cherished memories. "Your father ensured that you wanted for nothing from the day you were born until his last breath. He devoted himself to your well-being with a fervour matched by his immense love for you. We named you 'Zawadi' because you are a rare and precious gift, a beacon of hope and love destined to touch countless lives across generations."

"On the day of your birth, Zawadi, the stars aligned momentously for our family's future," Mum recounted, her words hinting at awe. "It was the day your father brokered a historic deal with a leading corporation from overseas, a deal that would forever alter the course of our family's financial destiny. We christened you after that company, a symbol of the boundless potential and auspicious beginnings that awaited you. Your Caucasian godfather, a man of his word, pledged to see you through to the pinnacle of educational success, a promise I have no doubt he intends to keep."

"Do you recall the tale of the elderly gentleman who gazed upon you as a newborn and imparted a solemn charge upon me?" Mum's voice took on a respectful tone. "He spoke of your unique gift, destined to illuminate the world with brilliance. I cling to those words to this very day, for you, my dear Zawadi, have always embodied the essence of your name—a precious gift to humanity. Your selflessness knows no bounds, always placing the needs of others above your own, a testament to the purity of your heart."

"We instituted your 'gifting day' from the earliest days of your education, extending through primary school," Mum reminisced fondly, her words tinged with maternal pride. "It was an opportunity for you to share your boundless love and generosity with your peers, a tradition upheld without fail. I vividly recall procuring an array of sweets, meticulously packed into cartons, to be distributed among the five-hundred-plus pupils of your school every month. And oh, how your compassionate spirit shone through, to the extent of dipping into our stores to assist classmates in need."

"And how many times did you pilfer from your dad and me to alleviate the financial burdens of your friends' education?" Mum's tone held a gentle reproach laced with a profound understanding. "Never did we harbour anger or resentment, for we recognised the purity of your intentions, though your methods were somewhat misguided."

"You, my dear, have brought immeasurable joy into my life," Mum affirmed, her voice brimming with unwavering love. "The dissolution of your marriage did not dishearten me; rather, I stood steadfast with open arms, akin to the father in the parable of the prodigal son, ready to welcome you and to propel you to greater heights than before. The revelation of the violation you endured shattered my heart, and I was profoundly disappointed by Ruhiu's lack of grace in handling such a delicate situation."

"And he should have shown you more compassion," Mum added, her disappointment palpable. "But despite it all, my darling, I know you are the goose, and those who have wronged you can steal just the eggs. You possess the resilience and strength to rebuild bigger and better, and of that, I have no doubt. Remember, pencils have erasers for a reason."

"Reflect, if you will, on the parable of the talents," Mum continued, her voice carrying the weight of timeless wisdom. "In this profound tale, the master entrusted varying talents to his servants according to their ability. Upon his return, he found that those who had invested and multiplied their gifts received abundant rewards. Yet, the one who buried his talent, out of fear or negligence, faced disappointment and rebuke from his master."

"Do not entertain the thought of burying your talents, Zawadi," Mum emphasised, her tone resolute. "For within you lie extraordinary gifts and untapped potential seeking expression. Remain steadfast in the smallest of endeavours, and I assure you that blessings beyond your wildest dreams shall be coming your way. Embrace your talents, nurture them with dedication and purpose, and watch as they blossom into a legacy of greatness."

"Life, my dear, is not a sprint," Mum reminded, her voice, a soothing balm to Zawadi's weary soul. "Do not fret over lost time, for the time God restores you, your journey shall astound those around you. Time is a fleeting concept; focus on embracing the world with the unique talents bestowed upon you. Just as the gentle flutter of a butterfly's wings can spark a tempest miles away, your steadfast dedication and unwavering spirit shall herald a storm of goodness for generations to come."

"No one possesses the radiant warmth and infectious joy that you do, Zawadi," Mum exclaimed, her pride evident. "Picture a child awakening to the radiance of your smile each day, a beacon of hope amidst life's tribulations. Your kind eyes and gentle energy have touched countless hearts, and it would be a travesty to deprive the world of such beauty. Do not forsake your dreams of changing the world with your gift; remember the lives you have touched and the hearts you have inspired."

"I want to reiterate, Zawadi, that should you require a procedure to restore your health fully, I shall be by your side every step of the way," Mum assured, her unwavering support evident. "Moreover, the right partner will enter your life, a companion with whom you will build a future brimming with love, joy, and fulfilment beyond measure. I do not doubt you will realise your dream of a family filled with warmth and happiness."

"I pray for you incessantly, Zawadi," Mum concluded, her voice imbued with love and devotion. "Your aunt is en route to your side as we speak, and I shall remain on the phone until she arrives. You are not alone, my darling; we are here for you, always and forever."

TOUCHING THE HEM: A MODERN MIRACLE

In the muted glow of her living room, the air thick with despair, Zawadi's suffering reached a zenith, a stark and harrowing moment when the full measure of her pain became unbearable. Each heartbeat was a drumbeat of agony, binding her upper body to her lower, compelling her to fold into herself as though her spine were stitched with threads of fire. The pain was both a jailor and a torturer, relentless in its intensity, causing her every movement to echo with sharp, gnashing torment.

The television flickered, a dim light in the gathering gloom, but its usual comfort blurred into the background as her pain crescendoed. With each wave that washed over her, her resolve crumbled a little more, leaving her breathless and desperate. She found herself brought to her knees, the cool floor a small relief against her fevered skin, as she folded forward, her forehead pressing against the ground. It was in this posture of utter defeat and supplication that Zawadi felt the heavy weight of her affliction pinning her down, an anchor dragging her to the depths of despair.

Around her, the room spun—a carousel of shadows and light, the walls echoing with the hollow sound of her laboured breathing. Memories of her mother's comforting presence and her melodic prayers in their native tongue swirled through her mind. The songs were a balm, yet the relief they offered was fleeting, overwhelmed by the torrent of her physical suffering.

As the pain carved through her, a story she had heard many times in church crystallised in her mind—the biblical account of a woman who had suffered for twelve long years with an issue of blood. This woman, marginalised and desperate, had reached out to touch the hem of Jesus' garment, believing wholeheartedly in the healing that could come from just one touch.

In her own moment of desperation, Zawadi felt a kinship with this ancient sufferer across the millennia. Like the woman with the issue of blood, she too was isolated by her condition, driven to the fringes of her own life by a malady no one could seem to mend. And now, here, on her living room floor, Zawadi reached out—not through a crowd but towards the flickering light of the television screen, where the image of her pastor appeared, his sermon a distant echo in her pain-fogged mind.

Her pastor spoke of faith, of healing, of reaching out in belief as the woman in the Bible had done. His words, usually a comfort, now ignited a spark of something fiercer in Zawadi—a desperate, burning hope. With trembling hands and a heart pounding with both dread and anticipation, she stretched her fingers toward the screen, her gesture mirroring the biblical woman's last resort to claim healing.

"Lord, if I could just touch, if I could just believe as she did," Zawadi whispered, her voice a raspy thread of sound. Her fingertips brushed the cool surface of the television, and in that touch, she poured all her anguish, her hope, and her yearning for relief.

As Zawadi reached out toward the flickering screen, her fingertips gently brushing against the glass in a symbolic plea for healing, she could almost feel the surge of power that had once flowed from Jesus to the woman with the issue of blood. In her heart, she envisioned that same divine energy emanating from her pastor as he spoke, bridging the vast expanse of time and space, reaching out to her in her moment of desperate need.

Yet, amidst this profound connection, a shadow of doubt crept into her mind. She felt akin to the tax collector who stood at a distance in the temple, overwhelmed by his own unworthiness, yet seeking mercy. In her humility and pain, she bowed deeper, a silent acknowledgment of her feelings of unworthiness yet a fervent hope that perhaps, even in her imperfection, she might still be touched by the healing and redemptive power she so desperately sought.

Tears streamed down her cheeks, unrestrained, as she imagined imbuing her touch with the power to heal, to change her fate. "Thank you, Lord, for not giving up on me," she sobbed, her voice breaking with the intensity of her plea. The room was still, the only sound her cries and the soft hum of the television, but in her heart, the tumult was slowly, subtly beginning to calm.

WAGING WAR

In the crucible of Zawadi's deepest pain, a flicker of possibility stirred within her spirit, a beacon shimmering through the veil of darkness. Reality itself seemed to warp, bending towards her in a divine caress. With each whispered prayer, the oppressive weight of her burdens lifted, replaced by an overwhelming peace—a tidal wave of grace engulfing her soul.

Yet, within this newfound sanctuary of faith, Zawadi found herself entangled in a profound contradiction. Despite her embrace of salvation, she often reverted to old habits of self-reliance and makeshift solutions, attempting to "tidy up" her life before she would allow herself to seek help from others. This inner conflict

233

underscored her ongoing struggle to fully surrender to the liberating promises of her faith, her spirit still shackled by the ghosts of past anxieties and uncertainties about the future.

Enveloped in divine light, Zawadi wrestled with doubt and her ingrained reliance on herself, while shadows from her past loomed, threatening to pull her back into despair. It was an epic struggle, a fierce internal war against the demons of her own creation.

Amidst this tempest of turmoil, Zawadi found solace in the transformative power of worship—a lighthouse piercing the stormy night. With each melodic heartbeat of her worship, the chains that had once bound her shattered, giving way to the expansive embrace of her faith, lifting her towards the dawn of true freedom.

SAVED BY A SONG

The song "Good and Loved" by Travis Greene and Steffany Gretzinger played softly in the background, its comforting lyrics wrapping around Zawadi like a warm embrace. At that moment, she knew she was not alone, regardless of the darkness of the valley. Zawadi felt her soul awaken from its slumber like a phoenix rising from the ashes of despair. In that sacred moment, she realised she wasn't alone, wrapped in the unfathomable depths of God's love.

And as the music filled the room, Zawadi felt hope ignite within her soul. A tiny spark, barely visible in the darkness, yet sufficient to keep her going. She would hold onto that hope at the moment, trusting that the sun would shine again one day.

Zawadi exchanged the dark cloud of suicide and depression for God's cloud, which showered her with love, peace, joy, and, above all, life. Zawadi knew then that her prayers were not bouncing off the ceiling; they had not reached critical mass. The cloud, finally full of rain, had begun emptying itself on her. And she received it. God's part of the equation is that he is good; all she needs to do is accept his love.

SURRENDERING AT HIS FEET: FINDING WHOLENESS IN STILLNESS

After years spent in a whirlwind of activity, constantly striving to do and fix, Zawadi reached a profound realisation: it was time to pause, to stand still, and to simply be. In the quiet stillness, she began to experience the gentle outpouring of God's love, a healing balm for her wounded soul.

Much like the biblical story of Mary and Martha, Zawadi had been consumed by the demands of her daily life, always busy with tasks and responsibilities. She identified with Martha, the diligent worker who sought to serve and please, but in her busyness, she had overlooked the one thing that truly mattered.

It was in the midst of this realisation that Zawadi found herself drawn to the story of Mary, who sat at the feet of Jesus, drinking in his words and presence. While Martha was busy with preparations, Mary chose the better part—to simply be with her Lord.

In a similar manner, Zawadi began to shift her focus from doing to being, from striving to simply resting in God's love. She understood that true restoration and wholeness could only be found in the quiet moments of intimacy with her Creator. Like Mary, she reached out and touched the hem of God's love, allowing it to envelop her in its warmth and healing embrace.

As she surrendered to this divine love, Zawadi felt the weight of her burdens lifted, her spirit renewed and revitalised. In the stillness, she found peace, joy, and a sense of wholeness that had eluded her for so long. It was a transformational journey, one that brought her back to the very heart of her faith, where love and grace abounded, and where she found the courage to embrace life with renewed hope and purpose.

THIRST: FINDING REDEMPTION BEYOND THE WELL

Zawadi's soul, long parched by a relentless thirst for acceptance and validation, found its oasis in an unexpected revelation, mirroring the ancient tale of the Samaritan woman at Jacob's well. This woman, notorious for her five husbands and her current lover, not a husband, received an extraordinary grace from Jesus, who saw beyond her societal labels to offer unconditional love and acceptance.

For Zawadi, this realisation washed over her like the first rains after a merciless drought. She was not damaged goods, despite the whispers and judgments that often followed her like shadows. In the eyes of her heavenly Father, she was cherished, wholly restored, her imperfections woven into a tapestry of redemption.

Though the earthly father she adored had been claimed by time, she had forged an unbreakable bond with a divine Father. His celestial embrace filled the void left behind, reminding her that her worth was not measured by her losses but by what remained. In the depths of her spirit, a miracle brewed—forged from the remnants of her fractured past, it was potent enough to launch her toward her destiny. This newfound strength was a beacon, guiding her through the uncharted waters of her future, promising not just survival, but a flourishing life sculpted by divine hands.

BANNER OF LOVE : THEN, NOW, NEXT

The song "Good and Loved" spoke to Zawadi that if she ever forgets about God's love, she should lift her head and see that God's banner over her is his love. She gradually lifted her head from the floor, having been bent down and crying. She felt incredibly light and free. Love had found her and lifted her.

Zawadi found it interesting that other people had taken a snapshot of her life and stretched the image out across her entire existence—her past, present, and future—falsely judged by friends and family as they assumed that they knew everything there was to know about her, including all that she would ever become.

The song mentions the One who was, who is, and who will be covering her. Knowing that she was dwelling within the shadow of the Most High, she had no more fear of the night terror, the arrow by noonday, or the pestilence that worked in darkness. Her past, present and future were under his control.

Zawadi contemplated the misconceptions that others held about her life, realising how people often projected their judgments onto her past, present, and future. Despite the assumptions made by friends and family, she found solace in believing that the divine presence encompassed her, shielded by the shadow of the Most High.

As she reflected on the significance of the song's message, Zawadi understood that the proof of love lay not in her sacrifices but in the sacrificial blood shed by Jesus. This profound realisation allowed her to embrace a profound shift in her spiritual journey—a surrender to Christ, accepting the salvation offered to her and relinquishing the burden of self-reliance.

WORSHIP AS A WEAPON

Zawadi delved deep into the transformative power of worship, discovering it as a profound experience that transcended language and human understanding, becoming her personalised emblem, and a formidable weapon in her battle against life's challenges.This revelation evaded her during the well-intentioned yet futile attempts of her friends to alleviate her predicament.

Transitioning from a breakdown to a breakthrough, Zawadi commenced a self-affirmation journey, embracing the profound truths of her faith. Affirming her worthiness and acceptance, she acknowledged her inherent value as a beloved child of God, forgiven and unconditionally loved.

RETURN OF THE GRATEFUL HEART

With those words lingering in her heart, Zawadi felt hope ignite. A small flame flickered, but it was enough to dispel some of the darkness that had clouded her mind. Despite the uncertainty surrounding the timeline of her complete healing, Zawadi solemnly pledged to be the one to return and offer heartfelt gratitude for the divine deliverance she had received, much like the one grateful leper among the ten whom Jesus had healed.

As she meditated on this biblical account, she drew a profound parallel: ten lepers had been miraculously healed, yet only one returned to thank Jesus. This lone figure, ostracised and marginalised like herself, had recognised the magnitude of his transformation and had come back to give praise where it was due. With an unshakable faith in God's ability to guide her through this trial, Zawadi held onto the belief that, in due course, her body and spirit would be fully restored.

Embracing this spiritual archetype, she committed not just to seek healing, but to nurture a heart of gratitude and recognition of the grace that flowed even now in her life. This commitment fortified her, granting her a serene assurance that her journey through suffering would culminate in a profound renewal, both physically and spiritually.

PEACE LIKE A RIVER

"Peace I leave with you; my peace I give to you. Not as the world gives do I give to you."
- John 14:27 (ESV).

As she hung up the phone, a wave of peace washed over Zawadi, subtle yet profound, a fleeting touch that reminded her of the enduring hope that flickered even in her darkest moments. With that hope burning brightly within her, she took a deep breath and silently vowed to keep moving forward, one deliberate step at a time.

Her mother's words echoed in her mind, a soothing anthem to her intrinsic worth and the boundless love that encircled her. With Aunty Afafa's comforting presence as a tangible manifestation of grace and love, Zawadi experienced a profound epiphany. She realized that neither her past missteps nor the uncertainties of her future were the architects of her path. Rather, she was guided by a transcendent faith, buoyed by the unwavering love of her Creator, propelling her towards a destiny woven with purpose and promise.

LOVE IS..

Zawadi's journey from brokenness to a vibrant sense of self was marked by the gentle but unyielding power of divine affirmation. Each scripture she embraced not only soothed her internal wounds but also reconstructed her external world, anchoring her deeply in her identity in Christ, who became the bedrock of her existence and a secure yet transformative place upon which she could stand.

"**I am loved**," she whispered, feeling the warmth of divine affection enveloping her.

"**I have the Father's love**," she affirmed, finding solace in the unwavering presence of her Heavenly Father.

"**Mum loves me**," she declared with conviction, grateful for her mother's boundless love and support.

"**My family loves me**," she acknowledged, drawing strength from the love that surrounded her.

"**I am forgiven**," she proclaimed, releasing the burden of past mistakes and embracing the grace of forgiveness.

"**I had the Father's love in my heart the whole time**," she realised, finding comfort in the enduring presence of God's love within her.

"**God doesn't make trash**," she declared emphatically, rejecting the lies of self-condemnation and embracing her inherent worth.

"**I am God's masterpiece**," she affirmed, recognising the beauty and uniqueness of her true self.

"**I am good, and I am loved unconditionally**," she declared boldly, embracing her identity as a beloved child of God.

"**I am love**," she concluded, embodying the essence of divine love that flowed through her being.

MASTERPIECE UNVEILED: REDISCOVERING IDENTITY IN DIVINE LIGHT

Zawadi's newfound perspective emerged as she embraced her identity in Christ, finding within each declaration a deep resonance that healed and shaped her. The following reflections illustrate how each affirmation transformed her internally and influenced her actions externally:

"**I am God's masterpiece**" (Ephesians 2:10) - As a divine masterpiece, she pursued her personal and professional goals with creativity and excellence, seeing herself as crafted for a unique purpose.

"**I am faithful**" (Ephesians 1:1) - This reminded Zawadi of her commitment to faith even in trials, reinforcing her resilience and influencing her to lead by example in her community.

"**I am God's child**" (John 1:12) - Recognising her identity as God's child restored her self-esteem and changed how she interacted with the world, engaging with others with the confidence of being loved unconditionally.

"**I have been justified**" (Romans 5:1) - Knowing she was justified by faith, Zawadi let go of her past guilt, allowing her to pursue future opportunities without the baggage of past failures.

"**I am Christ's friend**" (John 15:15) - This deepened her relationship with God and encouraged her to cultivate genuine relationships, bringing authenticity to her interactions.

"**I belong to God**" (1 Corinthians 6:20) - With a sense of belonging, Zawadi found a community where she could contribute meaningfully, enhancing her social bonds and community involvement.

"**I am a member of Christ's Body**" (1 Corinthians 12:27) - This realisation helped her appreciate her unique gifts and use them to serve others, strengthening her role in church and community projects.

"**I am assured all things work together for good**" (Romans 8:28) - This assurance fostered optimism and hope, even during setbacks, allowing her to encourage others with her steadfastness.

"**I have been established, anointed and sealed by God**" (2 Corinthians 1:21-22) - Embracing her divine anointing, Zawadi stepped into leadership roles, guided by a sense of divine purpose and security.

"**I am confident that God will perfect the work He has begun in me**" (Philippians 1:6) - This confidence allowed her to be patient with her own growth, inspiring patience in others as she led by example.

"**I am a citizen of heaven**" (Philippians 3:20) - This heavenly citizenship shifted her focus from temporal to eternal, influencing her priorities and decisions toward more spiritual pursuits.

"I am hidden with Christ in God" (Colossians 3:3) - Feeling protected, Zawadi became bold in her convictions and choices, no longer swayed by peer pressure or societal expectations.

"I have not been given a spirit of fear, but of power, love, and self-discipline" (2 Timothy 1:7) - Empowered by this truth, she tackled challenges with courage and initiated community outreach programs, spreading love and discipline.

"I am forgiven and free from condemnation" (Ephesians 1:7; Romans 8:1) - Liberated from condemnation, she forgave others easily, fostering reconciliation and deeper relationships.

"I am the salt and light of the earth" (Matthew 5:13-14) - Comprehending her role as salt and light motivated her to lead community improvement projects, enhancing the well-being and spiritual life of her community.

Zawadi's transformative journey, woven with the threads of divine affirmations, portrayed a vivid tapestry of change that not only healed her internally but also reshaped her interactions with the world. Her transformation was not merely a personal triumph but a shining beacon for others, illustrating the profound impact of embracing one's identity in Christ. Each affirmation, deeply rooted in spiritual truths, meticulously redefined her inner narrative and spurred her to engage in actions that mirrored her rejuvenated faith and self-identity.

With each declaration of divine truth, Zawadi experienced a palpable surge of empowerment. The chains of self-doubt that once ensnared her now lay broken at her feet, replaced by a steadfast confidence that elevated her stance. She sensed her destiny unfolding—a path marked by greatness and underpinned by the unwavering love of her Creator. This newfound realisation illuminated her: her past errors and future worries were mere echoes, not definitions.

Each step forward was bolstered by affirmations of self-love and acceptance, guiding her towards a holistic healing. Embracing the transformative power of her faith and the constant, nurturing love of her Creator, she found strength. This strength was not ephemeral but a continuous force, enriching her sense of purpose and intensifying her determination. Basking in the radiant glow of self-acceptance and the unconditional love of the divine, Zawadi was transformed.

Now, she stood ready to greet each day with an indomitable spirit, armed with courage, resilience, and a faith that did not waver. Knowing deeply that she was cherished beyond measure, Zawadi looked forward to a future brimming with hope and ripe with possibilities. Her life, once fragmented by despair, now danced to the rhythm of possibility and promise, a testament to the enduring power of faith and the identity found in the love of a divine Father.

Year 5

Chapter Twenty Two

BLOSSOMING FROM BROKENNESS

> *You can't transform the quality of your thoughts and emotions*
> *without transforming the consciousness*
> *from which they arise.*
> **—Barbara De Angelis**

As Zawadi's journey unfolded through a tapestry of challenges, from personal loss to profound self-discovery, each chapter of her life seemed written by the hand of a meticulous craftsman, intent on refining her through adversity. The absence of the traditional family she yearned for became a backdrop to her more intense personal trials, paralleling the endurance of those who survived wars or natural catastrophes. This perspective brought a crucial pivot, as she let go of her old identity, embracing the truth of her core self emerging through the pain.

Seated on her sofa, Zawadi's tears streamed down in private catharsis, mourning the person she once was—a complex mix of loss and love. Yet, amidst the tears, laughter began to rise, reminiscent of Sarah's incredulous joy in the Bible, transforming her grief into a lighter, freeing experience. This laughter marked a pivotal shift, a release from past burdens now viewed through the lens of gained wisdom.

Zawadi's metaphorical seasons of crushing and fermentation mirrored the winemaking process she witnessed in South Africa's vineyards. Each step, from the brutal crush of the grapes to their ultimate transformation into fine wine, symbolised her own seasons of transformation. Here, she learned to see these crushing periods not as destruction but as necessary for growth and excellence, much like Pastor T's counsel that patience crafts refined characters.

In the tactile and chaotic process of grape treading, Zawadi confronted the reality that from life's disarray comes a product of value—her own spirit being refined from the chaos of her experiences. She recognised that her personal pruning was not punitive but preparatory, enabling her to yield a richer, more fruitful life.

Zawadi's narrative wove through days of significant realisation: the day of her birth, which set the stage for her life's potential; the day she discovered her purpose, which directed her path with clarity; and importantly, the day she understood her limitations, liberating her from the burden of unsuitable expectations. These milestones shaped not only her self-concept but her legacy.

Her journey through singleness, guided by a relationship coach, reshaped her view of fulfilment beyond societal norms of marriage and children, fostering a robust sense of self-worth and independence. A poignant piece of advice to pause and reflect rather than relentlessly pursue goals reminded her to cherish each moment rather than merely accumulating achievements.

Through it all, Zawadi's struggle with self-prioritisation contrasted sharply with her generosity towards others. Her journey towards understanding that she deserved the same level of care and investment she so freely gave others was a crucial evolution in her narrative, teaching her the importance of self-nourishment.

Reflecting on her life choices in career and relationships, Zawadi embraced her identity as a late bloomer. Her path, filled with second chances, taught her the grace of timing and the beauty of life's unpredictable rhythm. She saw her life as a film—each scene, whether joyful or painful, adding richness and depth, illustrating that every moment contributes to the fullness of life's story.

Approaching her relationship with Aunt Flo with a new maturity, Zawadi was ready to engage in meaningful dialogue, recognising the growth and understanding necessary for healthy, evolving relationships.

DEAR AUNT FLO,

I am writing to express my deep gratitude for the countless lessons you've imparted to me. Though our journey together has of-

ten been stormy, I've come to understand that smooth seas do not create skilled sailors. As Rhonda Byrne wisely stated, "Gratitude will shift you to a higher frequency, and you will attract much better things."

In a world that constantly urges us to look upward and aspire for more by comparing ourselves to those at the summit, I've chosen a different viewpoint. In embracing gratitude, I've looked downward, recognising the incredible distance I've traveled and appreciating the myriad blessings that have enriched my path.

There were moments when I resented your arrival and the challenges you brought along with your three little companions. Yet, these challenges taught me to harness pain as a source of strength. Without your relentless presence urging me on, I may never have striven so fiercely during the moments you were absent. While suffering is a universal truth, and pain ceases only with life itself, I now choose to see the purpose hidden within my pain.

Looking back, I understand that you were the crucible intended to refine me. Today, I am profoundly grateful for the resilience I've developed and the gold I've become—feeling reborn through this transformation. You offered me a chance to grow profoundly, not merely to age, and for that, the power you've brought into my life is immeasurable.

You shifted my perspective from a plaintive "Why me?" to a proactive "What for?" and "What now?" Dwelling on why kept me trapped in victimhood, suggesting that this burden would be better borne by another. Yet, through your tutelage, I've come to embrace my challenges as uniquely mine, necessary for the cultivation of my rich soul and unbreakable spirit.

Thank you for everything, Aunt Flo. My journey with you has been indispensable to becoming who I am today.

With heartfelt gratitude,

Zawadi

Chapter Twenty Three

LIVE FULL, DIE EMPTY

> *Live your life by a compass, not a clock.*
> **- Stephen Covey**

The threads of authenticity delicately interweave in the intricate tapestry of Zawadi's extraordinary life, bearing witness to a profound transformative journey. It all began with her sister Kioni's seemingly unconventional plea for deliverance, igniting a metamorphosis within Zawadi. Zawadi's life mantra echoed in her mind, "*Live full and die empty*," Zawadi stood on the precipice of a revelation—not of the traditional religious kind, but of profound self-awareness. She realised that her deepest fear wasn't death but rather living a life devoid of purpose and meaning.

Immersed in the stifling expectations of society, Zawadi undertook a courageous journey of self-discovery, challenging the rigid norms that had long dictated the course of her existence. With the guidance of therapists and relationship coaches, she delved into her soul, carving out a path free from the shackles of societal conventions. The traditional milestones of life—education, marriage, family, wealth accumulation, and legacy building—came under her discerning scrutiny, revealing their hollow promises of fulfilment.

WOMANHOOD

Zawadi embraced a more expansive definition of womanhood, defiantly challenging the notion that femininity revolved solely around motherhood. She recognised the inherent value of her soul and spirit, redefining motherhood as a multifaceted expression that extended beyond biological ties. For her, it encompassed nurturing, support, and the boundless embodiment of love. Zawadi discovered her unique capacity to birth destinies, visions, and dreams, thereby challenging societal norms and leaving an indelible legacy of profound impact.

FAMILY

The conventional concept of family underwent a radical transformation under Zawadi's discerning gaze. Liberated from the confines of traditional familial structures, she found familial bonds in diverse forms—forging connections with strangers, embracing various tribes, and redefining the essence of kinship.

MARRIAGE

Previously idealised as the pinnacle of achievement, marriage underwent a profound reevaluation, transitioning from the culmination of her existence to a medium for self-discovery. Zawadi began prioritising soul-level connections over societal expectations, recognising that genuine love transcends mere blood ties.

TIME

Identifying her adherence to societal ideals as a form of idolatry, Zawadi embarked on a journey of self-discovery, purpose, and creativity. Formerly reserved for momentous occasions, time became a precious currency invested in the present moment. Her deliberate cultivation of self-love marked a departure from societal conditioning, redirecting the spotlight inward.

She bought a sand timer to bring her back to the present every 25 minutes, utilising the Pomodoro Technique. This simple yet elegant tool helped her focus her energies and manage her time more effectively, dividing her work into short, productive bursts followed by brief breaks. This method not only boosted her productivity but also maintained her mental well-being by reminding her to take necessary pauses and breathe, keeping stress at bay and her goals in clear view.

CONTROL

Guided by the Serenity Prayer, Zawadi found solace in accepting the limitations of her control, which empowered her to face life's uncertainties with grace and serenity. What Zawadi had perceived as an uncertain path transformed into an exhilarating adventure, with Zawadi focusing not on the unpredictability of life but on her responses to its twists and turns.

UNHEALTHY CRAVINGS

Recognising the profound impact of unhealthy cravings on her physical, biological, and emotional well-being, Zawadi embraced a fasting lifestyle and abstained from alcohol as an intentional choice, which played a pivotal role in improving her overall health.

MINIMALISIM

Embracing minimalism became a cornerstone of her stress-free lifestyle, freeing her from the relentless pursuit of material possessions.

EXTERNAL MEASURES OF SUCCESS

In an age dominated by the relentless pursuit of external success, Zawadi stood firm against the pressure. Her focus shifted from visible achievements to internal growth, self-mastery, and the wisdom derived from her journey. Undeterred by interactions with those who knew solely outdated versions of herself, Zawadi remained confident that her journey towards authenticity would be understood and appreciated over time.

In crafting a life beyond societal norms, Zawadi's journey transcended mere rebellion; a symphony of authenticity, self-discovery, and intentional living unfolded. Each rule challenged and revelation embraced meticulously contributed to the vibrant strokes of a canvas painted with the radiant colours of life genuinely, remarkably, and audaciously lived.

WORK LIFE IN BALANCE

Zawadi's journey at work had always been marked by her unwavering commitment and remarkable resilience. Her daily battle with health issues posed challenges that many might have found insurmountable, yet Zawadi's spirit remained indomitable. However, a turning point came when her condition threatened to disrupt her career trajectory. Her boss, witnessing her struggles, suggested she take time off whenever she felt unwell—a well-meaning proposal that unwittingly risked her becoming a near-permanent absentee.

Instead of resigning herself to frustration or accepting an indefinite leave as her fate, Zawadi chose to address the issue head-on. She requested a private meeting with her boss, where she laid bare the realities of her health condition and its impact on her work life. This candid disclosure was not easy; it required Zawadi to be vulnerable in a space where she had always strived to showcase strength. But it was necessary for forging a path forward that respected her needs and the company's expectations.

To her relief, the discussion was met with understanding rather than judgment. Zawadi proposed a flexible working arrangement that would allow her to work from home during her less severe days and come into the office when she felt more robust. This adaptive strategy was designed to ensure her productivity remained high while managing her health effectively.

Implementing this plan transformed not only Zawadi's work life but also began to reshape the workplace culture around her. Her successful negotiation set a precedent, showcasing how personal challenges, when met with empathy and flexibility, could lead to innovative solutions that benefit the entire workforce. It fostered an environment where openness and mutual respect flourished, encouraging others to communicate their own needs without fear of reprisal or stigma.

The ripple effects of Zawadi's arrangement were profound. Productivity in her department did not diminish; instead, it improved, as Zawadi was able to work in an environment tailored to her physical capabilities. This success story demonstrated that accommodating diverse health needs did not equate to lowered standards or increased costs but rather optimised each employee's potential and contributions.

Moreover, Zawadi's story became a benchmark for other departments within the company. Leaders who had observed her case began reconsidering how they could implement similar accommodations, promoting a broader understanding of diversity and inclusion. This shift was not just about making space for physical or health differences; it was about valuing what each unique individual could bring to the table when given the right opportunities and support.

Through her journey, Zawadi had not only safeguarded her career but had also championed a cause greater than herself. She had turned personal adversity into an opportunity for organisational growth, proving that the true strength of a workplace lies in its ability to embrace diversity in all its forms, including health. Each step she took further solidified her legacy within the company—a legacy of courage, innovation, and an unwavering belief in the dignity of every employee's journey.

As Zawadi reflected on the changes that had unfolded, she felt a profound sense of accomplishment and hope. Her actions had carved out a path for others in her company to follow, a path that acknowledged and celebrated each person's unique challenges and contributions. Her story was a testament to the power of empathy and adaptability in transforming not just workplaces but lives.

I AM NOT MY HAIR

After years of battling chronic health issues that left her often feeling drained and at times, disconnected from her own sense of self, Zawadi made a bold decision to undergo a hair transplant. This choice was more than cosmetic; it was a profound act of reclaiming her identity and exerting control over her body, which had so often felt like it was under siege from her illnesses.

The process began with her shaving off her remaining hair—a dramatic and symbolic shedding of the old. As her hair fell away, so too did some of the vulnerabilities and insecurities that had clung to her like shadows. She embraced this new look with a mixture of apprehension and exhilaration, aware that the road ahead would be challenging, yet hopeful for the renewal it promised.

For weeks, Zawadi walked around with a spray bottle, diligently misting her scalp to aid the healing process. Her appearance during this time was stark, almost alien to those who knew her best. Yet, this unusual routine added a new dimension to her daily life. Each spray was a reminder of her resilience, a small act of nurturing that mirrored the care she took in managing her pain and health.

Her friends and Mo, in particular, found her commitment and positivity during this time inspiring. Mo, who had always admired Zawadi's strength, now saw a new side of her courage. He joked with her one afternoon as they met for coffee, "You know, with that spray bottle, you look like you're about to take off to another planet!"

Zawadi laughed, her spirit undimmed by the comment. "Maybe I am, Mo. If dealing with everything has taught me anything, it's that sometimes, you need to be a little alien to find your way back to yourself."

As her new hair began to grow, each tiny follicle felt like a victory, a tangible result of her persistence and her faith. This personal transformation was not just about aesthetics but about growth and recovery—themes that resonated deeply with Zawadi's spiritual journey as well.

Thus, the hair transplant became more than a medical procedure; it was a rite of passage for Zawadi, marking both an ending and a new beginning. Her scalp, once bare and tender, now flourished anew, much like her renewed sense of self. Through this experience, Zawadi not only regained her hair but also reaffirmed her identity and her ability to shape her destiny, one small, deliberate step at a time.

INDUCED AMNESIA

As Zawadi journeyed through life, she adopted a practice that subtly reshaped her relationship with her past. With every snapshot taken, every joyful moment captured, she gradually nudged the darker memories to the corners of her mind, creating a visual archive of positivity that dominated her daily thoughts. This wasn't merely an exercise in photography but a transformative process, a deliberate act of focusing on the brightness of life, allowing the shadows to fade until they were barely whispers in the background.

This practice led to a peculiar kind of amnesia, where the intense pain and struggles of her past years became blurred images, difficult to recall without a conscious effort. When friends or events nudged these memories to the surface, Zawadi approached them differently. She didn't just remember; she dissected these experiences, extracting strength and wisdom like precious ores from the rock. Each memory, no matter how jagged, became a brick in the foundation of the formidable woman she was building herself to become.

Not all bricks were perfectly shaped; some were rough, misshapen, carrying the scars of her battles and the stains of her tears. Yet, each was essential, contributing to a structure robust and majestic, reminiscent of ancient edifices that withstand the test of time, preferred over the fleeting architectures of modern days. Her life, much like these timeless structures, was built to endure, its beauty derived from the resilience and stories embedded in every block.

Inside, her world was minimal yet vibrant, an inviting space that mirrored her inner transformation. It was playful and joyful, each room a testament to the life she had chosen to lead. The ambiance was a deliberate creation as well—infused scents filled the air, blending with the aroma of freshly baked goods. Every meal she prepared was a celebration, a simple yet profound act of love and nourishment, echoing the warmth and hospitality that anyone stepping through her door would feel.

In this crafted sanctuary, Zawadi not only rebuilt herself but also created a haven for others, a place where comfort and joy were as palpable as the walls that held them. Her home became a reflection of her journey—a blend of strength and softness, resilience and tenderness—a place where the past was acknowledged, not as a shadow that loomed but as a story that taught. Here, in her carefully curated haven, every visitor found a piece of home, and Zawadi thrived, her spirit enriched by every life she touched, every story she shared.

CBT - COGNITIVE BEHAVIOURAL THERAPY

The therapist Zawadi had been seeing remarked one day, "Miss Zawadi, judging from your scores on the Anxiety Scale, Depression Scale, IAPT [Improving Access to Psychological Therapies] exam, Phobia Scale, and WSAS [Work and Social Adjustment Scales], it appears that you've made significant progress. You no longer fall within the range of depression and anxiety, which is quite encouraging. "There's a noticeable difference since you first began CBT."

Zawadi responded, "I'm not surprised. I've achieved a kind of mental liberation. Your guidance has been instrumental, offering clarity and providing tools that have made a profound impact."

"In the two weeks since our last conversation, what's been going on?" the therapist inquired.

Zawadi replied, "Thanks to your assistance, I've pinpointed the vicious cycles and patterns in my thoughts and behaviours holding me and causing self-sabotage, especially my tendency to catastrophise. My previous coping mechanisms for dealing with depression were counterproductive. I used to withdraw, ruminate, and avoid people and activities, including those that benefited me. These behaviours no longer align with the direction my life is taking.

"I've learned to intercept my thoughts as they arise, ending potential issues at the source. It does require some practice, though. The battlefield, as it turns out, resides within one's mind.

"I grasp the intricate connections among my thoughts, emotions, physical reactions, and behaviours in the face of challenging situations."

"Remember the moment I shared about holding a baby, soothing it until it stopped crying, feeling like validation that I could be a good mom? And then, with the opposite outcome, it felt like a sign that motherhood wasn't in my plans.I used to avoid baby showers and events that reminded me of the heartbreak I endured. With the tools you provided, I allowed the emotions to surface, realising that suppressing them merely bred bitterness. It turned out that I wasn't jealous of friends and family with children; I was experiencing normal, albeit unfamiliar, human emotions. Journaling became my outlet; as I wrote, my heart felt lighter and my mind clearer. A friend asked me to be her son's godmother, and I felt ecstatic. I no longer dread being around mothers or children."

The therapist nodded thoughtfully, acknowledging Zawadi's growth and the transformation taking place within her. "That's a profound shift," the therapist remarked.

"It sounds like you've not only found peace within yourself but also embraced the idea of creating your own narrative—a narrative that reflects your values, your strengths, and your aspirations."

Zawadi smiled, her eyes reflecting the newfound sense of clarity and purpose that permeated her being. "Exactly," she affirmed. "I've come to realise that rebuilding isn't a sign of weakness, but rather a testament to resilience. It's about taking control of my own story, rewriting it in a way that honours who I am and where I want to go."

The therapist leaned forward, intrigued by Zawadi's insights. "And how do these videos fit into this new narrative?" they inquired.

Zawadi's smile widened as she reflected on the role her videos played in her healing journey.

"They're more than just recordings of happy moments," she explained. "They're tangible reminders of the life I'm building—a life filled with joy, purpose, and authenticity. Watching them reminds me of how far I've come and gives me the strength to keep moving forward, one step at a time."

The therapist nodded in understanding, recognising the profound significance of Zawadi's journey. "It's remarkable to see the transformation unfold," they remarked. "You've truly embraced the power of perspective and rewritten the script of your life. And in doing so, you've unlocked a newfound sense of freedom and possibility."

The therapist said, "I have no doubt you're on your way to success with this new mindset. I wish you all the best. And remember, you can find me if you need me in the future. Now, go shine like the bright star you are."

"I'll make sure of that," Zawadi said. "I'm going to let this little light shine ever so brightly. Thank you again!."

Chapter Twenty Four

AND STILL I RISE

> *Be still and know that I am God.*
> **—Psalm 46:10 (NIV)**

As the year waned, Zawadi stood on the cusp of a new dawn. Her home, once a sanctuary of solitude, now pulsed with the energy of rebirth. The final call from Dr. Mark, the soft glow of her surroundings, and the intricate tattoos marking her journey whispered of endings and beginnings. Each element spoke of the scars she bore, not as marks of defeat, but as medals of honour in the quiet battle she had waged against life's relentless tides.

In that serene moment, the old fears of an unfulfilled life dissolved into the ether. The dreaded medical tests and looming decisions no longer seemed like the monsters they once were. Instead, they appeared as mere steps on her path, necessary but not definitive of her worth or her journey's value. She understood now that every medical procedure, every scar, was just a small stitch in the broader tapestry of her existence.

The transformation was not just internal. The external validation she once sought had faded into insignificance, replaced by a profound connection with her inner self and the values she held dear. Her life was no longer measured by societal yardsticks but by the depth of her experiences and the authenticity of her existence. Zawadi's journey had taught her that the essence of life wasn't about adhering to prescribed milestones but about crafting a narrative unique to her spirit and her dreams.

DO SOMETHING! DO SOMETHING!

The echoes of her father's words, "Do something,Do Something!," no longer felt like a demand but a gentle nudge towards self-actualisation. She realised that her actions, whether big or small, were significant not in their scale but in their intention. Each step she took was a testament to her resolve to live authentically, moving beyond the shadows of doubt and into the light of self-acceptance.

THE PARABLE OF HOW A YAM GROWS

"When you plant a yam, if it doesn't grow through the head, it will find another way to grow"

Her mother's wisdom, a lesson in resilience, reminded her that growth isn't always vertical but often lateral, finding its way around obstacles, pushing through the soil of hardship to reach the sun. Zawadi embraced this notion, recognising that her life, too, could find new ways to blossom in unexpected directions.

JAILER IS A PRISONER TOO!

Now, as she gazed out into the fading light of dusk, her eyes were clear, her heart was light, and her spirit was unburdened. The horizon stretched wide before her, a blank canvas ready to receive the colours of her continued journey. She was no longer a prisoner of her past or a puppet of her fears. She was the author of her story, a story no longer written by the pen of societal expectations but by her own hand, guided by her heart's true compass.

LEGACY WORTH LIVING AND LEAVING

Zawadi's aspirations soared far above the conventional milestones of societal success—the longing for children, the naming of streets, or iconic buildings bearing her name. She eschewed the traditional "workflow" of life—a predetermined path of education, marriage, family, wealth creation, and the establishment of a tangible legacy. Instead, she viewed these conventional markers not as mandatory checkpoints but as mere options in the diverse landscape of existence.

Her quest was for a legacy of the heart, one marked by changed lives, healed souls, and the quiet, resolute strength of a woman who faced life's challenges with unwavering dignity and purpose. Her steps were measured and intentional, guided by an inner compass that directed her towards making deep, meaningful impacts rather than chasing superficial accolades.

In her journey, the metaphor of eagles—creatures known for their keen sight and majestic, soaring flight—resonated deeply with Zawadi. Like these noble birds, which do not follow the trodden paths but carve their routes across the vast sky, Zawadi chose to elevate her life's trajectory above the commonplace societal blueprints. She embraced a path marked not by the predictable patterns of the ground but by the boundless expanse of the horizon.

This selfless approach to life echoed aspirations she had harboured since high school, where she once contemplated a life as a reverend sister. It was a path steeped in service and spiritual fulfilment, focusing on the profound rather than the palpable. As she matured, these early inclinations evolved into a broader, yet equally purposeful direction. Zawadi's life became a testament to living beyond vanity metrics, embodying a commitment to enriching and uplifting others, aligning her daily actions with her most heartfelt values. This intentional living shaped not only her character but also left an indelible impact on those she touched, crafting a legacy far richer than any tangible monument could ever encapsulate.

As she stepped forward into the twilight of the ending year, Zawadi carried with her not just a legacy of resilience and a blueprint of authenticity but also a heart enriched by the profound sense of true fulfilment. Her life, a testament to living authentically and impacting profoundly, stood as a beacon to all who seek to define success on their own terms, guided by the courage to live deeply and truly.

EDUCATION TO THE DESTINATION

Zawadi's story was not about reaching a destination but about savouring the infinite sky of possibilities, each day a fresh brushstroke on the ever-expanding mural of her life. This realisation opened up a new realm of possibilities for her. Education was no longer just a formal process but a lifelong journey of learning that could take many forms—from books to travel, from classrooms to life experiences.

IT IS FINISHED

"It is finished," the words echoed softly, reverberating through the chambers of her heart with a weight and gravity that transcended time and space. She understood that her journey, with all its twists and turns, its moments of joy and sorrow, had led her to this precise point in time—to this revelation of truth and purpose.

For in those three simple words, spoken centuries ago by a humble carpenter turned Messiah, Zawadi found solace and redemption. She realised that her struggles, her pain, her doubts—all had been leading her inexorably toward this moment of clarity and understanding. And as she stood there, bathed in the light of a new dawn, she knew that her journey was far from over. But with those words ringing in her ears, she found the strength to face whatever lay ahead, secure in the knowledge that she was not alone—that she was guided by a love that knew no bounds, a grace that extended beyond the reaches of time and space.

PEACE LIKE A RIVER

As Zawadi reflected on the winding roads of her journey—the highs and lows, the twists and turns—she realised that each step was integral to the mosaic she was creating. The peace she now felt was hard-earned, painstakingly carved from the chaos of challenges and the solace found in her successes. Her journey, deeply influenced by Mo Gawdat's resonating wisdom, "The gravity of the battle means nothing to those at peace," served as a testament to the philosophy that true fulfilment lies not in the absence of adversity, but in one's ability to find peace amidst turmoil. Each challenge she faced and overcame added depth and colour to her life's mosaic, illustrating that peace is a profound achievement, forged in the fires of personal trials and triumphs. It was a peace that whispered of understanding and acceptance, a profound realisation that every moment held a purpose and every challenge a lesson. This insight allowed her to embrace her struggles with grace, viewing them not as obstacles but as integral parts of her journey toward self-discovery and inner tranquility.

STOP EXISTING AND START LIVING

Life, as Zawadi had learned, was not merely about the accumulation of days or the ticking of a clock; it was about the richness of each moment, the depth of every breath, and the vivid hues of every emotion felt.

Zawadi's story was one of transformation, not just of the self but of the very notion of living. She had dared to question the status quo, to defy the conventional, and in doing so, had uncovered a life of unparalleled depth. Her narrative was no longer confined by the expectations of society but was instead a bold declaration of independence—a life lived on her own terms, rich with the essence of truly felt emotions and experiences.

Now, as she stood ready to embrace the twilight of her story, Zawadi was not filled with fear or regret but with anticipation and hope. Her life was a beautiful testament to the power of resilience, the beauty of genuine self-discovery, and the endless possibilities that lay in the courage to forge one's path.

In her heart, she carried the eternal words of her mother, a reminder that every day holds a new dawn, every moment a fresh beginning. "Whenever you wake up is your morning." With this mantra, Zawadi looked forward to each new day, not just as another twenty-four hours but as a canvas awaiting the strokes of her continued passion and dreams.

And so, with a heart full of gratitude and eyes open to the beauty of her existence, Zawadi whispered into the calm of her tranquil home, "Live full, die empty." This was not just a mantra but a promise—a promise to herself to live every moment with intention, to fill each day with meaning, and to leave behind a legacy not of tangible monuments but of touched hearts and healed souls.

In this final chapter of her current volume, but certainly not her life, Zawadi understood that the best stories are those that continue beyond the last page, echoing into the lives they've touched, resonating through the ages. With a serene smile and a soul ignited by purpose, she was ready to turn the page, eager to discover what wonders the next chapter held.

LOST AND FOUND

Zawadi's story, deeply interwoven with the rich tapestries of biblical parables and modern-day challenges, is a profound testament to personal and spiritual growth. Drawing inspiration from the parables of the lost sheep and the lost coin, her life narrative beautifully illustrates the boundless love and relentless pursuit that defines her journey from feeling overlooked to becoming indispensable.

In her youth, constrained by societal norms and expectations, Zawadi often felt like the lost sheep, isolated and forgotten. The incident during a swim outing when her siblings left her behind epitomises this feeling of being lost. This moment, however, became a pivotal point in her life, as it taught her about her intrinsic value and the unwavering presence that continually sought her, much like the shepherd who leaves his ninety-nine sheep to find the one that is missing.

This divine presence, a metaphor for her realizatdion of her own worth and potential, lifted her from obscurity and placed her on a path of profound personal revelation and purpose.

> *"You're the One who never leaves the one behind"*
> **- So Will I (100 Billion X)**

Similarly, the parable of the lost coin resonates with Zawadi's journey. Just as the woman in the parable lights a lamp, sweeps her house, and searches diligently until she finds her lost coin, Zawadi embarked on an introspective quest to find her true self amidst the clutter of imposed identities. Each discovery and accomplishment in her life echoed the joyous celebration of the woman finding her coin, symbolising Zawadi's reclaiming of her lost parts and the joy of rediscovering her essence.

SO WILL I

As she broke free from the metaphorical grave of her past constraints, Zawadi found liberation, much like the themes in the song "So Will I (100 Billion X)", "If You left the grave behind You, so will I," reflects her determination to leave behind old confines and step into a life redefined by her own dreams and ambitions.

Her endeavours, from opening a community centre to launching a social enterprise and being a pillar for those in need, are not merely acts of altruism but a 'work of art called love.' Each initiative is woven into the very fabric of her community, impacting lives both practically and profoundly, illustrating her profound ability to love and elevate those around her.

Now, as she stands on the threshold of a new chapter, Zawadi embodies the ultimate surrender to life's journey, much like the final surrender to the will of the divine in the song. "If You gladly chose surrender, so will I," captures her readiness to embrace the future with hope and excitement, not with resignation but with a joyful acceptance of life's unpredictability. Each challenge she faces is viewed as an opportunity for growth, and every joy, a celebration of life's beauty.

THE PATH LESS TRAVELED

Confronted with a pivotal choice between the well-trodden path of life's routine and an unconventional journey of self-discovery, Zawadi stood at the crossroads. Recognising the impossibility of traversing both, she chose the less-trodden path.

The realisation dawned on her that the road less traveled required her to travel light. In the shadows of societal norms, she felt privileged in daring to explore uncharted territory, acknowledging the bravery needed to venture into the unknown. She aspired to gather lessons from this unconventional path and share them. She envisioned storytelling sessions akin to the *Tales by Moonlight* of her childhood—weaving stories for her mother and family and kindred spirits seeking solace in alternative narratives.

Freed from the buzz of chasing life's routine, Zawadi entered uncharted waters with a heart brimming with courage and joy. She embraced the adventure ahead, ready to face the unknown with a smile, albeit tinged with fear.

Life became a canvas for Zawadi to paint the portrait of her existence. She was grateful for the freedom to design a life aligned with her purpose, thus she explored diverse experiences. Simple pleasures—reading, attending gym classes, supporting friends, volunteering, learning to dance, and overcoming mishaps—became the focal points of joy.

Deviating from conventional pursuits of grandiosity, Zawadi revelled in small blessings. Rather than reaching for the stars, she found fulfilment in having the flexibility to wake up each day and pursue her heart's desires. Embracing her uniqueness, she acknowledged that standing out as a lone star was her design. The classroom of life became her workshop, a place in which she learned to number her days and apply her heart to wisdom. On this canvas of immortality, Zawadi painted a purposeful existence.

THE JOURNEY CONTINUES

Having discovered a renewed zest for life, Zawadi embraced each new day with gratitude and anticipation. With every step forward, she carried the lessons learned and the wisdom gained from her journey thus far. The road ahead may be uncertain, but Zawadi faced it with unwavering courage and a heart full of hope. For her, the journey was not about reaching a destination but embracing the beauty of the path itself. As she continued her journey, she knew each moment was an opportunity for growth, discovery, and transformation.

With each new day, she sees life as a magnificent movie, a tapestry woven with the threads of her diverse roles: daughter, sister, niece, cousin, friend, best friend, wife, divorcee, soulmate, godmother, leader, professional, and author. This is her legacy.

As the final lines of her current chapter fade, Zawadi leaves behind a beacon for all who find themselves lost in the shadow of conventional paths. Her life—a symphony of lessons learned, wisdom gained, and love shared—continues to resonate, a gentle yet powerful echo across the vastness of time and space.

"Itakuwa vyema mwishowe. Na ikiwa haitakuwa vyema, basi hicho sio mwisho" translates to *"It will all be well in the end. And if it is not well, then it is not the end."* - Mo Gawdat. With these words, Zawadi steps into the unknown future, her spirit alight with the promise that her journey is far from over. The roads ahead are many, and her steps are sure—for in her heart, she knows that every ending is but a precursor to a new beginning.

Thus, as the stars begin to sparkle in the night sky, painting the canvas of the cosmos with the light of a billion possibilities, Zawadi smiles softly to herself, ready for whatever comes next, confident in the journey, and ever hopeful for the future.

In this way, Zawadi's story does not end; it merely transitions into the next great adventure, continuing to unfold, one heartfelt moment at a time.

Chapter Twenty Five

DEAR ZAWADI

> *"Letters are among the most significant memorial a person can leave behind them."*
> **- Johann Wolfgang von Goethe**

My Dearest Daughter Zawadi,

As you embark on your journey through life, I want to share with you the profound wisdom and invaluable lessons I've gathered along my own path. You, my beloved, are a radiant expression of love, crafted with meticulous care by the hands of the Divine. In a world often clouded by superficial standards, I urge you to forge your own path with unyielding courage and authenticity.

Words hold immeasurable power; they can shape destinies and carve our reality. Cultivate a language of kindness and create a space in which emotions are welcomed and celebrated. Remember, your biology does not dictate your purpose; it is something far more profound and extraordinary. In many instances, obedience proves to be a wiser choice than sacrifice.

Choose your companions with discernment, for they have the potential to uplift or hinder you on your journey. Rejection, though initially painful, often serves as a redirection towards something far greater and more fulfilling. Your first love is your father, and death is but a transition—a doorway to another realm of existence.

Marriage, my dear, is a sacred union that can either blossom into something beautiful or dissolve like a mirage in the desert sands.Concealing dysfunction behind a façade merely prolongs the inevitable confrontation. Seek counsel from the wise and steer clear of violence in all its forms. Sometimes, we must descend into the depths of our souls to ascend to greater heights.

Beyond the physical traits inherited from generations past, I pray that you inherit not just my genes but also my spirit, resilience, and unwavering strength. May you carry forward this legacy with grace and fortitude, for while the visible may fade, the essence of who we are remains eternal. Let my life serve as a guiding light for yours, but always remember to infuse your unique essence into the tapestry of life.

Embrace the fractures of your heart, for they bear witness to a love that was genuine and profound. Sometimes, silence speaks louder than words, and discerning between fleeting chemistry and enduring compatibility is key in relationships. Heal your own wounds before attempting to heal others', and remember that hurt people often hurt others.

Find joy in the journey of life, my dear, and resist the temptation to fixate solely on distant goals. Embrace honesty, especially when it's uncomfortable, and prioritise your well-being above all else. Endure the trials of life with the resilience of a warrior, and never lose sight of your true self amidst the chaos of the world.

I wish for you one thing: to achieve the highest version of yourself. No matter what journey of life creates this transformation.

Above all, nurture a deep and intimate relationship with your Creator, finding solace and liberation in your mind and spirit. Guard your heart and tongue with vigilance, focusing on that which empowers and uplifts you. Cherish the precious gift of life, and be a beacon of love and strength in a world often shrouded in darkness.

May you spread your wings like an eagle and soar to unimaginable heights, leaving behind a legacy of love, resilience, and unwavering grace.

With all my love and blessings,

Mama Bear XOXO

ABOUT THE AUTHOR

.

Deutina Eseoghene Idisi is a captivating storyteller driven by a profound commitment to empowering women and reshaping societal norms. Her debut novel, *Five Good Years*, boldly reimagines the biblical masterpiece—The Woman with the Issue of Blood, paying homage to women's silent battles and unbeatable strength. With empathy as her guiding light, Deutina dedicates her work to every woman who has faced adversity, assuring them, "I see your pain and tears and lend my voice to you." She emphasises that her work transcends gender boundaries, acknowledging the profound impact of women's stories on all individuals.

As a fervent advocate for women's empowerment, Deutina courageously challenges the notion that a woman's value should remain confined to motherhood and marriage. Through *Five Good Years*, she delves into the journey of self-love, surrender, and acceptance, delivering a poignant narrative that celebrates individual authenticity and defies cultural expectations.

Beyond her literary endeavours, Deutina's life's mission is to assist girls and women in cultivating healthy hearts, souls, and minds. Through her writing and advocacy, she empowers individuals to craft fulfilling life experiences brimming with happiness and novelty, especially those who have weathered brokenness and embraced resilience.

In addition to her roles as a storyteller and advocate, Deutina is a passionate data and technology enthusiast, skilled at organising and building. Guided by her philosophy to "Live full and die empty," she immerses herself in research, constantly seeking innovative approaches to inspire girls and women to seize life's boundless opportunities.

Deutina lives by a set of guiding principles she affectionately calls her "Life Rules":

- ⚜ Be a voice, not an echo.
- ⚜ Turn a mess into a message.
- ⚜ Prioritise memories over material possessions.
- ⚜ Embrace a spirit of generosity: give, give, give.

Grateful for her unwavering support system and mentors, Deutina acknowledges their role in helping her navigate life's storms and harness the transformative power behind them. With her captivating storytelling and empowering message, Deutina continues to inspire readers to embrace their unique journey and create a life filled with purpose and authenticity. She views her literary work as a cherished gift, hoping that readers, especially the younger version of herself, see her heart through her words and carry forward the legacy of empowerment.

Connect with Deutina on social media and explore her website to join her community and engage further with her empowering message.#TinaTalks Website: TinaTalks.co.uk

XO Deutina.

Printed in Great Britain
by Amazon